Tyrants and Poets

By Steven R. Green

TYRANTS

AND POETS

Steven R. Green

Tyrants and Poets

Copyright © 2018 by Steven R. Green

CONTENTS

ANCIENT GREECE

INTRODUCTION

*W*hat is it that inspires an author to create a particular book? Is it a personal experience? A trait or idea of a certain famous individual? A question worth exploring about life or love or death, or some other existential factor?

Somehow, the strains of my life filtered my focus in this direction. I read a short article in a magazine about Sappho, the famous Lesbian poet of archaic Greece. More fragments from her work had been found. Who really was she? Her reputation has been modified and tarnished over the centuries. She was honored as a renowned Muse of the Hellenes, but was later perceived as a wicked tribate, and finally, an evil pedophile. The more I uncovered in my personal research, the more I came to my own conclusion: In a rigid patriarchal culture, she was the first real feminist. She set up her own consciousness-raising community and used her skill with poetry to spread the word! Some of the more liberated males of her time worked with her.

We all have a superficial knowledge about ancient Greece. But, before Ancient Greece, there was Archaic Greece. Before Socrates, Plato, Zeno, Diogenes, Epicurus, and Aristotle, there were the so-called Pre-Socratics of Miletus and Ephesus: Thales, Anaximander, Anaximenes, and Heraclitus. Around 600B.C., there were tyrants who ruled the various city-states. Some of them were benign and artistic; some had to be exiled. I also learned about the major political issues of that time: Oligarchy, income inequality, and the treatment of women. Oh my! Something very relevant here!

I used as much historical fact as I could to weave this tale. I hope you get to appreciate the people of that time as you read this novel.

1

THE BATTLE FOR SIGEION

The great general, Pittacus, stood with his legion at the shore of Signeion. He watched the warships of Phrynon, the arrogant Olympian champion, landing at the mouth of the Scamander. The reefed sails flapped in the wind and the triple rows of oars were set upright.

Pittacus was wearied of war. He had seen too many mangled bodies and heard the dying wails of young men who had proudly marched off to their own destruction. When he was called upon to defend his homeland of Lesvos, he fought with devotion. When he had to kill, he tried to make it quick, and found no joy in any sustained suffering of the vanquished. He hoped an enemy would be just as merciful when his own time came.

But Pittacus had grown more cynical over the years. Most of the wars involved aristocratic family feuds or conflicts over trading rights. He didn't care which one of a corrupt group took control and wondered why merchants couldn't just trade together. Such issues were not worth a man's life.

He also understood politics. Many favored him to lead Lesvos once Myrsilius was finally exiled. Phrynon was popular, as a result of the most recent Olympiad. Pittacus had no desire to be known as The Killer of Phrynon. Besides, he wanted peace with Attica. He and Draco had met when Pittacus made a visit to Athens. Although he was a hard-nosed leader, Draco was a practical man who did his best to restore justice and order.

As the Athenians disembarked, with shields glistening from the bright glare of the sun, they met no resistance from the Mytileneans. Phrynon led the army toward his rival with swords unsheathed. Pittacus stood his ground, with his own regiment around him.

The armies faced each other in tense silence. Pittacus raised his arm in a congenial manner. "Welcome to Signeion, noble Phrynon," he proclaimed. "I know of your victories in the Olympic Games. Our poets will sing about you." Pittacus raised both arms. Phrynon returned his sword to its scabbard.

Phrynon was confused by the friendly greeting; but soon regained his poise. He waved his arm toward his fleet. "Do you see those vessels? Do you know what that means?"

Pittacus responded with a hearty laugh. "And do you not see our navy, which has surrounded your ships?" He made a quick turn to his troops who began to laugh as well. Turning back toward the Athenian, Pittacus grew serious. "You have learned too many legends from Homeros. Do you plan to conquer Troy once again?"

Phrynon expressed his outrage. "You dare insult the gods!"

With a grunt, Pittacus stepped closer to his challenger. "You don't believe those myths any more than I do. We are competing for the trade route to the Black Sea, the north. But Lesvos has ties to Anatolia that are much stronger than yours. Just listen to

Sappho as she sings her poems to Cybele, the Great Mother, and Artemis, a favorite of the Scythian women. No one in Phrygia would deny our claims. Besides, Lesvos has a powerful navy. And you're far from home."

Phrynon remained stubborn. "You deny the great victory over Troy. But our victory over Signeion will not be denied!"

Pittacus snorted in disgust. "Our loyal soldiers will bleed and die to decide which tyrant and which oligarchy grows wealthier. We can resolve this another way."

Phrynon snarled at him. "Your poets are making you soft. Your skeptics are weakening your powers." But he was curious, and humored the general. "What is your proposal?"

With a nod, Pittacus made his offer. "Let your men sail home to their wives and lovers. We can settle this between us. You and I." Phrynon was taken aback by the suggestion. He paused to consider. He had proven himself in The Games. But Pittacus had gained fame as a general in real battles. "Where is your honor, Phrynon? We settle this trade dispute and your men return to Athens in peace."

The times were changing. The exploits of heroes through brute force were less appealing in life than in the epochs of myth. Finally, Phrynon made his decision. "Let it be so!"

As the two leaders drew swords and circled each other, Alcaeus, the poet warrior, slipped into the Mytilenean formation next to his brothers. "Where have you been?" asked Antimenidas with annoyance.

Stammering with contrition, Alcaeus mumbled, "I was attacked...I hid my shield and mingled with the peasants to avoid capture."

"Humph!" growled Antimenidas. "You were running from the battle." Attention returned to the battle at hand.

Both contenders were fleet-footed and skillful. Metal clanged and shields were employed with cunning. Finally, it looked like Pittacus was thrown off balance. Phrynon lunged. But Pittacus threw a net at his foe. Phrynon became entangled and tripped over the web of rope. Pittacus declared victory. The Mytileneans cheered; but the Athenians grumbled with discontent.

"Go home, Athenians!" Pittacus commanded. "The conflict is settled."

Phrynon rose and disentangled himself from the net. "That was not a legitimate victory," he declared.

Pittacus shrugged his shoulders. "The net is a regular weapon of combat. You know it's used in The Games. Go home, Phrynon."

Baffled by the legalities, Phrynon turned toward his ships. "This is not settled," he claimed as the Athenians retreated to the sea.

Pittacus then played his hand. "Phrynon, go back to Athens. Tell Draco that Pittacus will offer peace when he rules Lesvos. Attica will have free access to trade in The Black Sea if they make no attempt to colonize Scythia." Phrynon paused to consider the proposition. Realizing the economic potential, he pounded his chest with his fist to signal consent.

Alcaeus was inspired. "That was marvelous!" he exclaimed. "It was heroic, epic, dramatic!"

With a grunt bordering on a growl, Antimenidas said, "Go back to your poetess, Alcaeus!"

But Alcaeus grew serious. "Don't you see the opportunity here? After this battle, we will glorify Pittacus. He will be the hero of Lesvos. In our songs, we'll spread the news of his great victory, with some embellishment. It will give our cause great momentum. Peace with Attica weakens Myrsilius."

"I have to agree with Pittacus on one point. It's always another tyrant. Next time it will be Pittacus himself. He'll enrich himself and forget the people who supported him." Antimenidas grunted in disgust.

"Maybe not," replied Alcaeus. "You know Pittacus. He is a man of honor."

"Honor," echoed Antimenidas in contempt. "I find honor in whatever kingdom fills my purse."

2

CLEIS

*M*enares always worried about his sister, Cleis. She had a spirit that easily matched his own. She usually won their foot races and could climb the acropolis easily while he was gasping for air. Most of the time, he could best her in wrestling and swimming; but she reluctantly attributed those victories to his "man arms".

It would have been better for the family if Cleis had participated in the Arkteia when she was eleven years old. But mother was protective of her child and believed it was premature for her. Now, at a very rebellious fifteen, Cleis challenged everything. Several times, she threatened to run off to a temple and become a priestess. Menares worried that she could fall into options of a more ribald nature. He himself enjoyed one particular den of pleasure but shivered at the thought of Cleis in the profession of a hetaera.

So once again, she and father had plunged into a feverish dispute. Once again, she ran from their home into the maze of

Athens. And, once again, Menares was commanded to retrieve his sister.

He was torn because both father and sister had rational motives. The family needed a dowry to pay their debt. Father wanted desperately to remove the horos that signified a boundary to their seized land. Cleis was young, attractive and vigorous. She had inflamed the desires of several wealthy suitors. A strategic wedding would liberate their farmlands. But Cleis wanted to escape the trappings of women. She recoiled from domestic chores and actually preferred open air. There was the dilemma. They couldn't afford enough slaves. Fabric had to be made. Children had to be raised. Meals had to be cooked. Clothes had to be cleaned.

As Menares rushed through the avenues of the plaka, passing teeming stalls of green olives and golden apples, he took in the earthly whiff of fresh-cut grains. From scattered fires, the smoke of roasting vegetables, pigs and seafood aroused his hunger. Colors of gold and red, purple and blue, shimmered from rows of silk and woolen fabrics. Dogs barked and goats bleated. Children kicked up dust as they played between the stalls. Roaming musicians played their tambours and double-piped aulos and were rewarded with a satisfying meal. Menares usually dallied in the plaka to view the wares and take in the sights, sounds, and smells of the bustling marketplace; but he had to find Cleis before the family discord blew into a major catastrophe. Walking under the ancient stoa with its sanctuary to Zeus, he maneuvered around the architects who were planning a major temple to honor the overseer of the Olympian gods. Menares thought about ascending the Sacred Way to the altar of Athena, the Protector of the city. But, on a sudden insight, he turned westward, navigated the lush pine land forest, and climbed the stone steps of the Pnyx. That large rock was one of her favorite retreats.

His intuition was rewarded. Hearing the scratch of his sandals on the rock, Cleis turned and faced her brother. She made no attempt to run. Instead, she offered a slight smile and turned her gaze beyond the Rock of Ares, toward the Metroon of the Earth Mother, and awaited the crimson flush of another Spring sunset.

They sat silently as the sky shifted from an easy cerulean to a radiant coral and the sun made its eternal journey into the horizon. The Metroon turned pink while the Areopagus faded into shadow. Legend has it that the Amazons camped on that hill when they invaded Athens to rescue Antiope. The Trojan battle for Helen pales in comparison to that abduction. Cleis scanned the four Gates of the city that appealed to the wanderlust in all of us. Any argument between the siblings would be a weak echo of previous disputes. Cleis and Menares loved each other and had no intent to do further harm.

Finally, Menares rendered a resolution. "It's only a tradition, Cleis," he concluded. "It's a way to celebrate the maturing of young girls, the transition from innocent children to adult women. Think how many children don't even survive to this point."

With a grunt and a sneer, Cleis turned to face her brother. "You know it's more than that," she countered. "It's an announcement that I'm ready to be sold off, that I'm eligible to be someone's humble little wife."

Menares tried to soothe her with a casual wave. "Eh. One step at a time. Say the words, complete the ritual. Then, back home, you can talk with father."

"I'd rather talk with father AND mother. It involves the whole family."

Menares gazed upon his sister in bewilderment. "Strange request," he replied. "But we can make the suggestion. You know mother also wants you to complete the custom. It's long over-do."

"Mother does as she's told. She's a good wife." The sarcastic tone was not missed.

Menares stood up and extended his hand to Cleis. "Let's go home," he implored. "If you continue to rebel, father will take you away from the city and put you back on our farm."

"A logical solution," remark Cleis. "He can sell off some slaves, pay his debts, and I'll work in the fields."

With an annoyed grunt, Menares berated his sister. "You'd escape marriage to be a field worker? I seriously doubt that."

Cleis rose on her own power and stomped ahead of him. Menares smiled, shook his head, and followed his sister down the stone steps, and beyond the tribute to Tribal Heroes, beside the Hill of the Nymphs, to the Metroon. The Great Earth Mother called upon the moon, as it rendered a soft luminescence to the columns. Cleis stood by the old temple and chanted in muffled tones. "Gaia...Rhea...Kore...Inanna...Cybele". Menares grew apprehensive as the darkness of the evening covered them. When she completed her chanting, Cleis stared up to the acropolis, where Kore watched over the city. Cleis took several deep breaths and nodded to Menares. They walked solemnly through the town, past the agora, to their home.

****

As the merchant ship skimmed into the crescent-shaped harbor of Piraeus, crewmen climbed the mast to reef the main sail to the high bar. At the tiller, Charaxos skillfully maneuvered the rudder into the port. The fertile cliffs of Piraeus opened for him like an eager lover while determined merchants waited to exchange their commodities for his Lesbian wine, olives, and exotic goods from wild Scythia. As he docked the ship, Charaxos remembered his promise to his sister. She longed for the soft cotton fabrics from Attica. She was tired of the rough woolen himation, and the course strophion irritated her breasts. He was also determined to surprise her with silks from Anatolia.

It had been a long expedition beyond the Hellespont; but his affable style and honest bartering imparted him with a good reputation among the tribes of Scythia. The wild warrior women of Pontus were especially intrigued by his fruits and sandals from Lesvos. They could ride their horses and shoot arrows as well as any man; but, despite their tattoos and fighting skills, they were still women. And beautiful ones at that. But Charaxos always proceeded with caution when he negotiated with those proud and hot-tempered amazons. He anticipated a more accommodating experience in one of his favorite brothels in Athens.

His crew raised the anchor as Charaxos locked the tiller in place. The crew leader hopped from the ship onto the dock and a large sheet was thrown to him. He used it to pull the bow of the vessel to the dock, and then secured the boat to a post. A second sheet pulled in the stern. Lots were drawn among the crew to decide which two members would serve as first watch. It was a smooth operation which they had done many times before.

One merchant from the south displayed superb fabrics. Blue and purple cloths from Palestine. Shimmering red and gold velvets from Egypt and Ethiopia. The Egyptian cloth was embellished with depictions of their gods and goddesses with human bodies and animal heads. Since Sappho studied the diverse significance of the many goddesses, he guessed she'd appreciate those portrayals. Knowing his sister well, he picked out garments that were expressive but not garish. She preferred internal meaning rather that overt displays. Charoxos was on his way to Egypt after this stopover and he had a reasonable grasp of the Coptic language. But he chose to make the immediate trade at Piraeus since the fabric was extraordinary, the merchant was reasonable, and there was no chance he'd forget his promises. He still had to bring papyrus back to Lesvos since Sappho had acquired the art of writing. After a round of playful bickering with the merchant, the exchange was made. Charaxos carried the cloth to his quarters and carefully placed them in his personal chest. With his family obligation completed, he was ready for a well-deserved respite. His brother would be easily amused with trinkets from Pontus.

Charaxos had depleted his entire store of homeland wine. With all due respect to the Scythians, Charaxos had had enough mare's milk. After his days at sea, he could have walked the six miles to Athens and relish the company of its sophisticated hetaerae and proper wine. But he was too tired for a grand symposium; the local entertainment of Piraeus would suffice. He had a favorite venue along the Saronic coast and was ready to enjoy some leisurely and familiar comforts. With three crewmen, old friends who had shared numerous adventures with him, the shore leave began.

Pushing past the lewd pornes who shamelessly displayed their delights on the street, and left messages of invitation in the sand from their sandals, through the throngs of merchants offering garish trinkets and vulgar artwork, beyond the street urchins begging for obols with one hand while trying to pick your pocket with the other, they made it to their preferred residence of pleasure.

****

Everyone knew the old legend of Cassandra. She was the daughter of King Priam and Queen Hecuba, the rulers of Troy, and she had the gift of prophecy. But the gift was also a curse because no one would heed her predictions. People thought she was insane and often ridiculed her. So why would the proprietress of a salon of delights assume the name of a tragic chaste madwoman?

Lounging on a sofa, she sipped the local wine from her personal skyphos and laughed. "I remind you that 'Cassandra' also means, 'she who entangles men'". Then, with a sober expression, she put down her cup and elaborated. "When my village in Thrace was destroyed, I felt like Cassandra standing among the flaming ruins of Troy. The invaders took the women away in their ships and we passed the remains of Ilium." She turned to Charaxos with an accusatory glare. "Those pirates stopped in your beloved Lesvos to purchase your wines and olives with the spoils from Thrace." Charaxos offered his awkward apology. But she brushed it away. "It's the way of the world. Besides, slavery in Egypt worked well for me. See how I earned my freedom." With a sweeping gesture, she invited him to regard her premises.

"Impressive accomplishment for a Thracian peasant girl, eh?"

He scrutinized the fine tapestry that covered the windows and walls. The rugs were of thick Anatolian fabric with intricate designs and hypnotic colors of gold and purple and diverse browns. Musicians filled the air with skillful sounds of strings, drums, and winds.

With a sincere nod, he replied, "Indeed it is! You must have…". He paused out of respect but Cassandra encouraged him to complete his thought. "You must've labored for many years."

She laughed with a genuine freedom that few Athenian women would risk. "I'm glad you appreciate my struggles." With a ladle, she scooped more thick and fruitful wine from a large krate and replenished her skyphos.

Charaxos noticed the depiction on the vessel, a woman in armor with shield and sword. "Athena?" he asked.

"Why?" she replied with a sneer. "Because we're in Attica?" Charoxos wrinkled his brow in confusion and ladled more wine into his own cup. "Do you see a horse on her shield? Do you see an owl? No. In my homeland, the women battle with their men, not like these pale Athenian wives."

"I know," answered Charoxos eagerly. "I've been north." Their conversation grew solemn. Cassandra changed the tone.

"But come, my friend. It's time to sing, dance, feast, and love. Your mates have already found companions for the evening. She rose from her sofa, took his hand, and led him into the main chamber.

Charoxos meandered through the room, surrounded by the sound of lyra, flutes, and tympanum. Several musicians were harmonizing their double-piped aulos while one woman fingered a complicated kithara on her lap. She was accompanied by another woman playing an intricate hydraulis which relied on water pressure to create deep penetrating tones. Such instruments would have made a grand impression upon his sister.

Slaves and servant girls carried food trays, from which Chaloxos eagerly snagged portions of fish, pork, beef, fruits, and desserts. The flavors mingled deliciously in his mouth. Wine-bearers continued to fill his cup from skillfully painted amphorae.

Two brightly adorned hetaerae approached Charoxos. Their slender shoulders were bare. Their chiton tunics were shorter than usual and hung loosely with no belts. It had the effect of exaggerating their body movements and ease of access. With each casual motion, their breasts would alternate between exposed and concealed. Unlike the domestic wives of Attica, their faces were tanned and rose-tinted by exotic cosmetics. In fact, Charoxos suspected their aureolae were also enhanced with extra red. Bracelets and earrings jangled when they moved. Choosing to not make a choice, he invited them both to join him on a sofa. Charoxos spotted his two shipmates nearby, joking and drinking and laughing with other women and several young boys. Finally, one of his mates walked off to a private room with the consort he chose.

Charoxos asked the names of his companions and laughed at the answers. The younger girl who had a darker complexion and deep black hair, went by the name of Hestia. The Goddess of the family hearth and home! The other one, of fair hair and delicate features, called herself Echo.

"The mountain nymph," he noted. But the girl explained that it was a perfect name for a hetaera. She simply reflects what a man says to her while he worships his own reflection. Charoxos roared with delight and grabbed more grapes from a passing tray, which they proceeded to feed to each other. Charoxos asked them to play music for him. Of course, Echo displayed pan pipes. She leaned onto him and created the hypnotic melody of the satyrs as her flaxen hair spread across his bare chest. Sappho was right; the subtle gestures are the most enticing. Hestia accompanied her with her own aulos like a subtle zephyr enshrouding them. Her leg rubbed gently against his.

In the background, dancers were tapping their tympana and clicking crotala. Charoxos leaned back on the sofa and closed his eyes. His long journey was over. Soon he'd return to his home on Lesvos. But, at the moment, he was exactly where he needed to be. Echo stopped piping just long enough to kiss his chest.

Charoxos stroked her hair and offered his mouth instead. Hestia leaned toward his ear and the beads in her hair clacked as she descended. She whispered gently, "For one more drachma, you can spend the night with us both."

Charoxos laughed slightly. "Just a drachma, eh?" he replied with a sneer. "Six more obols when I already paid Cassandra?"

Hestia was not deterred. She purred as he and Echo continued kissing. "Any man with coin can purchase hetaerae. But for the right man, to share a night of pure love with us...who would put a price on that?"

Charoxos was moved by that remark. His sister spoke to him of her exploration of Love in all its varieties. Charoxos believed the force of Love is such a power in nature that no one Goddess could contain it. That's why he always returns to the Earth Mother, the origin, the first energy, the primal creatrix. But Sappho had a different idea with her cult to Aphrodite.

From a purse concealed within his cape, he produced a silver coin and handed it to Hestia. She studied the images engraved on the front and back. The weight was accurate. Echo then looked up at the coin, sighed, stared at Hestia, and nodded. Then she smiled at Charoxos. She whispered, "Thank you."

They rose from the sofa. Each grabbed food and wine from passing trays. Echo also grabbed a loutrophorus filled with fresh water. They would need hydration.

𝟥

SPINNING AND WEAVING

*C*leis sat next to her mother, who gleefully grabbed a bundle of flax from her basket. The family was fortunate to own a large field of the tall slender plant which provided for a great deal of linen. She watched as mother combed the bunch with a round kteis to separate the linseeds that would be used later for cooking and salad dressing. Mother directed Cleis to follow her lead, which the girl did with little enthusiasm.

"Trust me," said Mother as she attached a stone weight to the lower end of her spindle and hooked the other end to the bunch of flax. "You'll enjoy the Arkteia with all the other girls. You'll probably be one of the older ones." With the supple skill that came from years of repetition, Mother let the spindle slowly descend, pulling a flaxen thread with it. She could rival the faithful Penelope or the capricious Fates, weaving threads of contingency. "Most girls your age are already married. But you were so obstinate at eleven that I worried you'd be punished." She saw the frown on her daughter's face so shifted the focus. "Besides, Brauron is a beautiful place. I remember it well. You'll love the sacred spring and the cove and the cave of mysteries." Mother went suddenly silent, unable to reveal the mystery.

Cleis' spindle unhooked from her batch and fell to the floor. With a flush of embarrassment, she bent to retrieve it. Mother laughed gingerly. "Don't worry, child," she assured her. "A spindle drop is common. You'll have a lifetime to get the knack."

That comment did not soothe Cleis. If anything, it intensified her agitation. A lifetime! Father could only afford two slaves, a couple, who helped with the cooking and the farming. Spinning and weaving fell to his wife and daughter. Mother was very skilled in those labors; Cleis appreciated the soft chitons of summer and the comfortable himations of autumn. When she thought of the length of the himation, she tried to calculate how many hours of spinning and weaving went into that garment. Most of the winter, Mother was at the loom, joining the vertical stemon with the horizontal kroke, and beating them into a tight weave with her spathe. A lifetime! Mother was very pale, which the Athenians compared to statuesque beauty. Her only adventures beyond the home were trips to the agora to purchase foodstuffs or trade merchandise. She usually wore a cape or a hood to protect her ivory features from the rays of the sun. Only brutish porne, conceited hetaerae, and wild foreign women had rosy faces.

"It was so wonderful with all my friends," Mother continued with a bright smile. "We danced and sang. We were, 'arktoi', little she-bears!" But then her smile faded and she pursed her lips. "We bid farewell to childish things and learned to be mature women."

Cleis fetched her spindle while mother spun threads around her distaff. Cleis envied Mother's experienced dexterity but also feared the suffocating destiny it forebode. She wondered if it were possible to juggle Mother's skills with some option of greater freedom. With tears emerging from her eyes, she hooked the flax and let the weighted threads drop through her hand.

4

THE ROAD TO BRAURON

The journey to Brauron began when the carts left the Northern Gate of Athens, passed through a dense forest of olive trees, and the travelers stopped to pay tribute to the river god Cephisus. Dense green forest, of white myrtle, sweet yellow bay, and pine, opened to the foothills of the Egaleo mountain. The pilgrims stopped at a taverna in Athmonon near the plains of Marathon, surrounded by the omnipresent myrtle, tall cyprus, and wide-spreading cedar. The local dwellers had been expecting the annual pilgrims from Athens and welcomed them with servings of wine, goat milk, grapes, olives, cheese, and bread. Local spices and herbs further enhanced the repast. The payment of several drachmas was made to their hosts. Cleis could see the cliffs of Euboea across the narrow gulf and was told the tale of Amarynthos, the mortal man who pursued the goddess Artemis across that island. Cleis tried to imagine the pathetic man, enamored of the virgin huntress, in his vain pursuit. In commemoration, the people of Athmonon worshiped Artemis Amarysia and constructed a temple in her honor. The retinue visited the temple the evening before they left Athmonon. It was made of glistening marble from the quarry of Mount Pentelicus, the same source as Athenian temples. Within the temple, the hard, wooden statue stood proudly, with quiver and bow, surrounded by her nymphs and accompanied by two deer. The statue was older than the marble temple. Clearly, Artemis existed long before the columns and stoa that went up around her. The priestess and her adherents in the temple kept bee hives. Obols were exchanged for delicious golden honey.

As Cleis studied the statue of Artemis, a deep yearning gnawed at her stomach. Artemis resembled her favorite doll, a figure of the amazon Atalanta, the great huntress and the killer of the Calydonian Boar. No one could catch Atalanta in a foot race. She was independent and willful. Only with the help of Aphrodite, and her distracting golden apples, was Hippomenes able to win the race. Aesop recently made a children's tale from that; and called it The Hare and the Tortoise. He recited the tale in the agora to the delight of children and adults. But they knew he was really modifying an older tale. Atalanta consented to marriage with Hippomenes; but their union was more barbarian than Athenian. They lived as equal partners and remained fierce lovers. Finally, they were turned into lions!

Again, Cleis was filled with questions. She wondered why Artemis is exalted with deep devotion while the good women of Attica are limited to domestic chores within their huts. She began to consider the ambivalence of men: they demand a submissive housewife, yet dream of barbarian women. Is that why the hetaerae are so successful? Cleis smiled with a flash of enlightenment. Some of her thoughts she would only share with her doll of Atalanta.

As the sun rose the next morning, the company bid farewell to the people of Athmonon, packed their belongings on their wagons, and made the trek to the sea. Taking the trail along the bank of the Erasinor River, they arrived at Brauron by mid-day.

Sandwiched between two mountain ranges, the sanctuary was filled with scents of cedar, myrtle, and cyprus trees. From a high point, Marathon and Euboea across the narrow sea were clearly visible.

The girls were led to a sacred spring, where they were allowed to bathe and drink the crisp flowing water. A young priestess welcomed the company. Separating the girls from their companions, the priestess gave the "Little Bears" a quick tour of the sanctuary. Proceeding through the white stoa, the girls passed statues of beautiful young girls and boys in addition to nymphs, the ocean Nereids, and the Fates.

In one section to the side of the stoa was an altar for Iphigenia, the daughter of Agamemnon and Clytemnestra and the sister of Orestes. Cleis was confused about Iphigenia. There were conflicting legends. In one version, Artemis demands the sacrifice of the poor girl, who is burnt at the stake. But a second rendition has Artemis rescue Iphigenia at the last moment and substitute a bull instead. Some say she was an amazon warrior who was commanded to execute her brother for stealing a statue of Artemis. But ultimately Orestes is forgiven. The conflicting versions were confusing but, again, the ambivalence of men is revealed. Iphigenia is either an obedient daughter who is willing to sacrifice herself to honor her father; or she is a powerful warrior priestess.

Why would Artemis impose such a test upon Agamemnon? Why would she demand the sacrifice of his child only to stop the killing at the last possible moment? Artemis, the staunch protector of beasts and young girls, would so casually render a girl for sacrifice? Cleis was growing more skeptical. No god she knew would devise such a torture! Perhaps the legend comes from the eastern lands.

5

THE ARKTEIA

Cleis was self-conscious and awkward about the age differences. Most of the girls were between nine and twelve years old. The hair of these young pre-pubertal arktoi had been sheared to a short crop. But the older "bleeding" girls, the gynaikes, retained long hair. The young girls often romped and played in the nude, or rambled in their short chitoniskos; but the gynaikes were obliged to drape themselves in a more modest chiton or peplos. Cleis had never been sensitive about her body in the past. She and Menares frequently dipped in a spring, plunged under a waterfall, or ran through their father's field, with no concerns for modesty. But at Brauron, surrounded by naked short-haired nymphs while she was wrapped discreetly and displayed a long braid, she was conscious of the changes in her body. Fortunately, her roommates were of a similar age.

At the northern edge of the stoa, there were separated quarters, small rooms that smaller groups of girls shared for eating

27

and sleeping. Otherwise, the arktoi shared all the instructions and rituals in common. They also had ample time to explore the grounds at leisure.

Cleis often woke before the morning gong. Because it was facing westward, the portico could be cool before sunrise. It was the only time she appreciated the obligatory clothing. Letting her eyes wander the Sacred Spring, the stone bridge over the Erasinos River, and the moonlit hint of the dark mountains in the distance, she struggled to quell her restless twitching. The birds knew what they had to do as they soared and touched down, plucked at seeds and worms, and flittered off to their next destination. The flowers knew when to open their petals and release their scent; and when to close up and sleep for the evening. The entire earth understood the seasons. The crops died in winter but returned from Hades when beckoned by the stirrings of an awakening world. The bees knew when to gather pollen; the plants knew when to drop their seeds. Everything seemed to have an essence. Is that the work of the gods, she pondered? If it were, what then was the meaning of it all? Where was the endless eternal cycle going? Most painful for her, she seemed to have no divine essence. The rituals did not resonate for her. She doubted that Artemis would bring a plague to Attica if one girl from Athens refused to participate in the Arkteia. And yet, no girl could marry until she completed the tradition. She was complying, but with no sense of significance. She turned to her left to gaze at the Temple for Artemis just a few steps from the portico. Beyond that Temple stood the large Rock that the girls liked to climb in the afternoon. Some whispered about a secret Cave beyond that Rock. Nearby, a rooster made its screech.

There was motion near the great rock. As the shadows faded with the morning light, Cleis discerned the figure of one of the young girls. Her head was bowed into her hands and she seemed to be crying. For a brief moment, Cleis and the young arktoi took notice of each other; but then the girl hurried back into the shadows.

The great gong echoed through the stoa and the portico. Early hints of rose and crimson mixed with streaks of yellow as the sun returned from its daily journey. Cleis made her barefooted jaunt back to her room.

Antiope had just washed and emptied her water basin out the window. Psyche was brushing her hair and studying herself in her bronze mirror. Tryphaina, who kept her hair in a braid like Cleis, was applying olive oil to her arms and legs. The room was small but the young women shared a casual amity. Antiope noticed Cleis. "Welcome back, Dawn Goddess," she declared as she strapped on her sandals. "Apollo still shining over his sister?"

"Definitely," replied Cleis with a playful smile. "I think I saw his chariot moving this way."

"I hope so," Psyche griped as she examined a small blemish on her cheek. "I was chilly last night."

"You should've come to me," Tryphaina quipped with warm eyes and a smile. "We could've kept each other comfortable." She shifted over to Psyche and ran her hands through her flaxen hair.

Cleis took the basin from Antiope and filled it from the pitcher they shared. She splashed the cool water across her face to awaken from the trance of sunrise. "I'm hungry today," she remarked.

"Perhaps we'll finally get some catfish," said Antiope hopefully.

"I doubt it," groaned Tryphaina. "We'll probably be eating pomegranate seeds." Psyche giggled and tugged at the other girl's braid. Tryphaina stroked her shoulders.

"Well, then, in the spirit of Artemis, I'll go hunt for food. Just give me a bow and a few arrows. I'll find some rabbits."

Psyche turned to Antiope. "While you're at it, bring back some figs." She sniffed and grimaced. "And we could use some lavender incense in this room."

Antiope faced Tryphaina. "Hey, get your lover some lavender."

"Maybe I will," Tryphaina hummed in reply." She picked up Psyche's mirror to check her own reflection.

Two slave girls arrived with trays. Bowls of maza bread, grape leaves, olives, and sardines were served with an amaranth porridge filled with local vegetables. The vleeta was appealing with its soft grainy quality sweetened by honey. There were no figs but a small portion of dates. Hungry fingers scooped up the food.

"Figs are too sexy," noted Antiope with a sneer. "We're innocent things."

When the morning meal was done, the slaves removed the trays and departed discreetly. "They're so quiet and detached," said Antiope.

"They're frightened," explained Cleis. "If they insult the initiates, for any reason, they might be whipped, or worse."

"Hmm," grunted Antiope as she licked the meal from her lips. "I don't want them to be afraid of me."

"It's better this way," replied Cleis. "We can make mistakes. But now, under Draco, it's too risky for them." When Psyche and Tryphaina left to relieve themselves, Cleis spoke openly to Antiope. "You seem different from the other girls. You're so outspoken. I like it."

"My upbringing did not prepare me for the dignified life," she confided. "My family was poor when I was a child; but they recently succeeded as potters. They even have their own kiln now. My brother paints the pottery. He's very good. He knows all the old myths and depicts them in fine detail. So, we're now citizens, eh?"

"Your name. Antiope? The Amazon princess? You have her spirit."

With a grunt, Antiope wiped her mouth. "Like Helen, she ran off with Theseus, the founder of our glorious city! Then she defends him against her own sisters! Typical man, typical woman. My parents didn't give me the name to be a proud warrior; it was to teach me to be loyal to my husband no matter what he does."

"You disagree?"

Antiope leaned in toward Cleis. "And so do you. I can see it. Your restless mornings, your fidgeting during the lectures, your deep sighs when they speak of childhood's end."

The other women returned to the room. Psyche's face was flushed and Tryphaina avoided eye contact. Antiope could never resist a joke. "Are you two sweet innocent creatures ready for today's lesson?" After a breathless pause, all four roommates erupted in laughter.

----- ----- -----

Most of the young girls had crossed the stone bridge and were on the other bank of the Erasinos. One group played an energetic hide-and-seek. When the older pupils crossed the flat stone bridge, several girls raced to the "safe point" when the seeker found them. One of the girls bumped into Cleis and laughed. Two other girls were picking wildflowers, and banding each other's hair with yellow daisies, violet cornflower, purple foxglove, and bright red poppies. They giggled as they worked the stems. Three others were competing with stones, trying to hit a distant target. When the mark was hit, the winner howled in victory. One girl sat alone, cross-legged, and seemed deep in thought. Cleis recognized her as the girl by the rock during the sunrise.

The four long-haired older girls strolled north along the bank of the Erasinos with the small mountain range in the distance. Giving in to temptation, Psyche placed buttercups in the braid of Tryphaina, who took her hand. They walked through the field while Cleis sat on a small rock and wreathed flowers and Antiope tossed stones in the water.

"The little bears have a lot of spunk," remarked Cleis as she appraised her own handiwork.

"Indeed," replied Antiope. "That will soon be finished." She threw another rock with extra force and a grunt.

When the large gong resounded from the portico, the casual play came to a halt and the "bear cubs" hurried across the stone bridge, onto the portico. One by one, they scooped up water with their hands from a large krater, splashed their faces and arms, and proceeded through the stoa to the main courtyard. Torches were burning at the four corners: black lazuli at the North torch; white lilies at the West; blue foxglove East; and red poppies South. The redolence of blossom incense embraced their nostrils. The girls circled around the old priestess and her helpful acolytes. The adherents had their heads covered by a loose shawl and a flame rose in front of them from a fire pit.

The weathered crone adjusted her position on a small cushion and began the lesson. Her acolytes sang hymns in harmony to emphasize the words of their leader. "We live in a proud age. Theseus withstood the wrath of barbarian hordes and

Athena protects our glorious land." The chorus banged tambourines and raised their voices in praise of the Goddess of Attica. The crone lifted a warning finger. "But every age must honor the time before. Think back to when there were no columns and stoa; no cities and markets; no roads and farmlands." The percussion slowed to a deep grave tempo while the zils shivered. "The power of the Natural World prevailed. We hail Artemis, Goddess of wild things!" The pupils jumped when the acolytes howled like wolves and completed the measure with piercing ululations. The veils flew from them. They went into a wild dance, whirling and jumping, grinding their hips, and pulling at their hair. When the crone sounded the gong, the dancing ceased. They retrieved their veils and reformed into a chorus. The pupils were fascinated, with gaping mouths and widened eyes. Psyche instinctively grabbed Tryphaina's hand; but her lover was lost in a trance. Antiope braced herself in anticipation of the next outburst. Cleis absorbed the energy and felt a surge of something new and free.

The priestess continued. "Artemis, Eternal youth, Protector of the Wild Things, forgive us! Forgive the ignorance of children and men who would kill your Sacred Bear! Forgive Theseus and Heracles for taking what was not theirs!" The chorus began to wail and cry with honest tears and deep sobs. They beat their chests. "The war belt of Hippolyte! The Amazon Queen Antiope and her warriors, kidnapped by Theseus!" The pupils began to mirror their lead, crying and lamenting and pounding on the ground. Some rolled on the ground in clamorous remorse.

Antiope leaned toward Cleis. "My namesake? Kidnapped? Did you know about all that theft?" Cleis giggled and nodded. "I have a lot to learn," she realized at once.

"Most of all, we implore you to forgive Orestes, as Iphigenia did." The acolytes were pleading with painful pathos. "He dared to steal the image of you, Artemis!"

The acolytes screamed in outrage, "No! Blasphemy! Dishonor!"

"These girls before you today will display their reverence for you the way Iphigenia did!"

"Yes, they will," announced the acolytes. "Yes, we will," shouted the girls.

The crone stood and raised her arms to the sky. "Like Iphigenia, they will offer themselves as sacrifice!"

The acolytes howled in frenzy. The girls were less enthusiastic that time. The ululations sounded ominous and several girls trembled and cried. The mingling of devout wails and terrified screams filled the courtyard. Psyche sobbed in the arms of Tryphaina.

Antiope stared at Cleis with eyes wide and dark as lapis lazuli. "Sacrifice?" she asked with a tremor to her voice.

"No, wait…let me think." Was Iphigenia killed? Did Artemis save her? "It's not clear to me," Cleis stammered.

"Tomorrow!" shouted the Priestess. "Tomorrow we bid farewell to the little bear cubs!" After a pause, she hit the large gong. The lesson was over for the day. It was time for dinner.

----- ----- -----

The cry of Athena's owl was like a mocking jeer as it offered a lethargic hoot and followed it with a mocking screech. With its large eyes that could penetrate the darkness, it was a symbol of wisdom. But symbols often contradict reality. The creature is really a predator of the night that pounces silently on its hapless victim and seizes it in its sharp talons. Far from inspiring wisdom, it provokes nightmares!

Cleis stared at the kouroi that stood in their proud marble splendor along the base of the stoa. She wondered if those perfectly carved young boys were expressions of ideal form; or the memorials to youth offered for sacrifice. The kore girls were no more comforting. She stared at the statues of nymphs with outstretched arms. Were they votaries to a goddess or, like Iphigenia, pleading for mercy as the flames of the stake consumed them? Sacrifice. The word pounded against her mind like a great drum summoning adherents to the ritual.

The courtyard was empty. The Priestess and her acolytes never appeared after sunset. Sometimes she could hear them in their chamber chanting or reciting in subdued tones. Were they being reverent, or choosing which of the "Little Cubs" to offer the vengeful deity? Cleis gazed off to the northern horizon, beyond Marathon, and felt a deep yearning in her soul. She could hear the wind of the sea and the crashing of waves.

Suddenly Cleis realized she was not alone. The sound of bare feet on marble tiles was subtle; but once detected, clear and persistent. She turned swiftly and quietly. It was Antiope, standing less than a yard from her. They nodded together in wordless communication.

Finally, Antiope spoke in a whisper. "I was watching you," she confessed. "Looking beyond this pretty sanctorium. I feel it too." She raised her arm toward Marathon. "The hunger to travel, to go away."

Cleis lowered her eyes and stepped closer to Antiope. "Someone or something beckons me. I don't understand it. But the Fates are weaving a different path for me."

Antiope glanced at Cleis in supplication. "You're well educated. You understand the traditions better than I do. But I'm hungry to learn. When you follow that path, please take me with you."

Cleis stared at her new friend and recognized the same burning determination to soar beyond the gates of Attica, to sail the sea to other lands, to live a different life than the one decided by her family. "Yes," she decided with tears in her eyes. "Yes, I will." They embraced in the way of two comrades on a forbidden journey.

The young women heard soft sobs near one of the kores. It was the lonely girl again. She seemed to be chanting as she rocked in a corner. They approached cautiously and kneeled next to her. When the girl saw there was no danger, she whispered in a rushed tempo. "Zeus made Artemis forever young. She doesn't wear the belt." She was referring to the girdle worn by women who achieve menarche and complete the Arkteia. "I won't wear it either!" The girl began to scratch her arms and the women restrained her.

"It's our nature," explained Cleis to soothe her. "Mene, we are women, creatures of the month and the moon. No longer children, we become gynaikes." She rocked the girl in her arms.

"Our blood makes babies," added Antiope. "Like the sacred animals, women are a monthly sacrifice. Our blood strengthens the crops. We create life and food!"

The girl was not appeased. "Then why can Artemis run free while we must surrender to a husband?"

"The Triple Goddess," replied Cleis. "The stages of our lives. Maiden, Mother, Crone." But even as she sought to assuage the girl's distress, Cleis felt her own. The gong reverberated through the sanctuary and they made their way to the ritual.

----- ----- -----

As the arktoi entered the courtyard, each was handed a bear skin and directed to wrap it around themselves. The nervous protégés did as they were told and sat in a circle around the Priestess and the fire pit. The pelts were heavy and very warm near the fire. The acolytes surrounded the pupils with drums, tympanum, crotala, and several other instruments of wind or strings. They sang as they danced around the anxious girls.

The old crone began to speak and the singing of the acolytes diminished to a background mumble. "Tonight, as you entered at the portico, you came to the large round krater. You washed your hands and face in the water of that krater." With syrinx and aulos, the acolytes replicated the sound of water flowing in the spring. "When you are complete women, Gyne, you are like that krater." The acolytes splashed droplets of water on the faces of the arktoi. "You will grow large and round. You will carry a river of Life within your womb. Artemis will protect you." The singing of the chorus intensified. "But first, the Bear must run free! Rise, bears!"

Slowly, the apprehensive children stood with the bear skins wrapped around them. "Be the bear!" shouted the Priestess. The drumming intensified. "Be the bear!" echoed the acolytes, over and over. Modestly at first, the girls began to stomp on the floor, then wave their arms. "Use your claws!" the Priestess commanded. The girls began to play the bear with greater abandon. They swiped with their "claws", growled and danced with their bearskins swirling around them. "Be the Bear! Be the Bear!" Some began to crawl on all fours, some began to wrestle together, some ran around the courtyard, howling and grimacing. Antiope and Cleis imitated a bear with heavy lumbering strides. But the acolytes took their hands and led them into a frenzied dance. Soon the two companions were swaying and grinding and growling with the rest of the girls.

Tryphaina danced around Psyche, who pretended to fight her off. After a wild chase, Tryphaina caught Psyche, whirled her around and bent her over, in mock replication of bear love. Psyche laughed and broke free. They crawled on the floor, pacing around each other, snarling and clawing.

"To the Cave!" the crone shouted. "To the Cave," echoed the acolytes!" In wild abandon, the girls followed the procession beyond the portico, around the Temple of Artemis. They splashed into the Sacred Spring and moved onto the Great Rock, where the promenade came to halt.

Moving slowly to the front of the line, the Crone announced, "Soon the bears will be no more." The acolytes passed torches among the retinue and the flames created wavering shadows upon the rock. The redolence of moist soil and stone accompanied the procession into the depths of the sanctuary. The Priestess and her acolytes chanted repeatedly, "Birth to Death to Rebirth," as they descended into the bowels of the earth.

They moved into a smaller chamber filled with bones and ash. Suddenly, with the deep sustained clang of the gong, a fire burst in front of a large statue.

In the forefront of the statue, a man is on his knees with his arms in front of him in supplication. Next to him is a familiar Artemis statue, laying on its side. The man is pleading with a woman who stands proud with a veil on her head and a staff in her hand. Behind the woman is Artemis, with tiara in her hair, and quiver at her shoulder. Artemis has one hand on the shoulder of the woman. Her other hand is grasping the antlers of a deer. Her grip is firm; the deer cannot escape.

In a flash of sudden insight, Cleis recognizes the scene being depicted. Iphigenia was not sacrificed. Artemis saved her! Her brother, Orestes, pilfered a statue of Artemis. In the irony of fate, it is Iphigenia, who became a warrior queen, to pass judgment upon her own brother. For eternity, the myths of Iphigenia and Artemis will be entwined. The Crone spoke. "Attica is under the protection of Athena. But others are respected. Proceed!"

They departed from the Cave and continued their torch-lit procession under the gaze of the moon. The aulos made a deep croaking sound and drums beat slowly to direct the pace of their steps. Emerging from the Great Rock, they marched to the Temple of Artemis. "Now the bears will die," announced the Crone. She unlocked the great door and her acolytes opened the entranceway.

Again, a fire emerged with the gong's command. Two statues stood side by side. At the left was Artemis; but not the Artemis they recognized. The virgin Huntress and guardian of the wild things had transformed. She no longer wore a tiara but a round helmet that was flat on top. On either side of her head was a veil that contained the images of other gods and goddesses. Below her waist were renditions of animal creatures. And most surprising was the ornamentation of her chest. Were they numerous breasts? Or gourds? Perhaps a round fruit?

"Artemis the Wild One is changed. She nurtures. She oversees children and pregnant women. Now, girls, surrender your bear skins! Remove them!"

The girls dropped the heavy pelts from their bodies. Standing exposed before the flaming pyre, they turned their attention to the other statue.

"The bear cubs are dead!" proclaimed the Crone! "Hera will now command! The girls are gone, the Women emerge!" The acolytes sang and clapped in joyful celebration. Relieved to understand that the "sacrifice" was only symbolic, the girls joined the jubilee.

But Cleis once again stared into the face of Hera. She did not feel joyous. She felt defiant!

----- ----- -----

Despite her reluctance to attend the Arkteia, Cleis was sad when it was time to leave. Her philia with Antiope had grown into a true friendship. Psyche was a little too vain, but her wise quips and playful manner delighted Cleis. Tryphaina revealed to her that women have desire just as strong as men. Cleis was no longer ashamed of feelings in her body or fantasies in her mind. She was just like the other women.

Cleis had also absorbed the unrestrained spontaneity of the younger girls. She adored their dancing and running and singing, she laughed when they splashed each other at the Sacred Spring, and she admired their abilities to climb rocks as well as paint pretty pictures; to run freely as well as patiently read their lessons.

At fifteen, Cleis should already be married and provide the family with a valuable dowry. But Cleis didn't want to marry; she wanted to enjoy the freedom of the young girls. As she packed her belongings for the final ceremony, she reached into her sack and retrieved the figure of Atalanta, the Amazon princess. No one could tame her; Hippomenes never dared to try. They lived as equal partners, rode horses, shared in the hunt and the daily chores. Her very name, Atalanta, meant, "equal harmony." She studied her favorite doll with precision: the well-folded chiton with her war belt around her waist, the greave shin guards and cuirasses breastplate of a true warrior, the long straight javelin and the reliable quiver and bow across her shoulders. The doll had a removable shield and helmet that Cleis adjusted frequently since early childhood.

One last time, the gong sounded and the mournful melody of the diaulos played as the initiated neophytes entered the courtyard. The acolytes were young women who served for two years. The old Priestess was long past child-bearing age and retained the wisdom of time.

"It is time to shed the skin of childhood," the Priestess declared. "The playthings of youth must now be exchanged for the joys of full womanhood." The tambours were pounded and the flutes blown as the girls marched toward the fire pit. It was difficult to part with cherished objects and most of the girls cried and sought comfort from each other. With great misery, Psyche dropped her mirror into the flame, which grew as lotion jars, dolls, board games, old clothes, and numerous other remnants of a lost life were consumed in the blaze. The acolytes roamed among the pupils and passed out new gifts for the new women. Antiope was given an epinetron, a rounded clay cover for her knee and thigh. The contrivance was adorned in colorful print of a woman spinning wool. It made spinning more comfortable. Cleis was awarded her own distaff, the elakate, with hook and weight. Her weight, the sphondylos, was intricately embellished with miniature replicas of a peacock and a cow, favored animals of Hera. Psyche was enthralled by her weaving spatula, the spathe. Tryphaina was happy with a carding comb, the kteis.

Every arktoi received two final gifts. The first was a Phulakia for, "protection against". Some of the younger girls were confused by the cloth object and the older pupils explained and demonstrated how to use it. The girls never before were concerned about the monthly flow; but from then on, they had to practice modesty. The second final gift was the zone, the belt they would now wear as designation of their womanhood. They would learn how to create the folds in their chitons and peplos that would usually conceal the zone.

When all the souvenirs of childhood were turned to ash, the entourage moved to their rooms for dinner. The salad was fresh from the field and sardines were immersed in a warm porridge of barley and beans. In a surprise gesture in recognition of their new status, the women were served cups of diluted wine. The two slave girls sat patiently while the initiates fingered their repast.

Cleis called to the slaves and offered them a scoop of beans and olives. Coy at first, the girls finally relented and thanked Cleis with deep bows from their knees. Following her lead, Antiope tossed the slaves a bunch of grapes. Not to be outdone, Psyche and Tryphaina showed the slave girls how to dip their mazza into the porridge. The moist barley mixed with the herbs of the porridge. In time, the room was filled with laughter and relaxed conversation. The slave girls were sisters from Phrygia who were part of a barter. They accepted their fate easily and appreciated the chance to speak with actual citizens.

When the dinner was completed, the slaves removed the trays and the roommates prepared for bed. Cleis reclined on her mattress and hid her Atalanta doll in her satchel.

When the day was ending and the women were falling into sleep, screams startled them from their reverie. The acolytes were running through the stoa and shouting to each other. They ran to one of the rooms and the older pupils followed them. They paused at the chamber where several of the roommates were crying and wailing. The old crone lumbered to the entrance, stared into the room, and sighed.

Cleis stared fixedly at the familiar girl suspended from a rafter. She had used the zone as a noose. "There is often one," mumbled the crone as the sliced through the zone with her sickle.

"We will take her to Iphigenia. To be with the other lost babies."
The acolytes silently carried the body to the cave as the entourage
stood in silent lamentation.

6

WEDDING ARRANGEMENTS

*E*urybiades was a good man. He had served courageously as a hoplite in the Spartan infantry, when they successfully repelled the invaders from the Peloponnese. He had escaped the infamae of his family of wandering actors to gain the status of an Athenian dignitae. Although he was not awarded Athenian citizenship, he did well as a money-lender for traveling merchants and shared a reasonable commission from their imports. He was registered as a foreign metic and liked to display his pass when necessary. Now approaching forty years of age, he yearned to have his own family.

Eurybiades was fond of Cleis whom he knew since she was ten years old. He had watched her romping in the agora with her brother and running through the fields of her father's farmland. He had approached her father, Damiskos, when Cleis was at the typical age of twelve to request her hand in marriage. They were close to a dowry settlement when the spunky child displayed her rebellious spirit and her mother pleaded her case. But now Cleis had completed the Arkteia, had won her zone belt, and was almost beyond the age of marriage.

The Fates had been kind. The blight of last year and the current year's drought had resulted in a poor yield. Eurybiades had no choice but to place a horos upon the farmer's land, to demarcate an area that was being held until debts were paid. Draco, the new tyrant of Attica, had created a written code of laws to counter the whims of the oligarchy. The written laws had put an end to the chaos of the entitled class; but the code was strict and rigid. There was no grey area to negotiate. Consequently, a landlord had the full authority of the state to uphold his claim. An unpaid debt resulted in the seizure of land. The statute was like a double-sided battle-axe. The land is held hostage; but if the farmer couldn't work the land, he'd be unable to repay the loan. This situation conferred upon Eurybiades a significant leverage. Eurybiades preferred amicable relations with his potential father-in-law; but the periokoi of such land could easily become a serf, a helot, to a wealthy metic because of his debts.

Besides, the age difference was just about right and proper. He was thirty-eight and Cleis was fifteen. Competitors would probably be disinclined to pursue a maiden of such an advanced age.

The road to the Damiskos farm was less than a day's ride from Athens. With his two armed companions, all veterans of the Peloponnese battles, bandits would be ill-advised to challenge them. Nonetheless, a small encounter at a roadside tavern convinced the travelers to stay alert. Corinthian vassals with a grudge against Sparta noticed the lambda symbol on his shield. That particular symbol on his aspis provoked them like a loud insult.

Eurybiades sat in a corner with his mates. They wanted only to rest their horses, enjoy some fish stew with a rough bread of barley, and sip some adequate wine. When the Corinthians approached and sat down with dark sneers and sarcastic affronts, their leader banged his helmet, with its familiar horsehair crest, on the table. Eurybiades did try to resolve the situation. He knew the battles of which they spoke and noted that they fought gloriously. He reminded them that the battles were not personal. They were all hoplites and did their jobs with honor and courage. They clicked wine goblets, shook hands, and the Corinthians seemed to depart peacefully.

But when the trio retrieved their horses from the stable boy, and were ready to mount, their adversaries reappeared with their hands near their swords. The time for words had passed; weapons were unsheathed in a gleaming moment. After watchful pacing and circling, swords met with a jangle of bronze and iron. The reverberation of battle brought curious onlookers from the inn and the stable. The Corinthians fought with skill and never lost balance. But the experience of the Spartans, with their sharpened reflexes, proved decisive. Eurybiades parried a sudden advance with a javelin by maneuvering a slippery feint and following with a side thrust. The javelin deflected easily off his shield while Eurybiades swung his xiphos to a side glance on his opponent. The blade evaded the breastplate and found its mark.

His two companions readily dispatched their challengers, who suffered wounds to their arms and legs. The Corinthians yielded; but the Spartans did not relax until the vanquished withdrew on horseback through the forest. Fortunately, none of the injuries were serious. All the blood was from the surface. The victors sheathed their swords, accepted the compliments of the witnesses, finished their meal and wine, and, with a few bandages, resumed their journey. The simple confrontation added a spark to their conversation as they traveled the path north of Eleusis toward the Parnes range. At the foot of those mountains was the farmland of Damiskos and his family.

Eurybiades was almost grateful to the Corinthians for the minor skirmish. It renewed his vigor that had been drained on the rigorous journey. War was simple, he thought. Fight. Survive or die. Every one dies, Eurybiades conceded, and a glorious death is far superior to a protracted life that lingered to a feeble death. The priests tell tales of dead souls in Hades and of heroes returning from the Underworld. But Eurybiades knew better. The surge of life that flows with each battle is the only true resurrection. With a laugh, he thought of all the times he had been re-born. To fear death is foolish. To live every moment is true happiness! One more stop at a refreshing stream gave Eurybiades the chance to prepare for the arrival at his destination.

----- ----- -----

The family heard the horse hoofs pounding the dirt path like the grumblings of Hades when Persephone escaped with her pomegranate seeds. The slaves saw the dust and heard the snorting of the galloping horses as a field of birds flew from the incursion. Damiskos and Menares emerged from the farmhouse, with hands on their swords, to confront the xenoi and defend the women. Cleis and her mother peered from a window with curiosity and terror. Two loyal slaves grabbed staffs and axes, ready to fight to the death if necessary.

The leading interloper pulled his horse to a stop in front of the farmer. When the hoplite swept aside his cape, he revealed a gleaming panoply that was meant for intimidation. The helmet he wore was clearly Spartan. With its round head covering and visor, the man's face was completely concealed. His shield displayed the familiar lambda of Sparta. His bronze thorax, wrapped across his chest, held a depiction of the fearsome

Gorgon with her hair of whirling snakes and her expression of pure wrath. The greaves which covered his shins were embellished with bolts of Zeus' lighting.

When the warrior removed his helmet and shook his hair, Damiskos exhaled with relief. Eurybiades drop his head backwards and released a hearty laugh. The other vassals removed their own helmets and radiated large smiles. Damiskos and Eurybiades embraced and slapped each other's back. After the welcoming, introductions were exchanged.

Damiskos turned to his house and peered at the window. "Come out," he called to the women with a great wave. "There's nothing to fear. It's Eurybiades! Come!"

Reassured, Cleis and her mother stepped out from the shadows and stepped warily toward the visitors. When Eurybiades noticed Cleis, he was impressed.

"Is that Cleis?" he asked in joyful surprise. With roving eyes, he examined her veraciously. "A fine woman now. My patience has been rewarded."

The slaves brought the horses to the barn for a cooling wash and a well-deserved meal. Eurybiades approached Cleis and she stepped back from him.

"Don't dodge me again, girl," he exclaimed. "I've waited long enough for you." He spied the zone around her waist and the delicate fold of her peplos. "You have completed the Arkteia. Good."

He removed his glove and stroked her cheek. "Soft, beautiful," he murmured half to himself. "A man needs a good woman."

Confused and frightened, Cleis turned to her father with fear written across her face.

49

Damiskos casually explained to Cleis. "Four years ago, the arrangement was made. But you were young and defiant. Now it's almost too late. But Eurybiades has patiently waited for you. Now we can complete the arrangement."

Comprehension began its stranglehold around Cleis but she continued to cling to bewilderment. "What arrangement?" she snarled.

"Your marriage, of course," answered Damiskos with a wide-mouthed smile. Cleis felt panic surging from her groin to her head. A stab of deep emptiness cut through her stomach while air seemed to vanish from her body. She turned to her mother, who was nodding and smiling. Her expression seemed to communicate pride! The befuddled girl began to wobble as she became unsteady on her feet. The bright day was turning dark for her and she began to tremble as if she were cold.

----- ----- -----

The roses were bright red and their fragrance surrounded her. Deer were grazing in a large meadow and a gentle pool was filling with the cascade of a soft waterfall. Sparrows and doves landed next to her. She could hear the loud buzzing of bees. At a nearby promontory, a woman was seated upon a flat boulder. In her lap, the woman was strumming a lyre. Seven strings extended from the crossbar to a tailpiece that was a turtle shell. The shell had been painted black but with golden symbols. The woman held one of the two arms that were gently curved. With her other hand, she deftly played a delicate melody. As she approached the woman, Cleis took note of the golden symbols on the tailpiece: several doves, two geese, leaping dolphins, playful sparrows, and goats. Around the edge of the shell were wandering bees circling roses and grapes. The woman stopped playing and turned to Cleis. She then bit into a red apple. Cleis knew comprehension was emerging. The realization was coming to her... but she woke up too soon.

She was lying in her own bed and her chiton had been loosened. But neither mother nor father was sitting by her side. Instead, it was Eurybiades! With his panoply removed, she saw the older man next to her. She tried to bolt up; but the hoplite put his strong hand upon her shoulder and gently eased her back down. Cleis tried to stay strong but she couldn't suppress a whimper. Eurybiades placed a cool cloth on her forehead and spoke softly.

"Easy, girl. You need to rest. You'll recover soon." She made an effort to comply but her trembling and her sobs overwhelmed her willpower. "That's good," he declared. "Let the forces come out. Just like your lunar flow, women need to release their heat." He stroked her legs and studied the ample shape of her limbs. "A truly beautiful woman," he asserted with reverence. "You are the perfect wife for me." She remained silent and stiff on the mattress. "Let me show you something." He rose from her bedside and went to his panoply that was piled at the other wall. He brought back several articles and showed them to her.

"This is one of my greaves," he explained. "They protect my legs in battle. Touch it!" She touched the hardened bronze. Then he tapped it. "See? Strong and solid, eh? But watch." He turned the greave over to reveal the inside that would make contact with his leg. It was layered with lambskin and cotton. "Here. Touch that." She complied to his command. It was pleasantly soft and fluffy. "See, the greave is hard on one side to protect me, but it has a soft tender inside. Trust me. That is just like me. I am strong and hard when necessary; but I can also be very tender." He leaned in and kissed her on the lips. "I will be a good husband," he whispered.

As he continued to stroke her arms and forehead, Cleis turned her head and spied the Gorgoneia on his shield with glaring eyes and a mouth in livid fulmination. She recalled the myth of how Poseidon had raped Medusa in the Temple of Athena. The transgression led to punishment by Athena---of the girl! Her beautiful hair was turned into snakes. Athena again betrayed Medusa by scheming with Perseus to destroy the Gorgon. Perseus, the hero, was the ancestor to Heracles, another hero who raped and murdered and plundered his way across the known world. Heracles, who murdered his own family, killed Hippolyta, and ran off with her belt! He defeated Amazon warriors only because he wore a magic lion skin! The myths did not inspire pride for Cleis. Realizing the truth behind the legends, she felt a searing rage that matched the fury of Medea. Restraining the passion, Cleis was overcome with fever, a painful headache, blurred vision, and burning irritation across her skin.

Despite the cold compresses, Eurybiades could not abate the fires in her body. She began to scratch her arms with her sharpened nails, causing red streaks.

"I know what's wrong with you," he declared as he pinned her arms to the bed. "You're already fifteen and your woman heat has not been released sufficiently." Cleis squirmed and wailed but no one came to her aid. They knew the remedy as well. "Quiet, girl. I don't want to hit you. Stop!" She tried to calm down and pleaded with him to be merciful.

He raised his sword and, with a swift stroke, sliced through her chiton. Then he stood up but kept his sword pointed at her throat. He rapidly removed his own garments. "I've tamed wild horses with less spirit than you," he snarled. "Those horses learned to obey me. So will you. See how the gods embolden me!" He pointed to his engorged phallus, firm and ready to advance. "Look!" he commanded. "It is our destiny! Would you be like Myrrha, deny marriage, and doom Adonis?"

He dropped on top of her as she cried uncontrollably. "Stop fighting and you'll have less pain," he directed. "Accept your husband. Open yourself!"

Cleis repeated, "No, no," mostly to herself, as if in prayer. Where was Artemis now? Why did Athena not intervene? Perhaps it had to be this way, she concluded, as the full impact of Eurybiades' manhood pierced her defenses. His thrusts were like the cleaving of the priest as he sacrificed a bull. Would the augur examine her entrails, she wondered, to determine how well the crops would grow? Would her blood be spread to fertilize the fields? At Brauron, they spoke of sacrifice. Now she understood the greater implication. Must women always be the sacrifice to keep the heavens in order?

With a deep moan, Eurybiades stopped thrusting and fell upon her like a wounded warrior. She felt fluids mingling within her womb and dripping on her legs. Eurybiades rose slightly and removed himself from her sanctum. He looked down between her thighs and smiled. "It is done," he pronounced. "Look for yourself."

Cleis rose from her chest and followed his direction. She looked at the place of shame and saw patches of red blood staining the white sheet. She looked up at her conqueror who beheld her with sincere admiration. "You are a marvelous woman," he asserted. "Despite my experience with the hetairae and the bonds with the boys in my command, you impress me."

Cleis was not sure if she were complemented or offended. "So I'm better than the whores and the boys," she grumbled.

"Yes," replied Eurybiades with no hesitation. "But let me correct you. The hetairae aren't just coarse porne. They're intelligent, philosophical, musical, and poetic. For lonely hoplites, they are an oasis in a world of pain and blood and death."

Unable to render any other action, Cleis began to laugh. "You just took my virginity. You hurt me but I surrendered to you. I am bleeding for you like a sacrificial goat. And you choose to speak lovingly of the hetairae!" Her laughter bordered on hysteria and mixed with tears that gushed like the overflowing Nile. "I'm only to be your wife. I would never be intelligent or philosophical or musical or poetic like those well-trained professionals!" Her sarcasm cut like a concealed kopis with a sharpened blade.

"Do you want to?" asked Eurybiades in bewilderment. "Why would you need to? You'll be occupied with the duties of a wife."

She rose like a snake and hissed. "Get out!" She picked up his greave and threw it at him; then the other. Eurybiades dodged her throws easily and laughed happily. "You'll be happy in Sparta," he exclaimed. "Those women enjoy fighting just like you." Purposely taking his time, perhaps to demonstrate that he was the master and she could not make commands, he put his clothes on and affixed his panoply. "We've done what was necessary. Every woman must endure the first time. It is done. Your new life begins. Rejoice." While she whimpered in the corner of her bed, he continued. "We need to finish this wedding ritual. Mount the wagon and wear the veil. Come to me with joyful music and dancing. Bite the apple I will offer."

Her whimpering stopped. She crouched in her bed and glared at him. "I hate you," she hissed.

"Don't be a silly child," he retorted. "Your father's debts are cleared. His farm is liberated. You have a wealthy husband. I waived a dowry. What else do you want, woman?"

She wanted to answer his question, but was at a loss. Whatever it was she needed could not be readily defined. But she could sense something in her struggling heart, her forced breath, her racing thoughts, and some undigested clump in her stomach. Unable to voice her resistance, she continued to glower.

"Clean yourself," he enjoined. "Present yourself for the ritual."

Wedding Celebration

The women of the village were busy preparing the wedding feast. Cleis' mother was in command in her realm, the kitchen. She inspected the food as it arrived to assure freshness and purity. She supervised the cooks in how to cut meats and vegetables for eager hands, and how to properly dilute the wines. She watched the stew churning in the cauldron and directed slaves when and how to stir the ingredients.

Since the wedding party would not be traveling to the home of Eurybiades, it was necessary to improvise. The wagon with the bride would start from the stable and Eurybiades would wait for her in the farmhouse. Coming from Sparta, Eurybiades would have preferred a simple mock duel with his wife. Then, as the victor, he would've carried her to his quarters to consummate the marriage. But Athenians always sought to be more civilized in their public displays; so he consented to wait for his veiled bride with an apple instead of a sword.

Eurybiades, Damiskos, and Menares sat in the farmhouse pouring over a game of Mancala. Two played while the third waited his turn with the winner. At the moment, Menares was the observer as Eurybiades and Damiskos faced off. The smooth polished stones were moved deftly around the board as the contestants applied their strategies. Menares enjoyed ridiculing his father when blunders were made but Damiskos often disproved the criticism of his son. Eurybiades was skilled at concealing emotion when he made his moves; but displayed an open smile at the moment of victory. Damiskos grunted his concession and Menares took his position to face the Spartan.

While Menares placed his stones in their starting pockets, Damiskos joked with his new son-in-law. "From the sounds we heard, I believe the marriage has been consummated?" Damiskos laughed aloud.

Eurybiades replied in the camaraderie of men. "No more difficult than breaking a wild horse!" he exclaimed. His remark was met with joyous accord.

"It was past time," noted Damiskos. "Thank you."

"I know we reversed the tradition. I should've waited for my bride to arrive in the cart with a veil on her head. Then I would have given her the apple."

"It's fine," replied Damiskos. "I'm sure you gave her plenty." Uproarious laughter.

But Menares was reserved. He was concerned for his sister and felt he had somehow betrayed her. He made his moves automatically but his mind was elsewhere. He was thinking about the times Cleis had raced him up the hill to the acropolis. More times, she won the race. He recalled their evenings atop the Pnyx and shared stories about stars. They wondered if the nimbus of the night sky was really the milk from Hera's breasts. Some of the stars were the wandering planets, possibly Hermes, Aphrodite, and Ares. The moon, going through its monthly cycle of waxing and waning, seemed to mirror the path of human life. He loved the nature walks with Cleis, who knew the names of animals, plants, and trees and the goddesses affiliated with them. The spirit of Artemis flowed through her body. With his mind distracted, it was easy for Eurybiades to capture the stones. Menares congratulated him and then excused himself to get some air.

Resigned, defeated, and exhausted, Cleis washed her face and hair. She fastened her white chiton with the golden peronei Eurybiades had given her. She painted her face with white lead. She ran her fingers through the delicate veil her mother had made. She picked up the zone and planned to create a kolpos, the subtle fold of the chiton at the waist. Holding the zone in both hands, she thought about the poor girl at the Arkteia. Cleis sat on her bed with deep remorse. The girl was so sad and quiet. Cleis understood the girl's distress but never spoke to her or tried to comfort her. Cleis wondered who would comfort her at the moment of her own distress. She looked up to the ceiling and noticed several solid beams supporting the roof. At most, Cleis weighed about one hundred thirty pounds. The beams would easily hold that weight. If she stood on her bed, she could fasten the zone to the beam. Her neck was small and didn't require a lot of cord. Staring at the ceiling and burnishing the zone with her fingers, Cleis was at the borderland between life and death. She knew her death would disrupt all the family plans. Her father would be dishonored and Eurybiades would be vindictive. Under the code of Draco, her father would lose the farm and possibly be reduced to a helot. But, if she went on living, it would be a walking death. She wrapped the zone around her neck.

Menares walked into her room and saw a pathetic sight. His proud, assertive sister sat listlessly in her bed, her face smothered in white lead, with the wedding veil on her lap and the zone around her neck. She was staring at the ceiling in a dispassionate state. "Cleis," he stammered softly. "Don't make this mistake."

"Leave me, Menares. I need to be alone."

Menares nodded anxiously. "Like that girl you told me about, strangled by her own zone. No. I won't leave you alone right now." He sat next to her and removed the noose. "Listen to me. Complete the wedding. Bite the apple. In time, if the situation doesn't improve, then leave him. There may be some anger and noise but it will pass. But you'll have to..."

"What?" growled Cleis. "What will I have to do?"

Menares looked at the floor and took a breath. "You'll need to support yourself."

She laughed acerbically. "I'm musical and philosophical and poetic," she scoffed. "I escape one man to be bought by all others! That's my choice?"

"One step at a time," he replied. "First, we celebrate your marriage." He took her hand. "Cleis, I will always be your brother. We'll deal with circumstances together."

"You make a lot of sense," she conceded. "I know I confuse every one. I'm confused myself. I know the traditions. I know what's expected of me. But I can't comply. It's like a daemon has possessed me. Nothing fits for me."

"There is no daemon," said Menares as he embraced his sister. "But you are fighting some kind of war." He kissed her cheek. "The first battle is this wedding."

----- ----- -----

The groom stood by the portico of the farmhouse as the plow horse pulled the wagon toward him with his veiled bride who stood in the carriage. Behind the wagon, the procession played music, sang songs of celebration, and danced. The wagon stopped at the homestead and Damiskos took the hand of his daughter, who stepped down and walked to her groom. He was in full panoply with his longer cape and open helmet. She came to the portico and Damiskos handed her to Eurybiades. The hoplite lifted her veil and gazed upon her whitened visage. She offered the smile of a compliant slave. Eurybiades held out the apple. She thought of the golden apple that provoked a competition between the goddesses and caused the Trojan War. She recalled the apples that tricked Atalanta into marriage. She took the fruit, looked at her husband, gazed upon her family, and made the fateful bite. From that moment on, her husband would feed her.

8

CLEIS FLEES

Eurybiades frequently promised Cleis that he would take her to his estate in Sparta, but business concerns caused delays in that plan. As a money-lender, he needed to oversee his investments and negotiate regular trades. While awaiting their future journey, Cleis was confined to two gloomy rooms in a small apartment near the port of Athens. Although she was confined to the dark dwelling, the noise of the outside world disturbed her concentration and disrupted her sleep. Bacchanalian revelers sang and cursed and yelled, porne provoked and prodded potential customers, babies howled and dogs barked. Even worse, devious bandits and burglars could be heard whispering their incoherent schemes and slithering along the cobblestoned walkway. Cleis felt abandoned and unprotected. She kept sticks and knives nearby.

Even when Eurybiades was home, he wasn't really with her. They slept in separate rooms. Cleis spent most of her day wearing a veil and shopping for dinner. Eurybiades usually came home spent from the business, and pleasure, of the day. He washed quickly in the water Cleis had fetched from the local well and then warmed for him. Pouring his arms in the large krater and splashing his face, his daily hygiene was complete. For dinner, they reclined around a small wooden table and Cleis served the trays. He ate heartily and grunted his approval. Wiping his mouth with his sleeve, he proclaimed, "You're a good cook, wife. Your mother taught you well." Eurybiades removed his peplos and went to his bed.

Cleis followed him to his chamber and laid next to him. The smells of the marketplace, and the perfumes from other venues, emanated from his body. Like a dog, she could discern the story of his day from the various scents, odors, fragrances, and incense he emitted.

Before their marriage, his lust for her was unstoppable. He ravished her with the fury of a warrior in battle. For two months after their nuptials, he invaded, conquered, and colonized every detail of her body. Once her continent was despoiled, and all the mysteries exposed, he grew restless and sought new territory to exploit. Like depleted farmland, Cleis no longer sprouted with desire or bloomed with allure. Eurybiades was like a bee seeking new pollen and sweeter honey.

Cleis remained focused and was determined to make her escape. But first, she had to take the necessary precautions. She knew of women who had suffered painful childbirth only to lose their lives. Often the baby also died. She knew, of course, how infant girls were frequently discarded in the forest or the mountain to die of exposure, get eaten by beasts, or be confiscated for other uses.

In her regular jaunt to the agora, Cleis listened to the local gossip, spoke to foreign slaves, and confided to midwives. Her efforts led her a well-known mágissa. After a modest exchange of coins, the woman revealed the secrets of plants and herbs. The kindly practitioner took Cleis for a walk in the woods. Even in the age of Draco, there was no crime in taking a hike and picking flowers. Unripened acacia mixed with honey, a costly silphium from Africa, crushed juniper berries, and the lacy wild carrot were all known to be effective. Blending the flora with honey and cotton enhanced their power.

As they rambled along the forest of Athens, Cleis spoke of the turbulence in her life. The wise woman nodded attentively and assured Cleis of her compassionate understanding. When she shared her plan of escape, the woman paused and issued a warning. "Your husband, this Eurybiades, will soon be searching for you. Many a young bride seeks passage on a ship in Athens. But they're often captured and punished severely in public!"

Cleis was alone, with no family or confidants. She needed the wisdom of the mágissa. "Help me, I beg you. What should I do?"

The woman sat on a rock and considered the situation. "Do you have one friend who might assist you?"

Cleis remembered the Arkteia. "There was another participant at Brauron. She also seeks escape."

"Good. Stay with her. Hide in her dwelling for at least a week. In time, your husband will concede that you have eluded him. He'll move on to another pasture. But do not embark on a boat in Athens. Go to Piraeus instead. On your way, you can explain to curious strangers that you're on a pilgrimage to Delphi. Be convincing. Travel in a modest and pious manner. Piraeus is for merchants, seafarers, and hetaerae. You can easily get lost in the bedlam." It was prudent advice.

So far, the herbs, and Eurybiades' sudden loss of ardor, had kept her field safely fallow; but she knew it was just a matter of time. She had to act quickly.

Once Eurybiades left for his daily activities, Cleis packed a sack with as many items as she could carry. Folded chitons and peplos took little space. Extra sandals and under garments were easy to bundle. A water flask and some food would sustain her. She took several coins, rationalizing that her services garnered some payment. Atalanta was carefully included in the folds. That doll had become her talisman. Once she abandoned her marriage, Cleis would have no family, no clan, no tribe. The Little Atalanta would be her only clan. She would be a woman who had dishonored her family, especially her father. The punishment could be severe.

Cleis wore a peplos with a hood. She arrived at the statue of Hermes, always with an erect phallus, that marked the area of the agora. Porne with bejeweled sandals and inviting gestures were attracting male attention. The contradictions of Athens fascinated her.

Her simple plan was to linger at the market, and overhear the casual chatter of the merchants and musicians. She would make casual inquiries about her friend, Antiope.

As she wandered through the market, she came upon a mob of hundreds of boisterous people. Jeers and shouts passed among the crowd who, she realized, was a jury. A trial was in process. Peeking between heads and shoulders, Cleis caught a glimpse of the great Archon Draco, seated upon the bima. Instead of a laurel wreath, his was golden. His peplos was glaringly white as he slumped in his chair and listened to the plaintiff and litigant present their case. The defendant was caught in bed, in the husband's house, with the man's wife. The man could not deny that fact. But, according to the written laws of Draco, it was necessary to ascertain if the defendant was actually observed in coitus with the woman. If the cuckold proved they were having intercourse, the interloper faced instant death.

"Were they in the act?" demanded Draco, to the crowd's amusement. "Did you see him inside her?"

The husband was agitated. "They were in my bed!" he declared. "They were both naked."

Draco turned to the accused. "Can you explain that?"

The man anxiously replied. "I was consoling her." The crowd roared with laughter. Cleis was both astonished and amused.

"Consoling her, eh?" Draco rubbed his chin. "This city has many women you could have 'consoled'." The enormous jury was bursting with tears of hilarity.

The man's tentative reply was memorable. "With hetaerae, it's a business negotiation. But my relationship with his wife is personal and intimate. I care deeply."

Draco arose from his chair. "Enough! Let the jury decide. The sex act was not witnessed. But they were found in the husband's bed." Women were not permitted to testify so no one heard the wife's version. "If they had performed an act in the street, we could impose a fine and be done with it. But the man was in the marital bed. That's serious!" The massive congregation began to murmur and argue. The debating lasted twenty minutes.

With shouts and laughter, a verdict was rendered. The man was guilty of trespassing and non-consensual use of the other man's property. Two large hoplites seized the man and tore off his peplos. He was held standing naked before the throng.

Draco pronounced the sentence. "Because he made use of another man's female, the defendant shall now be the female for the offended husband." The husband pulled out a sharp knife and approached the accused. Cleis was terrified, anticipating a public castration. But the husband proceeded to shave the man's pubic hair. "Bald as a baby girl!" shouted a member of the massive jury. The shout turned into a repetitive chant.

Squirming and pleading, the man was placed on his stomach and pinned to the floor by the two warriors. The husband produced a rather large staff. The guilty man screamed in pain as the husband made the angry insertion. The man cried uncontrollably as the husband moved in coital oscillations. The mob laughed, whistled and clapped as they emptied their wine flasks and joked.

"Justice has been done," proclaimed Draco with a chortle.

The husband's vengeance was not yet complete. He stomped into the crowd and reached for his unfaithful wife. She was sobbing and wailing as he dragged her to the podium. When they reached the Archon, the husband began to slap the woman repeatedly until she collapsed on the bima. The drunken mob applauded their consent.

Cleis found her determination intensified. "This ignorant mass just left their drunken symposia, spent the coins of their labor on professional hetaerae, and now condemn two people who dared to love each other!" She pounded her fists against a stone kouris of a young boy. "The punishments served to satisfy the mob's perverse curiosity." She decided to leave Attica with no further delay.

----- ----- -----

The healer permitted Cleis to stay in her hut in the forest for one day. Any sojourn beyond that would have been too dangerous. The mágissa, in her work with many wealthy and powerful patrons, had worked as an herbalist, midwife, and sorceress. She knew many secrets of the dignita and their wives. This gave her tremendous leverage in her "magic". If a tradesman needed a favorable judgment from a magistrate, the healer would pay an evening visit. A simple reminder of a buried scandal could impact the magistrate's verdict. Of course, the tradesman thought it was an herbal concoction she threw in a fire, while chanting incoherent syllables, that caused the miracle. The woman's reputation grew; but so did her list of enemies. Hiding a man's wife could provide "evidence" of her malicious enchantments.

Cleis wandered through the agora and visited several temples. As she ascended the sacred path to the acropolis, wearing her modest himation and veil, she recognized Antiope just a few steps in front of her. Remaining discreet, Cleis increased the pace of her steps until she was aside her friend. Antiope turned her head to look at the veiled woman next to her but showed no sign of recognition. Cleis subtly moved her veil and Antiope's eyes brightened. With minimal expression, Antiope murmured to her, "Meet me at the Erichthonius," and rushed up the path. Cleis was confused but was growing less reactive to surprises or disappointments.

At the summit of the Cecropia, Cleis came to the Temple of Erichthonius and was struck by the columns that supported the structure. They were caryatids, sculpted female figures. Once again, the baffling ambivalence toward women intrigued her. Strong females, holding up a Temple to a legendary hero, oversee a city where women are of little value. Eurybiades told her it was different in Sparta; but Cleis had no desire to train for military action.

Antiope was dropping incense into a fire near an altar. When Cleis approached, Antiope remained aloof. Gazing into the multicolored sparks of the flame, Cleis addressed her. "I've been searching for you. I miss you." Antiope did not speak. Cleis made another effort. "Should I leave you?" she inquired.

Antiope's reply was sudden and firm. "No!" She gave Cleis directions to her quarters and added, "Don't touch me or embrace me. Come to my home tonight." She turned from Cleis and slipped quietly from the temple. Every loss, every hurt, every disappointment, was leaving a cleave on Cleis' heart. Wounds do heal but with hardened calluses. Cleis was hardening. A cold barricade was growing around a warm girl who used to laugh and dance with the seasons and play with the raindrops.

----- ----- -----

Antiope's humble dwelling was at the foot of the Acropolis near the Sacred Path. Goats roamed freely behind her home at the base and ridge of the citadel. Cats were chasing mice that scurried around slaves who were washing fabrics in boiling cauldrons. Horse-drawn carts moved carefully through the narrow alleyways, and left dung in their trail. Smoke rose from the flues of each hearth. The aroma of boiling soups, grilled vegetables, and honeyed cakes pervaded the domain.

Cleis remained veiled as she proceeded through the neighborhood and came to Antiope's address. When she knocked on the door, her friend pulled her swiftly into her abode. Antiope then quickly lowered the curtain of her one window.

Safely concealed in the shadows, Antiope turned to her friend, smiled with great affection, and embraced Cleis fiercely. "I miss you, too," she murmured secretively. Although Cleis was relieved by her friend's enduring fondness, she was surprised by her own lack of emotion. Loosening her hold, and with no hesitation, Antiope kissed her gently. "Please forgive my behavior. There's a reason."

They took seats near a small table and poured cups of water. Antiope spoke first. "I remember our plan during the Arkteia. It seemed so simple and so right at the moment." Her eyes darkened and her smile faded. "But since then, things have changed."

Cleis wasn't entirely surprised. "What happened?" she inquired.

"My father arranged a good marriage for me. I always liked him." Antiope couldn't conceal her enthusiasm. "He's a sculptor. He's working on the plans for the new Temple for Zeus!"

Cleis laughed sardonically. "I guess our plan to escape to strange lands is canceled." Antiope responded with an embarrassed pout. "It's fine, my sweet friend. If you're happy, then don't despair. I'm glad for you."

Antiope took Cleis' hands and kissed them. "Thank you. We'll always be friends."

"That's reassuring," replied Cleis. "I do need a favor. May I stay with you for two or three days?"

Antiope was confused. "I thought you lived on a farm and a small home in Athens..." Then she was hit with insight. "You're running away! How? Where would you go?"

"That's why I need three days, to arrange things," she explained. The silence between them grew until distant sounds seemed to blare.

"Yes," Antiope decided. "I'll need to say something to my husband."

"I'm a guest from the country, a friend from the Arkteia. For the people of Athens, generosity to a traveler or foreigner is a great value."

"True. You can sleep with me."

----- ----- -----

Antiope's husband was agreeable to the visit from an Arkteia friend. Having two women to shop and cook was a satisfying proposition. He spoke enthusiastically about the plans for the Temple in honor of the commanding god of the Olympians. The southeast corner of the city was comparatively vacant and that Gate deserved attention. Besides, some distance from the agora, the pnyx, and the Areopagus, would provide greater serenity to the supplicants. The sculptor knew the project might never be completed in his lifetime; but the work itself was just as satisfying as the attainment of a final goal.

Cleis liked him. His enthusiasm for his work was invigorating. His eagerness to share his inspirations with her, a mere woman, was refreshing. Nonetheless, Cleis was unable to relax and remained guarded in his presence. Antiope noticed the change in her friend and asked if they had offended her. Cleis reassured her and explained her behavior as anticipation of her abdication. When he invited her to his work site, Cleis declined politely. Antiope told him she was shy around men, a common attribute of Athenian wives.

The ruse began to unravel. He came home the second day and rushed into his wife's room while the women were weaving new chitons. He was nervous, put his finger to his lips, and spoke in a whisper.

"Today, in the agora, there was a hoplite from Sparta! He was proclaiming his displeasure for a wife who ran away. He demanded her return. He said his name was Eurybiades." Cleis felt a shock of cold run through her body. She was immobile, like a squirrel caught in a trap. The sculptor stared at her. "This hoplite, this Eurybiades, said his wife's name was Cleis."

The women embraced and tried to comfort each other. But they resonated with shared anxiety. Cleis expected no good response from the man. He would risk his entire career as a sculptor if he concealed a runaway wife.

His next remark surprised them. "What are your intensions?" he asked tenderly.

"I'm hoping to get to Piraeus," she stammered.

"I see," he pondered. "A merchant vessel, removed from Athens. Clever girl." He turned to Antiope. "My wife, prepare for a sojourn to Piraeus. I need to make some trades. My tools are worn." He smiled at Cleis. "Pack a lot of blankets. We'll need to keep our cargo safe, eh."

9

SKALA ERESSOS

The Vigla rises like the acropolis of Athens. From her veranda on that elevation, Sappho absorbed inspiration from the natural manifestation of Aphrodite that surrounded her. Beyond the coast, with sands painted grey by an ancient volcano, she could see tiny Psara with its gift of delicious slipper lobster. Further in the mist, she caught a glimpse of Chios and its valuable gum trees.

Well aware of her privileged status on the grand island of Lesvos, Sappho used her position to create a Temenos, a space removed from outside influences. The Vigla serves her well as a peribolas, a barrier against outside intrusions. Nonetheless, her loyal hounds, with the spirit of Artemis, serve as guardians. Within the separated space is her Hieron, her sanctuary. Within those layers of removal from outside disruptions, is her Thiasos, her cult to Aphrodite. Girls of high-rank, plus women with creative spirits, devote themselves to her service. In the cloak of piety, however, many initiates find the opportunity to unburden themselves of social expectations and liberate their expansive nature.

Peering through branches of the overhanging almariki trees, Sappho scans the valley and its busy harbor with its shimmering blue water. She can hear the distant bells of fish-mongers that mingle with the shriek of soaring eagles and the cawing of gulls. She longs to see Charoxos coming into port from his southern journey to Egypt. Her supply of papyrus is dwindling. Despite the expanding community of poets and philosophers on Lesvos, the local merchants have yet to grow accustomed to the written word. On the hilltop, goats are grazing and the mighty oaks of Zeus are withstanding the winds. Egrets find shelter in those strong branches, in nests that are concealed by a thick canopy of leaves. The oikia, or small dwellings, of peasants and tradesmen blanket the mountains that encircle the bay. Heliotropes in full bloom render their sweet honey aroma while roses, exploding with reds and yellows, are joined by purple lilacs dancing in the soft urgings of Zephyr.

Sappho longed for Anaktoria, the "army wife," who left when her husband returned from a Thracian campaign. A wedding and the domestic chores of a traditional family once again crushed the petals of a blooming flower. Anaktoria radiated with poetic abilities; but she chose a home life instead. Sappho knew about Glukupikron, the sweet bitter emotional turmoil of love's twisted pathway. She learned to accept that loss was an inevitable part of expansive love. She resisted possessive love, but still felt the agony of dissolution, and strove to comprehend the source of its pain. Such endless curiosity provoked Sappho to write lyrical sonnets.

Losing one of her "sparrows" to matrimony, Sappho was nonetheless facing the irony of performance at a royal wedding in

Mytilene, the capital of Lesvos. The music would play, the guests would dance, the performers sing; and then Sappho and the other poets would each present a monody, a solitary paean accompanied by lyre and flute. In full voice, Sappho would praise the bride and her lucky groom on their nuptials. She would sing of the joys awaiting the loving couple while she kept her personal opinions concealed.

In her romantic anguish, she was consoled by several of the adherents of her thiasos, her cult to honor and celebrate Aphrodite. The sacred gathering would join in songs of sweet melancholy. Abanthis would pluck her harp strings while golden-haired Gongyla accompanied the songs with her deep-throated flute, hinting of dreams and memories. Raven-haired Kallysta contributed a recent innovation: She applied a soft wooden bow to the strings of a barbiton, and created a scale which ran from harsh to ethereal. From Crete, the former slave, Dika, so impressed Sappho with her musical skills, that her mistress liberated her. The chants and melodies of this chorus aroused images of steep waterfalls cascading into hot thermal pools, of hummingbirds sipping the nectar of the beautiful but deadly delphinium, and of flaming stones racing across the evening sky.

Sappho explored the deep wound of departure like a botanist analyzing the petals and stems of a flower. But she accepted the contingencies of existence.

The philosophers of Miletus spoke of the impermanence of things. Thales saw life as water: ever-flowing, evaporating, raining, and shifting direction. The conquering Odysseus was lost in the throes of a sudden gale. The perfect Achilles defeated by an arrow to the ankle. And the power of a profound love can wane with circumstance. To be a worshipper of Aphrodite, or her alias of the ancient Cytherea, or the Kupris of Crete, is to accept her many moods and states. Where Eros would provoke and torment,

Aphrodite beguiles and intrigues. To truly immerse in the immanence of Love is to volunteer for a perilous journey, with its sanctuaries of sacred jouissance and its vortex of spiraling pain. At both extremes, the voyager is certain of being totally alive. Men spoke of the glories of war; Sappho explored the epic journey of the heart. For Sappho, it was always better to endure such pain than to sacrifice feeling at the altar of the commonplace. But the joy and pain are not separate. To think in such extremes is to take the mind of men. Women respect the subtle variations.

The women of her thiasos understood this and eagerly committed to a Goddess that was different from the other deities of either Olympus or Anatolia. Cybele kindles frenzy. The Palestinian Dionysus incites hysteria. But Aphrodite demands every transformation, each nuance, and total surrender to her natural immanence. She requires profound courage to confront the interior flames of your own soul.

Holding the plectrum in her fingers, Sappho plucked the strings of her barbiton, with its deep resonant tones. Alcaeus, grateful for the honor of being a male presence in her enclave, joined her with the lighter strings of his lyre. Gongyla, with her cheeks strapped, supplied depth with her diaulo. Abanthis met the instruments with a muted song that intensified to a proud proclamation of human resilience. The other girls provided the chorus, alternating west for the strophe and east for the antistrophe. As the music brought them into a state of reverie, Sappho began to recite. The words came from a sacred realm in the center of her vitality. She didn't know if she was creating the stanzas; or if she was a medium for the goddess. Perhaps it didn't matter. She and her beloved were one. Three long iambic lines concluded with a shorter fourth. It had an impact beyond description. Several stanzas of the same pattern spoke of her desire, her loss, her burning, and her eternal love. Alcaeus, the other poet of Lesvos, managed to copy her poetic structure; but he couldn't travel to her depth. The words for his interior experience alluded him. Despite his years of wedding poems, taverna ditties, funeral elegies, and seasonal descriptions, Sappho's descent was so much more personal and sensual. Rather than envy, he felt a deep longing to travel with her to that sanctum. Abanthis added dimension with her tambour as the creative improvisation reached its conclusion, and the chorus concluded with their epode.

Solon, an archon from Athens, observed the performance in silent appreciation of their spontaneous energy and fluid mingling. As an aspiring poet himself, he visited Sappho and Alcaeus on his return voyage from Lydia.

Sappho's hands were trembling and her brow was moist. Abanthis brought her a hydros to refill her kantharos cup with fresh water. Alcaeus nodded in appreciation. He sensed the epiphany. The thiasos retreated to the dining hall and reclined upon soft cushions. Trays were placed in the center of their circle and they feasted on the fine nourishment of Lesvos. Grape leaves stuffed with almonds and raisins were soaked in a spicy broth. Grilled fish pieces were filled with beans and surrounded by plantains and avocadoes. The wines of Lesvos were famous and had made her family's fortune. Gongyla assumed the role of wine-bearer and handled the amphora with dexterity. She reminded Sappho of her younger brother, Larichos, who served as a wine-bearer at the court of Mytilene, where he most probably developed other skills as well. Apples and pears were ripe and ready to slice. Honey was available for dipping.

Sappho needed a playful diversion and shouted out. "Alcaeus! Play us a song of the hetaerae! Give us a bawdy melody of drunken lust and sweet forgetfulness."

Alcaeus checked the strings of his lyre. "I have no wish to offend the delicate maidens present," he replied diplomatically.

The young nymphs giggled and encouraged him to proceed. "But if it would serve to relieve the tensions, I will obediently comply." The women nodded their encouragement. Alcaeus sang a rendition of a popular brothel melody. It was a tale of a naïve young peasant who visited one of the more cultured symposiums. The poor lad was planning to marry and needed to learn the necessary skills. Alcaeus' song contained several metaphorical allusions that made use of zucchini, cucumbers, figs, dangling grapes, and juicy peaches. At one point, a sensitive hetaera instructed the young man with the use of a sword and a sheath. The women giggled with pleasure as Gongyla, no longer able to restrain herself, embraced Abanthis and kissed her in a way that evoked a ready response. Lustrous Melora danced sensually with somber Kallysta, creating a spiral of paradox. Nerissa joined their undulations while Thalia listened intently to Alcaeus' ballad with earnest curiosity about meter and rhythm. The young girls approached Solon, who was sitting awkwardly in a far corner. They took his hands and he readily joined their dance. Outside, Sappho's dogs supplied a canine chorus. The four bulky black and white molossers howled and the four large brown Ionian molussus held their notes in deep lamentations.

Sappho smiled at her disciples, stood up, and approached Alcaeus. "You harmonized very well with me," she noted as she lay next to him.

"You inspire me," replied Alcaeus with sincere respect. "Our instruments are married. I think I'm learning more about Aphrodite. But I struggle to comprehend your idea about Transcendence."

Sappho tried to explain. "Some of the philosophers have learned from the priests of the east. It involves duality." She saw his bewilderment so elaborated. "When men compete in contests, they must either win or lose. The winner is elated; the loser is angry."

"Naturally," replied Alcaeus as he picked a few grapes.

"Perhaps not so natural," she countered. "What if the two men shook hands and complimented each other on a good game? Perhaps they are both reflections of something greater."

"So they shouldn't strive to win?" asked Alcaeus sincerely.

"Not at all," she answered. "The game must be in earnest." Alcaeus pursed his lips and pondered her words. Sappho found his expression adorable. "Oh, my poor Alcaeus," she laughed. "I'm not explaining this very well." She snuggled against him. "Right and wrong. Yes and no. Good and bad. That's an easy way to think. It's clear. But it's limited. Perhaps there is a reality above that."

"Friend and foe," replied Alcaeus. "If I try to understand the enemy, perhaps we reach amachos, eh?"

"Yes!" exclaimed Sappho. "Men usually solve conflicts with aggression. Amachos is a female method. The key to amachos is Love in all its variations. If I develop into philia, an intimate friendship, with another, I would be reluctant to fight."

Gongyla joined the conversation. "Old Archilochus spoke of love in his poems," she stated with expressive hands. "But he was reciting as a man and a warrior. For him, Love was always a battle. You had to conquer or be defeated. He never described his beloved; only the agony of defeat."

"Precisely!" exclaimed Sappho with a glowing smile. "You have learned well, my golden sunshine. Love is not just a desperate struggle. It's a many-sided journey. Even in loss, the sacred glow lingers."

Abanthis, emerging from her lethargy, stared upon Gongyla and stroked her brilliant strands. "I lay here exhausted and depleted. But I have no thoughts of defeat." Gongyla leaned into her. "Although depleted, I am also full."

"The Love poems of Archilochus derive from Machos. My endeavor is Amachos."

Alcaeus felt a light shine upon him and turned to Sappho. "Your search for Aphrodite is a search for peace among all people! Is it possible?"

Sappho's expression darkened. "Here we are in Lesvos just across the strait from Anatolia. I have many friends in Lydia. And yet, Lydia and Lesvos are often at war. Why? If they want my grapes, I'll trade with them."

Alcaeus picked a grape and brought it to Sappho's lips. She opened her mouth and tapped the grape with her tongue. Alcaeus inserted the sweet fruit.

----- ----- -----

The gathering collapsed on their cushions in the sleep of blissful exhaustion. The pottery and utensils were removed by house slaves. One slave, a young man of average build, collected the trays near Sappho.

The blade used to cut the melons and oranges was sharpened to an acute edge. It could easily slice through a fruit, or a throat. The slave held the blade and leaned toward the dormant Sappho. His hands shook and nausea built in his stomach. He looked upon his mistress, as she lay in blissful trust.

He felt the sharpened point of a xiphos dig into his back. Alcaeus hissed in his ear. "Drop the weapon, slave." The terrified young servant quickly obeyed.

Alcaeus turned him around and put his xiphos to his throat.

The youth stammered in fright. "I was only collecting the trays," he promoted as his defense. "I was trying to be quiet to not disturb them."

"Liar!" snarled Alcaeus. "I may be a poet and a musician, but I'm also a warrior. Don't insult my instincts. How much were you paid? Who paid you?"

Sappho was awakened by the ferment. As her eyes cleared, she saw Alcaeus, his eyes aflame, standing with his xiphos at the trembling servant's throat. When she saw the kitchen knife at her side, comprehension followed.

"Did you ever wonder why someone would buy your freedom in order to take the life of a wealthy, indulged poetess?" Alcaeus barely restrained the urge to plunge the weapon into the likely assassin.

"I didn't think about the reason," replied the slave. "I only wanted to be liberated, to keep my family safe. I couldn't do it. Never."

Dika approached the captive and stared into his eyes with fire. "In Crete, we would throw you in the Labyrinth and let the wild bull render punishment!"

Sappho rose and stood between Dika and the slave. "Easy, Dika." She addressed Alcaeus. "We have to interrogate him, get more information. For now, we lock him in the cellar."

"Amachos?" asked Alcaeus. "No," she answered. "Strategy."

10

AESOP

*H*e was accustomed to long walks, but climbing to the summit of the Vigla left him breathless and light-headed. He paused frequently at level sites to tighten the straps of his sandals, drink water, and resume regular breathing. A long sojourn in Samos had left him unaccustomed to the altitude of his current slog; but his mission was significant to three kingdoms. Besides, he wanted to meet the great poets of Lesvos.

Gazing down upon the harbor of Skala Eressos from his steep position, and taking in the fragrance of the blossoms that surrounded him, the wanderer considered the twists and turns of his life that brought him to his current destiny. As a child from Thrace, his only thoughts were the goats and sheep of his family's territory. Playing his Pan pipes, while tending his flock, he would conjure fantastical images and imaginative tales.

But pirates from the Macedonian region came down the Evros River and invaded his homeland with death and pain. He witnessed the slaughter of his family and friends. The horror of the trauma rendered him mute during the journey across the Aegean.

The pirates avoided the navy of Lesvos and landed in Samos to trade their bounty of livestock and captive children. He was separated from the last of his friends and enslaved by two men who served the pilgrims at the Temple of Hera.

It was in their service that he met Doricha, the beautiful slave girl from Egypt. She was also a native of Thrace but had spent most of her life in Egypt, where she learned of Isis, Osiris, and Set. She told him of the love between Isis and Osiris and how the murderous Set tried to destroy them. She sang of the descent of Isis into the Land of the Dead to rescue Osiris. He laughed when she described how Isis created a new organ to replace his lost phallus. Apparently, the device worked because they had the child, Horus. She drew a picture and explained it was the eye of Horus, and said the animal of the deity was the falcon of protection.

Doricha took pity upon the mute slave and freely shared her love with him. During a full moon, she appealed to Isis to relieve the boy of his horrid memories. They embraced through the night and, when they awoke, he had regained his speech! He laughed and sang and talked endlessly, making up for the lost months of silence.

In fact, the young man compensated with stunning oratory skills and learned to debate philosophers and negotiate with merchants for his masters. His service was rewarded with manumission. His reputation grew and he was made ambassador for Samos. His shuttling between Samos and Lydia resulted in reduced hostilities. The marvelous Temple at Ephesus was opened with secure passage for wandering pilgrims.

At symposia and banquets, kings and ministers, royal women and hetaerae, were entertained by his narrations. Often his tales of satire would bite at the sensitive edges of authorities. After some narrow escapes from the offended oligarchy, he modified his oratory. He told tales for children, who loved his renditions of grasshoppers and ants, foxes and hounds, or a hare and a tortoise. Of course, perceptive adults saw through the animal facades; but the arrogant aristocrats found his fables amusing.

No one knew his real name. It didn't matter since his past was dust. Besides, he liked the mystery ascribed to his slave name. Was it Egyptian? Ethiopian? The enigma enhanced his aura.

Taking one last draft of water, he resumed his ascent. A treaty between Lesvos and Lydia would be a proud achievement. He assumed the famous poets would assist another creative spirit in his endeavor. He yearned to celebrate such accomplishments with Doricha. But his lover was brought back to Egypt and served as a handmaiden to the pharaoh's daughter. His healer and lover with crimson cheeks was lost to him. He would never have the resources to purchase her freedom.

But neither would he ever forget his Egyptian priestess who restored his faith and showed him what love could do. Through challenges and victories, despair and joyfulness, success and defeat, a constant light would glow within. Despite an ocean of distance, Doricha would always be with him.

----- ----- -----

Sappho gave her servants a holiday. Occasionally she would organize a private ceremony with solemn rituals. She would tell her slaves she was either holding commemoration for her parents or paying observance to ancestors and local deities. Such activities were common in Lesvos, where ancestors were accepted as an enduring presence. Of course, slaves never complained about a day of rest.

Behind the veil of piety, she had further reasons for concealment. If an enemy was daring enough to bribe a slave and plot an assassination, it was clear that suspicions had been aroused. Safety required prudence for the survival of their coalition and the fulfillment of their objective.

While other members of her thiasos rambled and recreated on the grounds of her villa, Sappho led the inside guests in a meditation prior to their discussion. It was an impressive gathering of creative minds, serious philosophers, and out-spoken judiciaries. To an outsider, it might appear to be a private performance of her thiasos for the pleasure of a prominent archon. The common thread was poetry, but that profession wove a diverse tapestry.

In addition to Abanthis and Gongyla, Alcaeus wrote songs for every occasion: an elegy for a funeral dirge, a sublime love ballad in the voice of a sad girl, a libidinous call to revel while you can, or an epic poem proclaiming the heroism of his brother. But his poetry could be ambiguous, with a meaning that only certain ears would decipher.

Pittacus, the general who won the contest at Sigeion, when Phrynon thought an athletic trophy would match the skills of a seasoned warrior, was also a poet-warrior. Phaon, the boatman, provided transportation when necessary. Solon from Athens gave the meeting a sense of authority.

In addition to their poetry, another thread united the gathering: a deep sense of justice. The Penthilidae of Mytilene had grown arrogant and callous. If a tradesman complained of exploitation, a whip settled the quarrel. If an oligarch failed to pay for services rendered, nepotism defeated integrity. Taxes were collected with malice whether crops were plentiful or meager. When the tyrant Myrsilius and his conspiracy managed a successful coup, the citizens rejoiced. But, as tyrant, he was to be of little improvement. Pittacus had his own plans and plotted with the poets, philosophers, and artisans to organize another change. Pittacus vowed to bring objectivity to the courts and balance to the economy.

"There is a consciousness growing in the Aegean," announced Sappho. "We've taken a significant step in writing. The oral tradition requires extensive memory and cadence. But it has its flaws. We know that legends change with circumstances. History is modified to suit immediate intensions. But writing is permanent."

"Yes," concurred Pittacus, who pounded his right fist into his left palm. "What is recorded cannot be denied."

Phaon considered the implications. "We have Solon in Athens, Alcmon in Sparta, Arion in Corinth, and even Anacharsis from the Black Sea! Scribes copy the papyrus and we can spread the words, precisely, through every city."

"This is very true," said Solon. "The poems from Lesvos are very popular in Attica. The women read about the open female spirits on this island and begin to grumble."

"Poems are preserved," noted Alcaeus. "But so is news of events in every region of Hellas! Writing is a potent weapon."

"Which is why my girls are taught to read and write," said Sappho, who nodded to Abanthis and Gongyla. "My brother tells me of his trips beyond the Hellespont, into the Black Sea. Proud, strong women live as equals with the men they choose! Sometimes, they visit Lesvos. Meanwhile, in Attica, women must choose to be unpaid domestics or professional sex workers."

Pittacus pondered her suggestion judiciously. "Let us proceed deliberately but cautiously. Your poems and songs are less threatening to boorish rulers who miss the ambiguity; but they can penetrate."

"Like a gentle seduction with sharp point," said Alcaeus.

Solon was moved to clarify one point. "The women of Sparta are not like the Athenian wives. Oh no! They go to the gymnasium and learn military skills. They still marry but they are not ensnared like corralled cattle. They have freedom."

"True," noted Alcaeus with a snarl. "But Spartan women are raised to be war machines and to breed more war machines."

Before the debate escalated, Sappho reached for amachos. "Please! Fighting among ourselves weakens our cause. Every piece of Hellas has strengths and flaws. The liberation of women can only happen if we liberate Love and Justice as well!" Pittacus agreed and Alcaeus suggested they keep a clear focus.

"Our most pressing concern is the threat to Sappho," noted Gongyla. "We must protect her and uncover the plot that would do her harm."

Sappho agreed. "We will soon go to Mytilene. My younger brother, Larichos, is a member of the court."

"You'll need to establish a case," Pittacus advised. "We will interrogate the slave."

In the midst of their forum, the hounds began to bark and growl. A man's voice was heard pleading with the dogs. "Nice boy! Hold! Someone help me!" Girls and women screamed and yelled at the interloper. Pittacus, Solon, and Alcaeus rose from their cushions and drew their swords. They approached the alcove and confronted a man who, they soon realized, posed no threat. Four women had him surrounded with bows drawn and arrows aimed. Breathing heavily and sweating, he raised his hands in supplication.

"Please!" implored the stranger. "Draw back your dogs, and these women!"

Sappho went to her dogs to soothe them. "These women are skilled archers," she noted.

"Peace, my friends," he gasped. "I seek Sappho and the Great Poets."

"What is your purpose?" demanded Pittacus.

"Wait! I know this man," remarked Solon with a laugh. "We met in Lydia!"

"Peace and inspiration," he replied. "Please tell your lady that Aesop has arrived."

1

—

FROM EGYPT TO PIRAEUS

The situation in Egypt was tenuous. With Babylon dominating the region and Nebuchadnezzar moving into Judea, the royal family was in desperate straits. Necho's attempts to revitalize the Assyrians and repel the Babylonians were failures. Hostilities had intensified with Judea since the battle at Megiddo and the death of King Josiah. The Egyptian ruler was anxious to establish relations with the Greeks, which might also deter continuous raids from the Cimmerians and the Scythians. Charoxos was on good terms with the peoples of The Black Sea and could serve as mediator.

Necho was also in need of funds. Although Athens was suffering serious economic tension, Lesvos had done well. In his trades, Charoxos made sure to include a sufficient amount of papyrus and had grown favorable to the Egyptian beer from the marshland of Pelusium. Necho had plans to dig a canal through the Pelusian delta. Charoxos was enthusiastic about the project and believed it would significantly expand trade. Necho also was planning an expedition down the Nile and into Africa. Such magnificent ventures, and the constant necessity to maintain defenses, made Necho a motivated negotiator.

During several festivals at the royal palace, Charoxos was enthralled by a slave woman who performed the services of a hetaera. Her pale skin and distinct accent revealed her Thracian origin, but she had absorbed Egyptian culture extensively. Charoxos was reminded of Cassandra's tale in Piraeus. They called the enticing slave woman Doricha. She liked to enhance her whitened features with reddened natron from the hot salt beds of Africa. Consequently, she earned the nickname, "Rhodopis", or red-cheeks.

Like the Hellenes, the Egyptians valued physical beauty and Doricha applied their emollients and unguents with the genius of sophisticated finesse. Unlike Athens or Sparta but very similar to Lesvos, the use of cosmetics was a display of status. In fact, the gentler ladies kept their skin whitened. Only slaves and laborers got tanned by exposure to the sun. Upon that whitened surface, Egyptians applied black kohl in wide sweeps; eye paint in green, red, copper, and blue; red cover to lips and cheeks. In addition to beauty, another goal was protection from the burning Egyptian sun.

Charoxos thought he was immune from the arrows of Eros; but Doricha worked her magic like an irresistible Siren. He knew he might be thrown upon a rocky mythical shore and held captive in a misty cave; but he was captured in the web of her allure. Like an innocent boy, he lost his verbal skills whenever she poured wine for him or danced for his pleasure. When he heard her silken voice, he replied with a stammer or an awkward comment when he could speak at all. Her dexterity with unfamiliar stringed instruments had a hypnotic effect upon him; and the bells that jangled when she walked left him weak.

Despite her status as a slave, Doricha was a valued member in the royal household. She had gained greater prominence as a priestess of the deity that sounded something like, "Ee-Sat", and whom the Greeks called, "Isis". The only deity beloved throughout Egypt, Isis retained a loyal following and helped to unify the nation. The themes around her legend were unforgettable. As the sister/wife of a dying and resurrecting god, and the nurturing Holy Mother of the Sacred Child, Horus, her fable fascinated adherents. Forever struggling against constant evil, as personified by her other brother, Set, Isis resonates with her votaries who respond with both sympathy and awe.

In one festival, Doricha invited Charoxos to play the role of her lover/brother, Osiris. His body transformed into a raging spirit on the rugs near the altar of the Holy Couple. His passion burned his memory clean; but he had vague recall of music, chanting, incense, and strange beverages. Charoxos knew Sappho's celebrations were tender and sublime; but his rapture with Doricha was fierce.

After their erotic ritual beneath the gaze of Isis, Doricha brought Charoxos to the chamber of the sesh, where scribes worked on papyrus and stone. Charoxos was amazed at the expertise Doricha displayed in both the demotic and hieroglyphic scripts. Most of the sesh were the sons of wealthy men who had obtained their positions through inheritance. But Necho provided Doricha with a royal exemption. Pharaohs were allowed their eccentricities with no complaints; and a priestess of Isis was granted considerable respect.

Charoxos watched in awe as Doricha rendered the long oval of a cartouche and inscribed images within its boundaries. Arms and legs, snakes and birds, curves and feathers, emerged from her quill with apparent ease. With deep reverence, Charoxos asked her what she was writing. He had expected a prayer to a great deity or a royal pronouncement. To his disappointment, she said it was an inventory list of necessary food supplies that were dwindling in the palace kitchen. He stared at the intricate symbols and patterns. "A shopping list," remarked Charoxos with a smile. She nodded and they both laughed. The other sesh flashed serious expressions, and returned to their bookkeeping, letter-writing, and business calculations.

Necho was reluctant to part with his valuable slave, but he appreciated the strength of their bond; and the gold in Charoxos' purse. The price was steep; but Charoxos had never experienced any previous impact with a woman that could rival his consort with Doricha.

Once again, Charoxos and his crew put port in the harbor of Piraeus. The journey through the Mediterranean was challenging with strong winds and forceful currents. Several crew mates were departing and returning to families in Attica and Corinth. That would lighten the load on the Aegean and Charoxos was eager to resume his route home after the slight respite for fresh water and food rations.

Doricha emerged from the lower deck of the ship, stretched her arms and legs, took deep breaths, and smiled blissfully. Charoxos took her hand and she stepped onto the dock with the graceful movement of an exotic queen. "Walk with me," she implored her lover. Obediently, he escorted her into the town and ignored the curious gaze of the gaping throng.

A young woman approached the ship and initiated a conversation with the crew members left to guard the vessel. She was curious about their destination and how they sailed the ship. The men were eager to impress a woman who seemed truly interested in their vocation. She asked a lot of questions about Egypt and Lesvos. One of the men brought out some fish, wine, and corn. They were soon eating, drinking, and conversing amicably.

From a comfortable distance, Antiope and her husband scrutinized their friend's smooth management of the situation. Antiope shopped among the fabrics while the sculptor examined mallets, adzes, and chisels. But they kept Cleis in view. The men were drowsy from their voyage and the wine, with a philter of benign herbs from the mágissa, drew them into a deep slumber.

12

INTRIGUES

Sappho could no longer tolerate the interrogation methods of Pittacus, Solon, and Alcaeus. The screams and pleading of the would-be assassin served as repudiation of everything her temenos represented. Descending the steps of the wine cellar, she directed them to stop the torment.

The slave was stripped naked. His arms were tied to a ceiling beam and he was suspended a foot from the floor. His ligaments would burn and his arms grow numb as he moaned in pain. Sappho noticed the bruises on his face and legs. As a commanding hoplite, Pittacus knew how to retrieve information. With knives and burning torches, further trials were imminent.

Sappho approached the prisoner and looked up and down his exposed nakedness. She took his chin in her hand and forced him to face her. And yet, she spoke softly. "You have a good life here. For a few drachmas, you would betray me?"

Weary and defeated, the slave tried to explain. "It wasn't just an offer," he gasped. "It was a threat. If I refused, they would have to kill me. And my family…"

"Your wife and daughter had no knowledge of this plot," Sappho replied sharply.

"No!" he stated vigorously. "But they would be in danger."

Sappho nodded with comprehension. "I see," she conceded. Turning to her allies, she commanded, "Cut him down. Give him back his clothes. Then bring him to me."

Back on the veranda, Sappho's "flowers" had been chatting and pacing anxiously. When she emerged from the cellar, they ran to her like worried puppies. Dika was eager to make a strong point. "You always treat your slaves well," she said with moist eyes. "That man is an insult to all of us. You gave me a new life. I would never harm you."

Sappho embraced her darling from Crete. "I know, my dear Dika. I will never doubt your loyalty."

The men brought the culprit from the cellar. Sappho's "little sparrows" transformed quickly into vengeful falcons. They cursed and spit upon the villain. Their claws were out, but Sappho directed them to retreat. She instructed them to be calm and listen to his story. Alcaeus recalled that the man had paused, did not attack Sappho rapidly, and was probably in conflict.

The entire company reclined. Pittacus and Solon sat on opposite sides of the felon. Alcaeus sat directly facing him, alert as an eagle.

Sappho inquired, "What do we know so far?"

Pittacus led with the answer. "The slave was offered payment and freedom. He now begs for a chance to redeem himself."

He did as he had been instructed. Through the morass of Eressos, he traversed an open courtyard with thick green grapevines hanging from latticework. Artisans and tradesmen were enjoying an afternoon meal and were shielded from the sun's glare by the vines. Beyond the courtyard, he entered a thoroughfare filled with potters who were busily working their wheels. The scent of fresh clay and the smoke of burning kilns saturated the corridor. Turning left into a byway, he sauntered along a narrow artery that ended blind. The public house was on his right and he entered the noisy lodging that was filled with foreign wayfarers and detached figures with illicit plans. In the obscure shadows, and crowded din of the roadhouse, any secret was concealed. Someone pulled at his sleeve and he turned to a familiar face. Despite the hood, he was recognized as the man who had instigated the plot. Without a word, he led the way through a portal to a dim vestibule.

They sat on a wooden bench in a small niche of the vestibule. The familiar instigator removed his hood and spoke in a low growl. "Is it done?"

From the folds of his chiton, the slave retrieved a package wrapped in woolen cloth. He handed it to the conspirator, who unwrapped the package that held a bloodied blade. Quickly re-wrapping the knife, he concealed the weapon and grumbled, "Hold out your hand." The obedient servant followed his command. Coins were dropped in his palm, which he closed in a fist. "I'm leaving. Don't follow. Wait ten minutes, have a drink, and leave quietly." Having completed his business, the mole retreated through another penetralia.

Left alone, he sat calmly and scanned the crowd. Anyone in the taverna who spied the exchange of coins might be tempted to approach him in the dead-end. When the tavern maid brought his drink, he made a display of searching for an obol like a man of poverty. He finished his drink and flirted playfully with several women, staying alert to pick-pockets. When a sufficient period of time had elapsed, he slowly departed from the public house and made his way back through the narrow artery. Back at the courtyard, he was met by Alcaeus and Solon who were casually consuming a bunch of grapes. The poets rose and greeted their "friend". The three left the agora and mounted their cart.

"You did well," said Alcaeus to the slave.

"Thank you," replied the suspect. "I deeply appreciate this chance to prove myself."

Alcaeus nodded and turned to Solon. "I've never seen him in Lesvos before. None of the banquets or festivals."

"I have," grunted Solon. "I know him well. He an agent for Draco."

"Draco!" Alcaeus chilled. "The great archon of Athens?"

"Indeed," Solon snorted. Then turning to the slave. "Show us your reward." The slave produced his bounty: four silver coins with images of Athena on one side and an owl on the other. Solon was surprised. "Four dekadrachm! That's forty drachmas!"

"I couldn't hold any more," the slave noted.

"By all the gods!" Alcaeus barked. "For the average worker, that would be twenty day's work! Even for a busy doctor, it would be almost seven days."

The slave spoke out. "It wasn't worth my reputation or my deep remorse."

Solon pondered the implications. "It would appear your Poetess of Lesvos has unsettled the oligarchy of Athens."

----- ----- -----

Solon was deeply embarrassed. "Attica and Lesvos have a tense history. But this outrage is shocking!"

"Apparently, I'm quite a threat to Draco," she considered.

Alcaeus pondered the circumstances. "Here on Lesvos, our women are relatively free. They like fashion, colorful paint, and shiny jewels. They can move about unrestrained and their ideas are received well."

Sappho agreed. "We have strong relations with Anatolia and Scythia. We know the free warrior women. We are far from Athens."

"True," noted Solon. "But the women of Attica are growing restive. Many girls resist the Arkteia. Some even commit suicide. Athens has suffered economic turmoil and the oligarchy won't budge. Tradesmen and farmers are trapped in debt. Draco's new written laws are severe. He uses ink and pen to justify sadism."

Aesop noted the irony. "So, this new communication, writing with paper like Egyptians, is a two-sided axe. We can share our songs, our stories, and our poems. But we can also strangle people with unreasonable rules."

"We are in a time of change," added Solon. "Thales, on a mission from the Ionians, remains in Lydia with Croesus. Aesop and I left that kingdom with great hopes."

"I know of this Thales," announced Sappho. "He is the philosopher of water. He believes it's the primal element."

Aesop jumped back into the conversation with renewed enthusiasm. "That's very true! He's also a mathematician and a skeptic. He seeks to disprove divine causes and seeks natural explanations." Aesop saw Sappho's expression and dropped to a more reticent tone. "My lady, Aphrodite's realm is different, I believe. The nature of Love is different than an earthquake or a thunderstorm."

Sappho laughed at Aesop's disquiet. "Your blasphemy is forgiven," she replied. "Besides, Aphrodite is immanent in the very nature around us. Perhaps your Thales will actually prove her power."

Solon provided an anecdote. "Thales predicted a solar eclipse. But, rather than giving the scientific explanation, he used the occasion to end that foolish war between the Lydians and the Medes. On the field of Halys that very day, the adversaries made a blood oath."

"Yes!" exclaimed Aesop. "With the Persians on the march, a grand alliance, throughout Anatolia, Hellas, and Scythia, could guarantee an era of sustained peace. The Cimmerians have already complied. Their connection to Pontus will help."

Sappho laughed. "It looks like you have another tale to tell, Aesop. Alcaeus and I will compose a grand epic poem. With Alcaeus' allusions to heroic battle and my emphasis on the gentler things, the poem will resonate with the world!"

Kallysta ran her bow across her barbiton, getting their attention. "Haven't we forgotten something?" she clamored. "Someone from Athens tried to kill Sappho! Why?"

"I think I understand," replied Alcaeus. "I've learned many things from Sappho. Her greatest lessons are how to love like a woman." The men bolted upright with startled expressions. But the sparrows smiled at Alcaeus. "It actually threatens the Athenian order of things. The power structure..."

"Humph!" grunted Abanthis. "You mean the men!"

"Yes. The men," Alcaeus conceded.

Pittacus was intrigued. "When you speak of loving like a woman…"

The meeting was interrupted by more barking of the hounds. But, that time, the bellowing had a familiar and happy resonance. The dogs stopped their clamor, and the voice of Charoxos issued from the entranceway, laughing and conversing with his pets.

The entourage ran to the entrance with Sappho in the lead. As usual, Charoxos returned home with several surprises. Next to him, holding his hand, was an Egyptian hetaera in full attire. On his other side was a girl of about fifteen who stared at the impressive gathering in astonishment.

Sappho shouted out, "Charoxos!"

Aesop followed her with his own shout. "Rhodopis!"

----- ----- -----

Charoxos knew his sister would be surprised when he returned with the two passengers, but her reaction to Doricha was painful for him. "I've struggled to maintain the sanctity of my temenos and you bring home an Egyptian whore! How could you do this to me?"

"That's not fair," replied Charoxos. "You disappoint me, you votary of Aphrodite. You're being hypocritical."

Sappho, the poet of sweet poetry, paused to find words that would match her emotions. "You don't understand anything I'm trying to accomplish. The women in my sanctuary are growing powerful in a free safe hieron. You bring a foreign hetaera with a foreign god. You heard Aesop. She's a 'Rhodopis', a rosy-faced whore!"

Charoxos tried to counter her attack. "Stop saying that! Aesop was addressing her with affection and admiration. It's merely a name."

"A tradename! She's in league with Eros, the Limb-Loosener!" Sappho proclaimed with emphasis. "Her influence on my acolytes could be very harmful. Besides, Myrsilius could turn your love into a scandal. He could rouse the polis. Or bribe an oracle to denounce us. People have been stoned for less! Between the angry rants of Alcaeus and my political satire, Myrsilius needs little motive to make us pharmakos, scapegoats! Is that what you want?"

Charoxos laughed but with anxiety. "You're over-reacting, sister. In many ways, she's perfect for your community. She brings pleasure; and she is also a priestess for a beautiful goddess. I've been with her. She's closer to Aphrodite than Eros. Your Aphrodite and her Isis are kindred spirits!"

Sappho slumped onto an armchair and crossed her arms. "Don't plunge into blasphemy now," she murmured in exasperation. "Doricha must remain in your separate quarters until I learn more about her."

"Fair enough. I understand that you need time to consider."

"And you will not attend the royal wedding with her."

Charoxos' jaw dropped. "You ban me from the Mytilene castle? Outrageous! This was not the welcome I expected after my long absence!"

"Nor I!" she rejoined firmly.

Aesop appeared at her portal and nervously clenched the fold of his peplos. "Excuse me, my friends. If I may have a word with you?" Sappho waved for him to enter and he stood between the siblings. "May I have some water?" he beseeched, partly from thirst and partly for time to gather his thoughts. Sappho nodded and waved her palms upward with impatience. He quenched his thirst and his angst. "I suggest we all be seated." Charoxos took a chair and Aesop found a foot bench that was sufficient.

The siblings awaited his discourse. "Could it be," Sappho asked, "That the great story-teller is at a loss for words?"

"I once was," replied Aesop. "Before I met Rhodopis." He turned to Charoxos. "When you arrived with her, I was shocked, joyful, and extremely covetous. You see, I loved her once." He lowered his gaze. Looking at Sappho, he added, "It wasn't just an erotic attraction."

"I see," Charoxos granted. "You've known her. I hope that won't create a tension between us."

"No, my friend." He shifted to Sappho. "I remember one of your poems of a similar dilemma, the pain of watching a woman you loved flirting amorously with a man." He turned back to Charoxos. "I know that pain. There's no one to blame." Then, with a playful smirk, he added. "But I remain envious."

Sappho was curious about one of Aesop's remarks. "You said something about having no words until you met her?" Aesop bowed to her and presented a rendition of his life journey, which included the traumatic events in Thrace, the abduction, his loss of speech, and how Rhodopis cured him. "You do make this woman sound quite exceptional," she acceded.

Aesop made a bold reply. "My lady, you live in privilege and entitlement. You sympathize with the polis and you dream of a better society. But, from your position, you may be unable to grasp the full extent of desperate poverty or overwhelming circumstances."

Sappho was impressed. "That may be true," she realized. "I speak for the poor, but as a wealthy woman."

Encouraged, he went on. "Rhodopis and I are both refugees from Thrace. We suffered humiliation and terrible losses. We both survived by our wits and gained the respect of our masters. Beyond judgment, can you find the honor in that?"

Sappho's body jolted. "Honor," she pronounced as if in prayer. "That is something poets acclaim frequently. There is honor in the courageous hero who overcomes his fear and subdues a powerful foe. But there is also honor in surrendering to the call of Love, to being faithful to your most sincere desire, to showing the courage of gentleness."

Charoxos joined the discussion. "I am being honorable. I love Doricha despite the judgment of family or tradition."

Aesop nodded. "Warriors praise Honorable Death in battle. I also praise an Honorable Survival. Rhodopis and I, orphans from Thrace, survived without doing further harm. That girl, Cleis, survived despite the constraints of Athens."

"Yes," exclaimed Sappho. "The survival is honorable when you preserve something inside yourself. Something pure and honest and natural."

"Indeed," noted Charoxos. "When the polis rises up, they know the risks of punishment and reprisal. And yet, they take action. The philosophers speak of something in the human heart that values justice."

"So, there is an essence," Sappho deduced. "Something that makes a creature human."

"Perhaps," replied Aesop. "Does it come from a god; or is it something in us?"

"You speak of 'sofia'," said Sappho. "I'm reluctant to discount the Muses," she added.

"The discussion is beyond me now," Charoxos confessed.

"Let me explain," Sappho replied. "If you believe the Muses send you a gift, you are in opposition to this new concept. 'Sofia' is a personal inner strength, not a divine gift."

Charoxos was intrigued. "You believe this?"

With humility, she answered, "I'm reconsidering everything."

13

MYTILENE WEDDING

The castle rested with massive dominance atop the island's acropolis and maintained an unobstructed view of Mytilene Strait with Anatolia on the horizon. Along the parapet walk, sentries were able to view the entire domain from all directions. This was useful for a ruler who suspected enemies from all sides.

The towers, balconies, and stairways were festooned with garlands of roses, lace, violets, and buttercups. Musicians filled the air with festive melodies while the large scullery was buzzing with anxious cooks, kitchen help, and nervous slaves. From the pinnacle, flags of every state, clan and tribe were librating in formation.

The epithalamia of poets from across the Aegean would proclaim the joyous celebration that was uniting two prominent families of Lesvos. In wagons and on horseback, they came to Mytilene from Sparta, Corinth, Megara, Athens, Crete, and

Ionia. Beyond Hellas, guests arrived from Thrace, Scythia, Pontus, and Lydia.

Croesus of Lydia had acquired wealth from the gold which flowed in the Pactolus River, and had established a unified peace through Anatolia. But Solon of Athens had cautioned him about the impermanence of life and the whims of the Fates. Anxious about the Persian empire, the Lydian King consulted numerous oracles, conferred with the philosophers of Miletus, and established alliances. When Aesop offended Croesus with the tale of Midas and the golden touch, the king sent that lector out to sea on royal missions. Their reunion at the wedding was imminent.

Sappho arrived in a small caravan that carried her thiasos to Aphrodite. It was an arduous journey from Skala Eressos; but her sparrows were resilient. The voices of twenty females --chattering, laughing, singing, and rehearsing – emerged from the covered wagons and aroused curiosity among the peasants and craftsmen they passed. Several hoplites encountered the train. But, with escorts like Pittacus, Solon, Alcaeus, and Aesop, the encounters were respectful. Several nobles who were also on their way to the castle, joined the company. Some of the girls chose to ride horses instead of traveling as passengers in the wagons. One of the riders was Cleis, who had learned quickly from more experienced women. When they befriended the girl from Athens, and learned of her talisman doll, they often called her, "Atalanta."

"I am not a strong free Amazon," noted Cleis with prudent embarrassment.

But one of the woman corrected her. "You resisted family, husband, and tradition to preserve your integrity. That means you're very strong." They galloped off ahead of the caravan as Sappho watched them from the seat of her wagon and Dika held the reins next to her.

"She was meant to be here," Dika stated with certainty. "She flourishes in her freedom."

"Yes," Sappho concurred. "Like wild mountain laurel." She liked the purple headband Cleis used to restrain her blond hair. Such bright blond, Sappho thought, rivaled Gongyla's flame. Sappho grew more pensive with Dika. "She is determined. She wants passionately to conquer life, to have control over her own destiny. Never again will she be a victim. And yet…" She trailed off without completing the sentence.

Dika had a sensitive intuition. "Too much the conqueror?"

Sappho smiled at her loving cohort and stroked her cheek. "You know my poetry very well. I'm glad you came to me. Charoxos made a beautiful purchase."

Dika looked back with a coquettish smirk. "Would you have me bound to you again?" she teased.

"Never," replied the poet. "I only want you here of your own free will."

Dika countered. "And in my free will, I choose to be bound to you."

They arrived at the foot of the acropolis of Mytilene and were greeted by horsemen in full panoply. They recognized Pittacus readily. They had fought with him in several battles; but they also knew of the tenuous bond between Pittacus and Myrsilius. The guards were also familiar with the two famous poets of Lesvos, Sappho and Alcaeus, and bowed in respect. The women were advised to disembark from the wagons. It was a challenging climb to the castle and loaded wagons would put serious strain on the horses. No one complained. The acolytes were eager to stretch their legs and get the exercise. In like fashion, Cleis and the other horse-riders dismounted.

"Climbing another mountain," Aesop sighed. "I'm getting used to it." With a jovial laugh, they made the ascent.

----- ----- -----

The company moved through the main gate and entered the green bailey surrounded by large stone walls and wooden beams. The bailey was filled with musicians, acrobats, orators, and merchants. Water krates were located at each corner and Sappho's thiasos rushed to refresh themselves. Sappho wondered if her younger brother, Larichos, had to accept the burden of water-bearer from the coastal wells to the summit.

The current tyrant of Lesbos, Myrsilius, arrived in the bailey, surrounded by family members who served as his security. When Myrsilius overthrew Melanchrus, he made many promises and had the enthusiasm of the people. Sappho grew weary of the repetitive pattern: A strongman posed as a champion of the down-trodden, attacked the corrupt elites, promised an equitable distribution of wealth, and the elimination of debts incurred through usury. But the hero soon grew complacent and complicit. The next round of resentments began to fester. She knew that Pittacus was biding his time and waiting for his own opportunity. But he had a tarnished history. He originally plotted to obstruct the ascent of Myrsilius but later relented. Charoxos and others felt betrayed by Pittacus; but he explained that the time for them was not yet ripe. He managed to soothe some followers; but not before Alcaeus had written some critical poetry. An oral presentation can end, but papyrus lingers. The memory of his reversal left scars. Skilled poets can impact reputations.

Myrsilius glowed with a sunny smile as he approached Sappho and her entourage. His peplos was adorned at the rim with gold threads, probably to rival the style of Croesus. He wore a long cape made from fine threads with purple tints. The wreath in his hair was embellished with semi-precious stones from Egypt and lands to the east. His eyelids were painted Phoenician blue, which would rouse the envy of artisans. Walking with Myrsilius was the agent who had paid Sappho's slave. The two men were surprised to see Sappho but soon contained their emotions.

"My dear Sappho! And Alcaeus! Such an honor!" Myrsilius kissed Sappho and embraced Alcaeus. "The most renowned poets of Hellas!"

Alcaeus feigned modesty. "You're too kind, my liege," he replied. "Even here in Lesvos, Terpander preceded us. He gave the lyre seven strings."

Myrsilius was intent on flattering his guests; Alcaeus was careful to keep Myrsilius friendly so the compliments were accepted with apparent gratitude.

The encounter between Myrsilius and Pittacus was cooler. "My good Pittacus," pronounced the tyrant. "Your presence honors my castle." The message of, "my castle," was spoken with emphasis. The customary phrase was, "*the* castle". The people had carved every stone and carried them to the summit. Masons had carefully aligned them. But, as ruler, Myrsilius was legally entitled to call it, "my castle".

"I live to serve," replied Pittacus with strained poise and a lowered head.

"Good! Good!" affirmed Myrsilius with impatience. "Please, enjoy the comforts I lay before you!" He swept his arm across the bailey at the food and entertainment. "Our island is united. We are at peace. The time has come to celebrate!" He moved on to other guests.

Sappho embraced the tyrant one more time. She whispered in his ear. "My servants are very loyal. I also keep written records on papyrus, just in case something were to happen to me." Myrsilius pulled away and stared in her eyes.

The agent paused and glared at her. Sappho stared right back at him. Myrsilius waved his hand and his entourage slowly walked away.

"I hate that man," Alcaeus murmured. "Instead of relieving the burdens on the poor, he raised taxes, increased the leverage of landlords, and positioned magistrates in positions that would enhance his own power. He lied to us!"

"Easy, friend," whispered Pittacus. "Not now."

Alcaeus glared at Pittacus. "When will the time be right?"

"Despite your beliefs, I saved your life by changing strategies before we took action. Trust me. The right time is coming."

With a grunt, Alcaeus moved off to the banquet hall. Sappho watched him leave and then turned to Pittacus.

"Mistress, I understand this dangerous game. Alcaeus is an idealist. But you have to move your pieces carefully."

At that moment, a slender youth in bright colorful costume came to them. He wore a short chiton in the female fashion. Holding a silver-tinged amphora in one hand and a basket of skyphos cups in the other, he inquired, "Shall we pay homage to Dionysus?" He then recognized his sister. "Sappho!"

"Larichos!" exclaimed Sappho. They gave each other a hearty embrace. When they disengaged, she noticed that Larichos' hair was tinted with touches of gold and he was wearing jeweled earrings. "I see you've done well for yourself."

Larichos laughed. "I was never meant to be a wandering seafarer like my brother. I've developed other skills, suitable to my disposition." Larichos fluttered his eyelashes. Pittacus grunted and took a deep draught of the wine.

"I'm proud of you, brother," she replied. "You rival Ganymede himself!" Pittacus almost choked. "You've applied yourself to your circumstances." Pulling him aside, she asked, "How goes Myrsilius?"

With a casual air, he readily hissed, "He's a self-serving liar and thief. They all are. But he pays me well for my services?"

"Services?" asked Pittacus with a growl. "So, Ganymede, he's your Zeus?"

"He's my lord," countered Larichos. "I attend to his needs and desires." He leaned closer to the general. "I might even pose for a statue," he whispered.

Pittacus grumbled something incomprehensible. He then remarked, "You would do very well with those well-bonded hoplites of Sparta and their retinue."

"Yes, I probably would," replied Larichos. "But I'm not really a fighter. That's why I love my sister's poetry."

Sappho pondered that comment. She wondered if only a man such as Larichos could appreciate her heart-felt sonnets.

She felt a sadness at her core. Alcaeus and Solon seem to understand. But there is a wall, an obstacle, they have to surmount. Sappho can travel both worlds. She can entertain the general public at weddings, funerals, and festivals; but she can also speak a deeper language of intimacy with her thiasos. Can men acquire that flexibility?

A great gong was rapped and the resonance filled the bailey. She could feel vibration in the stone walls. The celebrants were being summoned to the grand dining hall.

Passing into the castle, they entered a grand hall with three sets of oak beams, bound at an angle, forming the ceiling, from which hung large chandeliers with over twenty blazing candles each. On both sides of the hall were arching walls painted in gold and bedecked with paintings of all the gods of Olympus and local deities. Famous swords and shields from legendary heroes were fixed to those walls, in commemoration of historic battles. Atop both walls were walkways that guards and servants could traverse without interrupting the celebration. Additional candles on freestanding candelabras brightened the artwork and the path to the next room.

Passing through a triple archway, the guests arrived at an atrium with several windows cut into the stone that offered a view of the Strait and the mountains. On the right side of the atrium was a grand stairway that spiraled up to the second tier. Proceeding up the escalier, the company entered the royal dining hall. Chandeliers and banners from all the nations were suspended from the rafters. Tall arching windows encircled the entire hall. Long tables were lined up through the room and the seats for the royal retinue were at the head of the tables on a raised dais. But Myrsilius insisted that their travel thrones be placed upon the dais instead of mere chairs. Servants removed the chairs and struggled to carry the heavy thrones upon the dais. When the thrones were appropriately positioned, Myrsilius and his bride took their seats and the company followed suit. Croesus of Lydia was seated to his right, while Periander of Corinth was to the left of the bride.

Sappho examined the royal thrones and was impressed by their fine engravings of leaping dolphins, helmeted Athena, dancing nymphs, lions, goats, triremes, and the twins Artemis and Apollo.

Alcaeus leaned toward her. "I see an image of Aphrodite on the back of the bride's chair," he reported. "Or is it an engraving of you?"

With a gentle smile, she replied, "You're too kind." She then produced several Lesbian coins from her pocket. "Look!" Her face was clearly engraved on the electrum coins, with a pair of dolphins on the other side." Alcaeus was speechless. Her reputation, and the clans that supported her, provided significant leverage. It was obvious why an enemy would find it convenient to employ a slave as a scapegoat in the event of her demise.

The ceremonies began with solemn formality. The assembled poets offered their Makarismos to bless the royal couple.

In deference to his Lesbian hosts, Alcman, the famous Lydian who lived in Sparta, presented a poem in the Aeolic dialect. He sang of the joys of maidenhood and the duty of marriage. In pleasant tones, he described the delights of marital bliss and the miracle of motherhood. He beseeched Artemis to protect and preserve mother and child. He received a respectful ovation.

Upon completion of his own poem, Alcman introduced his consort from Sparta, the marvelous Megalostrata. In addition to strong physical attributes derived from the Spartan gymnasium, Megalostrata was a fine poet herself. In her presentation, she called upon the bride and all her future daughters to stay strong, and find honor in their lives as women. She received polite applause.

Callinus of Ephesus spoke of the Great Temple to Artemis in his home and of the Goddess' many-breasted nurturance. He called upon the Fates to nurture the betrothed with the generosity of that chaste goddess. Sappho was intrigued by the blend of virginity and lactation; like a virgin forest that renders fine fruits.

Alcaeus soon turned from the conventional wedding tribute to calls for celebration. He chose a solitary nomos while Sappho accompanied him with minimal strums from her barbiton.

Now let us drink while day invites.

In mighty flagons hither bring,

The deep-red blood of many a vine,

That we may largely quaff, and sing,

The praises of the god of wine,

The son of Jove and Semele,

Who gave the jocund grape to be

A sweet oblivion to our woes.

The crowd soon called for the poetess from Eressos. Sappho modestly rose, with Alcaeus to accompany her on his lyre.

Some say the most beautiful thing

Upon this black earth, is an army of horsemen;

Others speak of infantry and ships,

But I say it is whatever one loves.

Raise high the roof beams; Sing the Hymeneal!

Bridegroom, never again will there be a woman like this!

Sweeter than the bee's honey,

More tender than the hyacinth.

Once the attendees were becalmed, she sang a more suggestive stanza.

Carpenters! Raise the roof!

The Bridegroom is a very large man.

With his controlled sophrosune,

He opens Love's Door.

The poets laughed and applauded at Sappho's praise of male size and control, which allegedly served to contain the wild fires of the woman's lost maidenhood. Myrsilius understood the underlying sarcasm and sneered. His queen flushed and looked down at her sandals.

Solon used typical symbols to serve as metaphors for the wedding night. He spoke of conquest, of ploughing a virgin field and peeling a ripe fruit. When he sat down, he hoped Sappho would appreciate the poetic structure he had learned from her. But she was agitated by the content of his erotic poetry.

The wine was having its effect. The ceremony grew more playful and risqué. Archilochus, the poet of blame, who once drove a disloyal lover to suicide, sang praises to Dionysus and warned the groom to keep his filly in her stall. Mimnermus, accompanied by the young Nanno with her aulos, sang of how life without Love is worse than death. He celebrated "amorous assignations and tender bedrooms," and lamented the wilting of attractiveness with old age." As the celebrants applauded, Solon encouraged him to tolerate change and live a long life.

When civility was at its nadir, the gathering clamored for Semonides and his infamous satires. Sappho cringed when he wobbled to the center of the tables. In his popular brothel song, he talked of the various kinds of women. Zeus made one type from a pig and she keeps her house a mess and her clothes filthy. From a fox came the woman who instigates trouble. The dog-woman is an intrusive gossip. Semonides went on with his cruel rendition of labile women, lazy women, vindictive women. He concluded his diatribe by announcing that woman is the worst thing Zeus ever created. Sappho clenched her fists and seethed.

Myrsilius found his opportunity and went straight at Sappho's grand devotion. "You praise Aphrodite, the great goddess of Love. You encourage your disciples to honor her.

Have you forgotten her faithlessness? She deceived her husband, Hephaestus, and slept in his bed with Ares. Hah! The goddess of Love with the god of War!" Nervous laughter twittered around the hall. Myrsilius smiled with victory.

Sappho composed herself and responded to his provocations. "Perhaps the wine has impaired your memory. You conveniently forget significant parts of the story. It was Eros who gave Ares the gift of his charmed javelin. In that way, Eros bound Ares and Aphrodite. The tale serves as a warning. It's typical of a man to confuse Eros with Love. Your bitterness probably resulted from erotic traps in your own life. If you'd seek an antidote, I invite you to learn more about Aphrodite's magic."

The crowd roared with delight and Myrsilius feigned humility in defeat.

"Well done!" Alcaeus replied to her. Solon nodded in deep appreciation of her logic.

Returning the banquet to a more entertaining mood, Aesop told several tales. Thinking of Rhodopis, who worshiped the feathered kite in her Isis ceremonies, Aesop recanted the fable of the kite that was sick. The poor bird was dying and asked its mother to prayer for him. But his mother berates him: a lifetime of ill deeds is never redeemed on a deathbed confession. The revelers laughed in delight; but Myrsilius did not appear to be pleased. Aesop tried another tale. He tells the tale of a flock of doves who are terrified of a predatory kite. To pacify the kite, the doves make him their king. However, as he proceeds to kill one after the other, the doves realize their mistake. The crowd grew restive and Myrsilius sat still on his throne. His bride took his hand to console him. Aesop decided it was time to leave the festivities and adjourn to his chamber.

Concerned for Sappho and Aesop, Alcaeus offered the gift of an extra song.

Feed the man who hungers for a loaf of bread.

Do not enslave the pauper who cannot pay his debts.

Do not torture those who are forced to embrace in secret.

Aphrodite beckons, Love is the way.

Drink your wine and eat your bread!

Ignore the farmers of the grape and the wheat.

Ignore the baker who rises early to supply your loaf.

Once again, the flood will come.

The banquet went silent. Myrsilius and Croesus whispered to each other. Pittacus approached Alcaeus and Sappho and spoke softly.

Semonides stood, clapped his hands, and held up his goblet. "Musicians, play! Singers, sing! Dancers, make your moves! Let us honor Dionysus and his alluring maenads! Drink!"

Periander of Corinth, who was seated by the queen, seized the opportunity. "Yes! Agreed!" He stood up and gestured to his chosen poet. "Arion, son of Lesvos, and inspiration of Corinth! Tell again your Tale of The Dolphin!" With happy relief, the crowd roared for his popular epic. "And you, Sappho's thiasos! Will you be his dithyramb?" Sappho understood Periander's gesture; and encouraged her cult to dance for Dionysus."

To please his patron, protect his fellow poets of Lesvos, and render a memorable performance to the assembled aristocracy, Arion gave a dramatic rendering with all the fabulous details. After winning a grand poetry contest in Syracuse, Arion was reportedly abducted by pirates. He was about to be cast into the sea when he played a final song on his lyre. A great dolphin was drawn to the music which was a tribute to Apollo. When Arion jumped into the water, the Dolphin rescued him and brought him home to Corinth. The Fates brought the pirates to Corinth in a storm at sea. Arion revealed himself to the marauders at the statue of the Dolphin, who is now a constellation near the Summer Triangle.

Sappho's entourage played the role of satyrs very well. They sang and danced with their instruments as they circled around Arion, fell to their knees, leaped in the air, and spun around with goblets of wine. Dika and Gongyla approached the royal dais and happily gestured to the bride to join them in their merriment. She awkwardly looked to Myrsilius, who was intoxicated beyond the ability to dance. He waved his permission and the young queen left the dais and joyfully engaged the playful satyrs. Her hair came loose, her tiara was slipping, and her royal persona was disintegrating; but she didn't care. For the moment, surrounded by wildly circulating nymphs, she was a playful girl once again. In such a performance, Sappho's sparrows were not a threat. When the music stopped and the young bride returned to her throne, Myrsilius fell asleep in her arms while she smiled radiantly at the jubilant crowd.

----- ----- -----

The sun was barely emerging with orange radiance over the mountains of Anatolia, and pouring early light onto the Strait of Mytilene, when Sappho and her entourage were packing their wagons for the return home. To their surprise, Periander of Corinth, accompanied by Arion, came to them. After casual morning greetings and several jokes about Arion's dolphin, Periander addressed Sappho.

"You are a beautiful and bold woman," he declared. "You have strong allies. Your women are powerful, free spirits." He

124

came closer and spoke more intimately. "But the Fates are capricious." Sappho stopped her packing and faced the tyrant directly. "You know I created a walking bridge over the Saronic Gulf?" She nodded prudently. "If you ever need a short route to the Ionian Sea, remember that bridge."

Sappho was deeply moved by the sincere concern of the aging ruler. "Thank you, my lord," she said with appreciation. "Times change rapidly. A proud leader today may require exile in Corcyra or Syracuse tomorrow."

Periander smiled knowingly at the wise woman. "You know of my pain, eh?" As if pleading with her, Periander went on. "You know the gossip. Oh, Sappho, I swear to you by all the gods that I did not kill my wife. I have had my moments of fierce anger, and we had frequent arguments. But I did not push her. My wife fell down those stairs!"

Sappho gazed at him and saw not a powerful tyrant but a vulnerable man filled with painful remorse. A flow of compassion rushed through her veins. "I know about your son in exile in Corcyra. My brother is often at the Ionian Sea."

"Yes. He knows of you and your brother. I want him back in Corinth, dear Sappho."

She placed her hand upon his shoulder and made a solemn vow. "Perhaps, when I'm there, I'll visit the cliffs where Aphrodite mourned for Adonis. Even a Goddess feels the torment of separation."

----- ----- -----

Aesop was carrying his sack to the wagon when he encountered Lydia's King Croesus and Solon on a morning walk. As they approached, he anticipated a tense exchange.

"Good morning, Aesop," Croesus called to him. "Did you recover from the evening's amusements?"

The King was in good spirits and Aesop was relieved. "Yes, your majesty. I pray the fates are being kind."

"The Fates have truly blessed me," replied the King, as he placed his hand on Aesop's shoulder. "With advisors like you and Solon, I have learned to contain my hubris."

Aesop was amazed. Solon interceded. "The good King understands the capriciousness of life. With a sober reflection, he is looking forward to a long era of peace."

"Indeed!" exclaimed Croesus. "Your tale of Midas helped put my value on the proper things. And Solon warned me to never be too confident. Your advice may provoke me at times; but your honesty has kept us all out of trouble. If the Persians do cross into Anatolia, I will need sincere advisors."

Aesop was euphoric. "Thank you, great King! I live to serve." He bowed his head.

"And now I'll give some advice." Croesus pulled both men in close. "These poets of Lesvos --- Sappho and Alcaeus and Arion. They have great power in their words. Those words are now being put to papyrus and spread throughout Hellas. No longer do they only entertain local aristocrats. Words are powerful weapons."

"Yes," replied Solon. "I admire Sappho. I strive to replicate several of her poems. I'm trying to master her structure."

The King went on. "They must be careful. Words provoke thoughts and thoughts provoke actions. Tyrants may be threatened. Their songs may intend to inspire beauty, but they can also encourage rebellion."

Aesop was at a loss. "I don't understand."

Croesus offered examples. "When Sappho sings of a woman's desires, the wives of Athens grow restive. When Alcaeus offers a biting satire, a tyrant's authority is weakened."

Solon comprehended the warning. "We'll talk to our friends," he replied. "But I doubt we could suppress their spirit." "Of course not," said the King. "But channel it wisely. And make use of the Aeolic dialect. The message will be less overt." Solon nodded in agreement. Croesus added a final warning. "There are several clans on Mytilene in continuous conflict. It is common for the poets to voice their loyalties to their own clan. Often it is done in satire. But we have larger goals. We have the opportunity for regional peace. Sappho and her brother have strong trading relationships with Scythia, Crete, Egypt. Myrsilius would be wise to keep his head and show the wisdom to be judicious."

14

A COMMUNITY OF SPARROWS

From his view on Sappho's veranda, Solon enjoyed a wide panorama of the property. At a circular courtyard with a statue of Aphrodite, several members of her thiasos were practicing on their flutes and stringed instruments. Some preferred a solitary practice while others united in a communal effort. Solon was impressed by their intense focus and their lack of competitive nature. They were not reserved about asking for help and were eager to share any technique they had acquired. Beyond the courtyard, women sat on boulders or lounged under ancient oak, ash, and sycamore trees while they spun yarn, painted on vases, practiced writing, and engaged in energetic conversation. In the meadow, Cleis was among a group that was walking horses at a relaxed pace. He could identify Cleis by the purple headband that had become her style de rigueur.

"I'll be returning to Athens soon. Draco needs the information from Croesus. But I'm glad I came to your beautiful island and got to meet the famous Sappho. Your property is a magical realm, a piece of Olympus brought down to earth for mere mortals. Your acolytes are very special women with fine skills. But I am troubled. I have questions."

Sappho sat next to Solon and was drinking tea of sideritis and lavender. "What troubles you, Solon, on such a pleasant day as this?" She offered him some of the tea and he readily accepted.

He sipped slowly, preparing his words to avoid offense. "Do the members of your cult remain here indefinitely? Do they stay for a required time span? Do they pass an initiation or celebrate when their interval is completed?

Sappho nodded and smiled. "Those are the usual questions," she assured him. "I'm sure you've heard many rumors." He nervously concurred. "I have been fortunate to have inherited a marvelous estate on an island where some women are relatively free. It was convenient for my brothers to support my endeavor. Charoxos is often away on a trading mission and has no time or inclination to manage an estate; Larichos has his duties in Mytilene and has too gentle a disposition to be a farmer. My third brother, Erigyius, left the family and chose to wander the world in search of knowledge and adventure. I agreed to maintain the family property if I could do it my own way."

"I see," Solon remarked. "You never married?"

She replied wistfully. "Actually, there was a man called Cercylas. Yes, like the island in the Ionian Sea. He was a wealthy merchant and a friend to Charoxos. We had warm feelings for each other. But, Cercylas wanted me to live with him in his homeland in Rhodes. It was very convenient for him, being close to Crete, Egypt, and Palestine."

Solon frowned with comprehension. "But it was not convenient for you."

"Precisely," she replied with a sad tone. "I'm not a woman who exists only to satisfy a man. He understood that. I had a mission."

"Ah, yes. The mission. This school for women?"

Sappho grunted sardonically. "Some people do call it a school. They do learn many things here. But it's really a very special hieron, a sacred place cut out from the rest of the world." She saw the expression of wonder on his face and clarified further. "There was a time when Woman was honored, when the metroons for the Great Mother were the center of communal life. In Hellas, we sang paeans to Gaia. In other lands, Inanna was the First Great Goddess to descend into the Underworld, to rescue her lover, Tammuz. When Inanna emerged in Phrygia, she became Cybele. In Phrygia, her male adherents were driven into fanatic seizures. Desperately striving to be one with Cybele, they would un-man themselves!"

Solon shifted uncomfortably in his chair. "Yes, I know. Cybele and her eunuch priests of Attis exist in Athens. Very often, when they recover from their trance, they suffer deep remorse."

Sappho agreed. "So I'm told by the warrior women of Scythia. These poor men make a terrible mistake. One doesn't join the goddess through mutilation, but through submission and love."

Solon struggled to comprehend the connection. "We agree. Before the Olympians, before the Titans, there was the Mother. From her Body and from Her blood, all was created. Men admired women as a divine miracle. They bleed with the moon. From their loins, new life emerges. From their breasts, that new life is fed."

Sappho went from there. "Then came the Great Upheaval. Men refused to be children of The Mother. They craved battle and conquest. Instead of sacred chants, they chose the battle roar. At Delphi, the navel of Gaia, Apollo overcame the Pythia and claimed the Oracle for himself. In another myth, Zeus held Hera from her feet, and kept her dangling from the clouds of Olympus, until she submitted to his domination. Since that time, Hera has been a bitter and vengeful goddess. Of course, she punishes the women who are seduced by her husband. Zeus is never harmed."

Solon experienced a degree of enlightenment. "I think I'm beginning to understand. You want to restore the glory of The Great Mother."

Sappho clarified further. "I want to restore the status of women. In Athens, your wives are basically domestic servants. Women have only three choices: humble wife, seductive hetaera, or temple priestess. Cleis could be my child; she rebelled as I did. But she's even stronger than I am; she did it with no family support."

Solon kept trying to put together the fragments of her explanation. "In your thiasos to Aphrodite, you seek a hieron for women with no definite duration."

"Exactly! Some stay until they choose to leave and marry. Some remain with no clear objective until the Goddess delivers inspiration. All the time, they learn, explore, debate until they're ready."

"Ready? For what?"

Sappho's expression turned firm and determined. "There is a great change coming in our world. The time of heroes, like the impetuous Herakles or the arrogant Theseus, is drawing to a close. Women are feeling a deep discomfort in their lives. They come to Eressos with only a vague sense of disquiet. They're restless and confused. They need this hieron to step out of their time and rediscover something in themselves."

"But you worship Aphrodite. Isn't she a rather impetuous goddess. She can also be vengeful and fickle."

Sappho pursed her lips and took a deep breath as she tried to remain patient with her guest. "Solon, you're a victim of Homer and the other myth-makers. Their tales of the Great Love Goddess are modifications. Just like Pythia and Hera, Aphrodite was re-created in the minds of men. She used to be Moira!" Solon was jolted with surprise. "That's right. She was one with the Fates. The Egyptians spoke of Ay-Mari, the Goddess from the Sea! In Lydia, near Caria, there remains a great temple that honors Her ancient glory."

"Yes," replied Solon. "I heard of it in the court on Croesus. But Artemis in Ephesus is more popular."

"Yes. Artemis," said Sappho ponderously as she stirred another cup of tea. "I teach my girls about a special trinity which helps them understand the full implication of Love. "Aphrodite's consort, Eros, is the fire of lust and passion. Of course, he's male." She laughed and Solon joined the joke with his own chuckle. "Then you have Artemis, the free virgin goddess who resists all chains of convention. She protects wild nature, young children, and pregnant women. She loves the vulnerable creatures as she remains strong. She's immune to the arrows and javelins of Eros."

"And Aphrodite?" asked Solon.

"The most mature and purest Love. It is a bond not born of necessity or custom. It transcends gender, tradition, divine belief. Some call it agape. To describe such love, I wrote poems about Helen. Alcaeus thinks Helen was a disruptive woman who caused the Trojan War. I disagree with him. Helen and Paris were deeply in Love. That kind of Love cannot be contained by marriage vows, family commitments, or political necessities. It's a Pure Love."

"And how do you know when you are in that kind of pure Love?"

"You no longer need poems. You don't have to practice the words to say; they come naturally. You won't need instruction in how to make Love. Your bodies will know. It's the Love that lives in the earth and the sky. It's the Love of the Universe."

"Oh my," was all Solon could express.

"Do you now understand?" she asked.

"A safe space, a hieron, where a woman can come and stay until she determines her true destiny."

"There also are men," she noted. "Sadly, only a few. Being from the dominant and privileged side, it's very difficult for men to see the joy that could be theirs."

Solon wanted to believe everything she said; but, certain realities pulled him from the heavens and back to the hard earth. "Sappho, you speak of a changing time. But the Babylonians threaten. The Persians are planning to march upon Lydia. Tyrants continue to plot and scheme."

"That is what makes my mission so urgent. My acolytes don't just sing and dance and recite poetry. They also milk the goats, care for the horses, weave clothes, carry water, prepare meals. They are also taught self-defense."

"Really?"

"I have Scythian friends who sometimes travel from Pontus into Lydia. Those women visit Lesvos. They train my sparrows well."

"Amazons!" exclaimed Solon.

Sappho laughed. "The old Circassian name. Amezane! 'Forest Mother'. Look at the geography of Lesvos. Much closer to Anatolia than Attica. We have a long history with the peoples of The Black Sea."

Solon was humbled. "You have much to teach me. I am eager to learn."

Sappho gazed into his eyes. "Someday, you would make a good Archon in Athens."

Solon brushed aside the notion. "Nah! I'd rather learn the lyre and improve my poetry." They both chortled happily.

"I can understand. But, if you are called to serve your city, you will."

15

THE ADONIA AT THE WATERFALL

"Please, Sappho, I would very much like to attend your Adonia." Rhodopis looked into her face with the eyes of a supplicant. "I have been to Byblos as well as Egypt. This festival is familiar to me. Perhaps we can share the experience and compare our traditions." Sappho studied the new member of her household and contemplated possible consequences.

Rhodopis continued her plea. "I know your great devotion to Aphrodite. I know the story of Adonis, whom the Goddess loved. When he was killed by a boar, she mourned deeply. Some say she even went to the Leucadian Cliffs, to the Temple of Apollo. She leaped from those cliffs to prove the sincerity of her love." Sappho was impressed by the wealth of the Egyptian's knowledge.

Charoxos grew impatient with his sister. "Rhodopis has been respectful and cooperative since her arrival. Your obstinance is not justified. She's a priestess and you treat her like a criminal."

"Calm yourself, Charoxos. I'm not refusing." Despite herself, Sappho had grown to like the foreigner. Her dedication to Isis and Osiris was sincere and Aesop's tale of her curing him piqued Sappho's curiosity about her medicinal skills. She addressed the Egyptian. "Why does he still call you 'Rhodopis', rosy-cheeks? The Athenians, who keep their wives pale white, use that term for porne!"

"Sappho, I would like to walk with you. This interrogation is not necessary." Charoxos protested, but Doricha raised her hand for serenity. "It's a beautiful midsummer day. I am growing fond of you. Women of Aphrodite and Isis can certainly find a gentle compatibility."

"The hetaera is shrewd", Sappho realized to herself. "She knows I find her intriguing and she's trying to seduce me." Sappho tried to resist but her passion for strong, assertive women left her vulnerable. "A good suggestion," Sappho conceded. She looked at her brother who was fidgeting nervously. "I won't bite her," she said to him. "Unless she bites me first." Doricha nodded to Charoxos and he acquiesced. He watched them leave the portico and descend the stone steps on their way to the courtyard.

The two powerful women sat next to the statue of Aphrodite. A young acolyte was strumming her barbiton and inquired if she should leave. Sappho told her it was fine and urged her to continue playing. For a sweet moment, the women sat quietly and absorbed the sound of the barbiton strings, the twitter of nervous birds, and the splattering of the fountain. "

"Red is a very significant color in Egypt," Doricha stated calmly. "We use red ochre for many occasions. It can symbolize many things. Red is Ra, the Sun God. Red is life. Even in death, a mummy is given a necklace with a red amulet to assure life after death. As a priestess for Isis, I honor her with red."

"I see," replied Sappho. "The color is part of your dedication."

Doricha nodded with a grunt. "There's more. The evil brother Set has red hair. Anger is red. I use the red for the goddess before Set can appropriate it. I'm sure you know there are two Egypts. Pharaoh wears the double crown, one red and one white. White is purity. The red and white crowns, bound together, stand for unity. The nation is not complete unless they are joined."

Sappho realized Doricha's blush was complex. "I'm sorry. I only knew the symbols from Attica."

They rose and thanked the girl for her pleasant music. As they strolled along the grounds, many girls and women acknowledged them with waves, nods, and smiles.

"The humble wives of Athens are kept pale, so the hetaerae use the red as a contrast," Doricha further explained. "Red is also a symbol for danger. The red sun can be warming and help crops grow. But too much sun can burn and destroy. It is the same with water. If the Nile is kind, we have sufficient food. But too much drowns our grain and too little is a killing drought. In Egypt, we appreciate the value of the middle way."

Sappho was deeply attracted to the Egyptian priestess with a Thracian origin. She felt a powerful need to join with her force. Would Charoxos understand? "You know the Adonia?"

"I believe so. It reminds me of the Judeans when they speak of a Lord, an 'Adonai'. But in my land, your Adonis would be Tammuz or even Osiris."

Sappho considered other parallels. "The seasonal return from the Underworld does also resemble Demeter and Persephone."

Doricha agreed. "The cycle of the crops, dying in the Fall and re-emerging in Spring, remains a deep mystery." She took Sappho's hand as they walked. Sappho did not resist.

----- ----- -----

As the group hiked to the waterfall, Sappho explained the myth. "Your Adonis is a child of incest," Doricha grasped with a sarcastic laugh. "Just like Isis and Osiris! Only a coincidence?"

"Perhaps not," replied Sappho who was growing more relaxed with Charoxos' consort. "His mother was hidden in a tree."

"Of course," noted Doricha happily. "Osiris was trapped in a tree by the evil Set."

"This is fascinating," Sappho stated with enthusiasm. "When Aphrodite found the infant Adonis, she left him in the care of Persephone. But when Adonis grew into a beautiful young man, both goddesses wanted him. Zeus had to resolve the rivalry."

"Of course, the powerful male god had to settle the battle between two raging goddesses." Doricha's sarcasm was obvious. "And how did the wise Zeus resolve it?"

"Adonis spent four months with Aphrodite, four with Persephone, and four with his personal choice."

Doricha pondered the implications. "And how did Hades feel about Persephone's young mortal lover? And why did Persephone agree to condemn Adonis to a fate so similar to her own?"

Sappho side-stepped her questions with more information. "Adonis soon chose Aphrodite, the goddess of Ultimate Love."

"And how did Ares, or Hephaestus, feel about that?"

"He did get killed by a wild boar," answered Sappho. The two women paused. Doricha began to laugh and Sappho found her mirth contagious. Soon they embraced joyfully. "I hope you'll find the respect to mourn for Adonis," Sappho chuckled.

Struggling to reclaim restraint, Doricha assured her host. "I always respect tradition." The other women giggled as they passed them. The roar of falling water was gaining volume as they proceeded to their destination.

"In Hellas, women climb to rooftops with their shallow bowls of lettuce for the ritual. It's their little Adonis Gardens. But my thiasos climbs to different levels."

----- ----- -----

Cleis walked the path in the company of Dika, Abanthis and Gongyla, skimming through tall grasses, twisting tree roots, and floral clusters. Curious rabbits would pause to observe the parade and then scurry to their shelters. Summer birds flew beyond the caravan. While the three older friends gossiped and joked on the journey, Cleis was more reserved. The others shared personal feelings readily; Cleis remained a closed secret.

When they stopped to sip rapidly gushing water from a narrow stream, Dika playfully splashed Cleis, who smiled and resumed her walk. "Hey!" shouted Dika. "You're supposed to splash me too."

Cleis turned back toward Dika but kept walking. "I'm not a child," she shouted in retort.

Dika rushed up to Cleis and touched her hand. "Yes, you are!" countered Dika. "A young, agile, strong, versatile child!"

Cleis stopped with annoyance. "What do you want?" she demanded.

Dika walked directly in Cleis' path and faced her. "I like you. You're strong and smart and eager to learn every skill. You're not easily frightened. I want you to trust me, play with me, be my friend."

Cleis tried to apologize in her own way. "Dika, I don't mean to offend you. I'm just not a very friendly person."

Dika persisted. "I don't believe that. You've been hurt. I can tell. But it's safe here. Take the chance. Open up."

Hoping to end the encounter, Cleis replied, "Alright. I'll try." She turned back to the path.

"Start now!" Dika's lips were trembling and she felt a cool chill in the midsummer heat. Her eyes were moist. Her voice did not communicate anger but, rather, determination. "I won't let you give up."

Gongyla caught up with Abanthis right behind her. She found the two girls staring intently at each other. "Are you ok?" she asked anxiously. Abanthis pulled up as the confrontation was ending. "What's happening?" she queried. But Cleis just turned silently and resumed the hike. Dika looked at her two companions with anguish. "I'm going to crack that hard shell," she remarked and continued her ascent.

----- ----- -----

The endless chatter of birds harmonized with the turbulent clamor of the crashing water to create an enclosure of thunder that surrounded the expedition. Passing through a thick blanket of ferns, and proceeding carefully across slippery moss, they arrived at the foot of a steep waterfall with a wide curtain of water. The plunge was interrupted at one point by a flat rock terrace which many group members reached from an air space behind the curtain. The rock face behind the water offered natural steps to the terrace that had been an integral part of the Adonia for many years.

When Doricha arrived at the gully and peered up to the crest of the cascade, she was rendered speechless by the imposing mixture of breathtaking beauty and intimidating danger.

Sappho spread her arms. "That is the roof for our Adonia," she declared. "Aphrodite's Platform! Can you feel her immanence in the formation?"

Doricha continued to stare at the waterfall and trace the drop from the rocky crest to the babbling pool at the base where some of the girls had disrobed and were swimming. "Perhaps I do sense a presence," she sighed.

Sappho called to the swimmers, reminding them to climb the rock face with their "Adonis Gardens". The girls emerged from the pool and wiped each other with their chitons.

As Cleis was about to ascend the rock stairway, Dika took her hand. "Come with me. I want to show you something." Cleis chose to humor her and walked beyond the stairs. In the rock face was a cave that was hidden from casual view by the curtain of water. They entered the cave and sat in the cool damp enclosure as the water plunged in front of them.

"I often come here when I need solitude," Dika confessed. "There's a time for community and a time to confront your personal landscape." She leaned back on her elbows and glanced at Cleis. "Would you take off the purple headband?" she asked. "Let your yellow hair fall as free as that water."

Cleis wanted to express annoyance at the persistent entreaties; but, instead, she chose a different option. Removing the headband and tying it around her wrist, she shook her hair free and studied Dika's expression. She wasn't panting with erotic lust; she was admiring Cleis as she would a fine sculpture.

"May I touch your hair?" pleaded Dika. Cleis consented with a nod and Dika ran her fingers through her damp golden strands. With deep sincerity, she said, "Cleis, I suspect you have been hurt. But I would never hurt you. I want to know you, your story, your dreams."

Cleis took in Dika's words like a soothing salve. Reaching out to stroke Dika's hair, she said, "I escaped from Attica to find a new life. I suppose that also means new friends." Dika smiled and Cleis leaned in tenderly to kiss her. It was a subtle, gentle graze of affection. "I think we're going to miss the Adonia."

Dika jolted out of her reverie. "Oh no, we mustn't. Sappho would be hurt." Standing up, she took Cleis' hand. "Come! The ritual does offer some release. The noise of the water drowns out all the howling." Before leaving the cave, she added, "Next time, we'll bring torches. I want to show you some other things in there."

Cleis laughed and hugged her new friend. "Lead on," she replied.

As they left the cave, they met Doricha, who was waiting at the entrance. "Sappho told me to wait here and make sure you didn't miss the ceremony."

----- ----- -----

The terrace jutted out beyond the cascade. To be on that ledge was both thrilling and terrifying. With close-up views of the bursting crest and the chilling plunge, an acolyte stood with the curtain of roaring water at her back. Dika was right. The experience of streaming vitality and fantastic terror, wrapped in a chrysalis of noise, provoked release.

"The gardens are dying!" the votaries screamed. "Adonis is dead!" They threw their clay pots in the stream, tore at their hair, ripped off their clothes, and pounded on their chests, crying and moaning in lamentation.

Cleis found the catharsis of the ritual contagious. She started to yell and cry. She mourned deeply but not for Adonis. A cascade of memories flooded her consciousness. She cried for her mother who taught her the art of spinning. She cried for Menares who was probably haunted with despair for his lost sister. She cried for the farm with its meadows and fields and streams. She even cried for her father and Eurybiades, both good men who just couldn't understand.

As the light of Midsummer turned pink on the western horizon, the weary entourage made their descent. At the pool, they washed their faces and moistened parched throats. Silently, solemnly, they walked the path back to the temenos. Occasionally, they would embrace or hold each other for support. Cleis readily let Dika hold her. It stopped the shivering.

16

COMMUNITY MEETING

Every week the entire thiasos gathered for a women's symposium. New members tended to be shy, cower in the corners, or stammer a few awkward words. The more seasoned acolytes lounged comfortably, often in each other's arms, or massaged the backs and shoulders of companions. They talked eagerly and stared anxiously as private confidences were whispered in the ears of trustworthy friends who reacted with dramatic gestures or squeals of delight. It was common for an adept to approach a novice, reassure her, and offer an adjacent seat.

The large ballroom was used for the intimate conclave. Fireplaces carved into the stone walls provided comfortable heating. Windows were swung open to allow for soft breezes and the sound of crashing ocean surf. If a bird happened to fly into the chamber, the event was viewed as a sign from Aphrodite, whom the congregation would then welcome with hearty paeans.

Such interruptions served to ease the tension that would build from multiple personal disclosures.

To commence the meeting, Sappho led them in her popular Ode to Aphrodite. After a brief time, every acolyte learned the words and happily sang with her. The harmony created Beauty in every season. Sappho put a lot of emphasis on Beauty; but she spoke of the different levels of beauty. The overt physical beauty of a young woman is something to admire. But the transience of that level is a subject often explored. Sappho spoke of The Good as another kind of Beauty. Compassion, empathy, honesty, fair compensation, impartiality, and justice are all part of The Good that renders a person Beautiful beyond the winds of time.

Servants brought water, wine, and trays of fruit to the ballroom. Sappho allowed the servants to participate in the community. Their various life experiences provided further insights and wisdom.

At this particular gathering, Doricha sat at her side. When she was introduced, several acolytes interrogated her about her profession. With no shame, Doricha spoke of bodily pleasure as a gift from the gods. The congregation shared their opinions openly but not in judgment. Instead, they expressed their own fears and fantasies. When she could, Doricha reassured them or rendered blatant advice. She made it very clear that women also contained the keys to personal pleasure; in fact, she noted that women were capable of sustained pleasure whereas men required "rest periods". Some girls blushed and giggled; others nodded and smiled wisely.

Then Doricha went on to speak of Isis, Osiris, Set, Nephthys, and Hathor. Several acolytes noted similarities and differences between the Egyptian and Olympian deities.

One girl, a new member, asked about the incest among the gods and goddesses. After some discussion, the young girl began to sob. Others rushed to comfort her and encourage her to share. She spoke of her own experiences involving a brother and an uncle. Several women made it clear that her experience was not uncommon; they told of their own family betrayals. Often, they were told to never speak of it. Some had been threatened by their perpetrators. For many, the thiasos was the only time they ever revealed the violations they had endured. The girls shared a collective lamentation; but they weren't grieving for the fallen Adonis. They were crying for their own losses: of naïve innocence, of trust in her family, of a vision of a world of purity. Some mourned but with anger. They dreamed of vengeance and divine justice and released tears of rage.

Dika, Gongyla, and Abanthis were holding Cleis' hands and rubbing her shoulders. They were gently encouraging her to speak. Finally, she took the risk. "Doricha, you said women can experience sexual pleasure."

"Yes, dear," replied Doricha. "Sexual and sensual."

"I never did," she confessed. "I felt attacked, powerless. He hurt me. It was something I just had to do." She began to whimper.

Many of the girls groaned and cursed. "Your husband was a terrible partner," Sappho pronounced. "You should look forward to the conjugal union with joy."

"I don't want another lover," Cleis asserted with anger.

"You have not yet had a lover," Doricha stated. "You had a husband. He did not know how to be a lover. The hetaerae of Athens were bad teachers. They lied to him about his erotic skills. So, he thought he was wonderful. He was a fool who only made the hetaerae wealthy."

Cleis was confused and proceeded with caution. "You were one of the hetaerae," she said.

"Yes, child, I was," replied Doricha. "But I never deceived men; I taught them. I reminded them that every woman is a reflection of the Goddess. I showed them how to approach a woman's body as they would an altar. My old friend Aesop told a tale of a contest between the wind and the sun. His conclusion was that force will only bring resistance, but warmth will bring comfort. I like to think I inspired that tale."

"You were attacked," added Sappho. "Invaded, violated, desecrated. As a result, you pulled up the drawbridge, you bolted the doors. You wear armor day and night. You've protected yourself from pain. But you also locked out the bliss of natural gratification. You're not giving Aphrodite the chance to heal you."

Cleis attempted to protest. "I've given my life to Aphrodite. I dedicate myself to her."

"In ritual," replied Sappho with tender compassion. "Reciting the prayers, singing the poems, you made a perfunctory commitment. You have protected yourself very well. But you find it difficult to remove the panoply when the war is done. It's safe here. You will not be harmed. Open the doors."

Dika leaned into her friend. "When you're ready," she said softly, "I'll help you."

----- ----- -----

Charoxos was packing his wagon when the women emerged from the ballroom. Solon was helping him carry merchandise from the storage bins. Solon would help to crew the vessel on the journey back to Attica. Krates of wine, fine linen cloth, barrels of anise, bags of olives and amaranth, and pottery from Sappho's thiasos were loaded carefully below deck. Some lavender and honey were secured on shelves.

Both men were relieved to learn that Sappho and Doricha had developed a friendly relationship. "So Isis and Aphrodite have come to a settlement?" asked Charaxos.

"It was never their problem," replied Sappho. "It was my own foolishness. Can you forgive me?"

He embraced his sister. "Nothing to forgive," he replied. "It's my fault. I startled you with an Egyptian priestess and a runaway wife from Athens."

Sappho laughed happily. "And both have worked out very well." Then, on a serious note, she asked, "Can I trust you to be cautious in your pleasures?"

Charoxos leaned into Sappho. "As much as I can trust you with Doricha," he answered.

Nicely cornered, she parried. "My pleasures are always tender," she appraised.

"I see," he teased. "Men are always insensitive louts."

"No, dear brother. You've had good teachers. But tell me this: A male has numerous erotic adventures and is praised for his capacity. A woman enjoys pleasures of the flesh and is met with disapproval. Why such a discrepancy?" Solon leaned in to hear the answer.

Charoxos looked at them and gave a sly grin. "A man makes his deposit and leaves. A woman carries the seeds and the consequences." He winked.

"Love between women is so much safer," Sappho countered. "I've taught you many of the skills."

Solon began to feel uncomfortable with the sibling exchange. "Perhaps we should get to the pier and catch the winds before sunset," he suggested.

"Agreed," Charoxos replied. Then, tenderly, "Be kind."

"Always," she murmured.

Doricha sauntered to the wagon and embraced her lover. She then acknowledged Solon. "When you return to Athens, remember what you have learned here."

"I'll do my best, Priestess," he replied. He turned to Sappho and embraced her. "You and your thiasos have impressed me deeply. From now on, I will try to love more like a woman. Thank you."

The poetess and the priestess watched as the wagon disintegrated into the horizon. It was time for dinner. After an exhausting symposium, the sparrows were hungry.

Sappho always worried when Charoxos left on his voyages. His journeys were dangerous; and the home was left more vulnerable. Words came to her:

Cypris, and you, Néreïds, Bring my brother back to me unharmed: let him sail home safely: Grant that every one of his heart's desires, all be accomplished Once he makes amends for the present straying of his ways, Return him to his friends and protect him from our enemies. No longer a worry to his sister, let him consent to do her honor.

17

MAKING LOVE LIKE A WOMAN

Alcaeus tossed his lyre on the lounge, crossed his hands in front of him, and stared into the void. "Please don't mock me, Sappho," he implored her. "I have trained myself to use your stanzas of four lines. I've taken up the plectrum you devised. I try to share honestly as you do." He took a sip of sweet dessert wine and sighed heavily. "But my mele, my songs, still sound like taverna ballads. I don't have your genius."

Sappho sympathized with his frustration. "You're at a disadvantage," she tried to explain. "You're a man." He grunted whenever she took that line of reasoning. "It's not an insult."

With irritation, he asked, "Why should my gender be such an obstacle? I learn from you."

Sappho rose and stepped next to him. Standing directly in front of him, she stroked his shoulder while her leg brushed against his thigh. Her soft chiton opened slightly at her knee. "You have to learn more about loving," she imparted with sensitivity.

"You've never complained," he replied defensively. "We've had loving moments."

She leaned into him closer. Alcaeus placed his hands on the inside of her thigh. "Are you aroused?" she asked.

"Why must you ask? You know me better than that."

"How do you know?" She rocked gently.

"Why are you taunting me like this?"

She took his head in her hands and joined their foreheads. "How do you know I'm arousing you? "

Meeting her challenge, he stared directly at her and answered. "I'm growing. I'm throbbing."

Matching his stare, she asked, "What do you want to do?"

Bewildered but persisting, he replied. "I want to spread you open. I want to push myself into you."

"Yes. Exactly," she replied. "Your penis is directing your action." She backed away from him and returned to her lounge. "Do you understand?"

Flushed and agitated, he retorted. "You've never been this cruel before."

"How do you feel right now? Be honest." Her gaze was intent and sincere."

"I feel...humiliated...overpowered...defeated."

Sappho chose her words carefully. "You wanted to invade me, force your way inside me. Then you felt defeated. Your love-making has the manner of a military battle. Your phallus is used like a sword."

Alcaeus protested. "You initiated!"

"Yes," she replied. "With touch and strokes. You responded with aggression. You had to either conquer or be defeated. My dear Alcaeus, love is not war!"

He tried for more comfortable ground. "I was frustrated about my poetry. Now I'm also frustrated about our sex."

She laughed at the irony. "Don't you see? It's the same thing. You write poetry as a man but you want to express yourself as a woman. To sing like a woman, you have to love like a woman."

----- ----- -----

With Sappho's permission, the young women took the friendliest molussus with them on their trek back to the cave behind the waterfall. The large brown guard dog knew the familiar path and pranced easily along rutted trails, muddy byways, and craggy routes. He was alert to all sounds, scents, and motions of the woodland while the band of acolytes could focus their attention upon the blossoms and fauna of the journey. Gongyla took the lead position with the hound while Abanthis brought up the rear. Dika and Cleis walked quietly between them and studied the changing terrain. When they arrived at the natural pool at the base of the falls, the small group refreshed themselves and refilled their water flasks.

They advanced behind the water curtain with the molussus sniffing every moist stone and swaying fern. At the cave entrance, Dika and Gongyla lit torches made from flax and oil. Abanthis and Cleis carried pottery bowls and philters of oil.

"I made this discovery in early Spring," Dika told the others. "Since then, I visit often." A current of air kept the smoke from the torches moving out toward the waterfall, leaving the air of the interior fresh and clear.

They followed Dika to an inner chamber of the cave. The labyrinth of stone walls began to muffle the sound of the waterfall until they arrived at a closed circular cavity, which was quiet enough to amplify the sound of heartbeats and breathing. "This is it," Dika announced. "Light the bowls." The clay bowls were filled with oil that was ignited with the torches. The dancing illumination revealed walls filled with artwork depicting numerous scenes.

On some walls were depictions of communal hunts for wild boars and deer. There were also paintings of social gatherings around fire pits with people eating and dancing. A leader stood by some of the fires with raised arms. Perhaps the leader was an oracle. Significantly, the figures depicted in all the scenes were both male and female.

Dika took Cleis' hand. "Come over here," she directed with excitement. "Look." Cleis looked where Dika was pointing. It was a set of illustrations. In the first scene, a baby is left alone; but Artemis spies the child from her tree perch and, with her bow, is pointing at her. A she-bear approaches the infant. In a second scene, a woman warrior is in the lead of a group of men and confronts a Giant Boar with her spear. A third section displays a young man running and a woman stooping to pick up apples. "I knew you'd like this," said Dika.

Cleis stared in wonder. "It's Atalanta!" she gasped. "As a baby, she's abandoned, but Artemis sent the she-bear to nurture her. And there she battles the Calydonian Boar. And Hippomenes distracts her with Aphrodite's golden apples. They marry!" She gazed at Dika in amazement. "How is this possible?"

"There is a long history to Lesvos," replied Dika. "These are ancient paintings."

Gongyla approached with the hound. "There was a time when the Warrior Women of Pontus crossed the Strait of Mytilene and came to Lesvos."

Abanthis joined the conversation. "There are fantastic myths about our island. It wasn't really mermaids. It was these women. Lesvos has an old relationship with Anatolia."

Dika added more information. "Their men were comfortable along the Black Sea and in Anatolia, so the women left on their own. But before departing, they established kings, The Penthilidae, to maintain order among the clans. Sappho still uses their Aeolic dialect in many of her poems."

Cleis sat on the cave floor and continued to study the wall paintings. Dika shifted behind her and wrapped her legs around Cleis. She blew on Cleis' neck and explored her ear with her tongue. Cleis let nature be her guide. She rested her head backward onto Dika's chest. They began to breathe in unison as one. Dika slowly glided her hands onto Cleis' breasts and embraced them tenderly. There was no pain and no fear. Cleis felt a warm affection for Dika that was completely alien to her experience with Eurybiades.

----- ----- -----

Alcaeus followed Sappho's lead as they laid naked together in her bedchamber. When she gently stroked his chest, he mirrored her behavior. She caressed his hips and kissed his waist and stomach. He ran his fingers through her hair and down her neck. On her direction, he gave no mind to whatever his penis was doing and let their bodies patiently meld together. She explained her method. They were separating Eros from Aphrodite, allowing sensual exploration to intensify their mutual pleasure. Ultimately, they would experience a joining to the Goddess of Love with the full force of the natural world. She emphasized patience and fine attention to each contact.

Alcaeus experienced a shift in his longing. No longer did he endure a desperate desire to satisfy a seething hunger. Instead, he felt the serene composure of an experienced explorer discovering an uncharted land. He held her breasts with profound admiration and the need to give as well as receive fulfillment.

The women of Lesvos had a reputation for their oral skills; and Sappho did not disappoint. She also encouraged him to experiment with his mouth, tongue, and teeth. Waves of body electricity surged through them like a rapid current. When the tide reached it crescendo, Sappho mounted him and he easily slipped inside her. A volcanic eruption overwhelmed them as they merged into the hot lava of their shared passion.

When they consummated their love-making and fell back upon her bed, the air seemed fresher and the birdsongs were crisper. The floral scents in the room were mesmerizing as they sensed their bodies returning to their usual levels.

Sappho smiled and snuggled next to Alcaeus. His bemused expression caused Sappho to chuckle until she realized something was troubling him. Still merged, only an inquisitive visage was necessary.

"It was wonderful, my sweet lover," he explained. "And yet, I feel frightened. I think you took something from me. I'm confused. You have power over me."

Sappho tried to comfort him. "It's the typical reaction of a man who enters Aphrodite's realm. You feel vulnerable. Let me assure you: there was no victor or vanquished. We both were totally engaged in her essence."

"A total surrender," he pondered.

"Precisely. We both surrendered. We were equal participants. No conqueror, no victim."

Alcaeus was filled with insight. "I made love to a free woman who was my equal. It was wonderful."

Sappho returned the compliment. "You loved me like a free man; freed from your need to control and to be in control."

Alcaeus was troubled by one final question. "In Attica, they have a term. 'Tribate', a woman who loves other women. They spit when they say it."

"They're ignorant," replied Sappho. "If no penis is necessary, they deem it to be evil. So, when women make love, they think it's unnatural. But a man, with his penis, can leave his wife home and enjoy the pleasures of both the brothel of hetaerae or young boys."

Alcaeus considered her explanation, liked it, laughed, and kissed her. "So, making love like a woman is threatening for some men. It also happens to be wonderful." He laughed again and louder.

They wrapped themselves in their own chrysalis. Both considered poems of butterflies and bursting seeds.

----- ----- -----

"Cleis, you're being too passive." Dika caressed her body as they lain together. "You're not an Athenian wife any more. Move. Touch me too. Enjoy yourself."

Cautiously, awkwardly, Cleis examined her friend's anatomy like a scientist analyzing a newly discovered species.

Dika kissed Cleis and mussed her hair. "My sweet girl, you have my permission to satisfy your curiosity. I'm not fragile, I won't break. I want you on top." She shifted and prodded until

Cleis was peering down upon her. "You ride a horse so well," she joked. "Why can't you ride me?"

Cleis took the challenge. Glaring down at Dika, she began a rhythmic undulation which gradually increased. Cleis felt a great release throughout her body as they both started to breathe heavier and moan with a love that was no longer contained. This is not what she was taught at Brauron. This is not the way she engaged Eurybiades. This was freedom.

She could hear Gongyla and Abanthis at the other side of the cave. They were whispering and laughing and kissing. They readily accepted what was happening and finding their own pleasures in the cave with painted walls and glimmering torchlight. The big molussus was relaxing near the entrance of the alcove, and not the least disturbed by his human companions. The walls told her Atalanta was there! Cleis was finally where she was meant to be.

18

THE HERAION OF SAMOS

Phaon, the ferryman, was an interesting fellow. With his facial scars and twisted stature, he might be Charon guiding the souls of the dead across the Styx. Yet his poetic wit and skill as a boatman appealed to Sappho. His hands perfectly synchronized the sail and the tiller as he brought his passengers into the sheltered cove of southern Samos on the shore of the Makale. Sappho stood proudly at the bow with one foot on the gunwale for balance. Dolphins playfully emerged from the water and seemed to welcome her with their squeals. Seagulls circled overhead to announce their arrival.

Alcaeus studied her in a way only a lover would. He was inspired.

"Poetess of Violet hair, Skin that hints of dark Mystery,

Draw down the Moon within your lair,

Trapped in your perplexity."

Antimenidas lowered his head and groaned. "Please, Mistress, make him stop."

She simply smiled. "When the Muse inspires you, it must be expressed," she replied.

"I'm not so sure about the Muse, but I can see that *you* inspire him." He grew more pensive as they approached the inlet of Pythagoreion. "Your brother would never approve this mission."

"We must not lose this opportunity. It's the month of Thargelion, the birthday of Artemis and Apollo. There is peace among the kingdoms of Anatolia," she noted.

Cleis eagerly agreed. "One of the original shrines for Artemis of the Amazons! Atalanta took a vow to Artemis and was rescued by a she-bear!" Her enthusiasm was contagious and the crew showed increased interest. "Also, Ephesus may help us understand how Artemis and their Cybele are fused in their worship."

"The Lydian people are like any other good folk," added Sappho. "They're philosophers and poets, not invaders."

"True enough," said Pittacus, who was honored throughout Ionia as the victor of Sigeion. Nonetheless, his hand kept a firm hold on his sword. Pittacus noticed their boat taking a detour, landing in Samos. "Phaon, where are you taking us?"

"Before Ephesus, we must visit the Heraion," answered the ferryman. "Any pilgrim to Cybele-Artemis, should first pay homage to the birthplace of Hera." The boat slid onto the soft beach and Phaon quickly disembarked. "Both the Heraion and the Artemision are very old temples, from the time before the Olympians." Alcaeus also jumped into the shallow beach and helped Phaon pull the vessel ashore. "With Hera's blessing, we will then ferry to Anatolia. Reliable scouts will then take us through the Mycale range."

"The Birthplace of Hera," Sappho murmured. "How can a god be born?" She struggled with a deep strain of skepticism. Yet she eagerly planned to perform for the birth of Artemis. Removing her simple sandals and pulling up her himation, she stepped into the warm water of Samos. In the distance, across the Strait, the mountains of Lydia's Mycale range were visible.

----- ----- -----

They made a powerful impression: Three armed warriors,

three local guides, a delicate but capable poetess, her acolyte, and the awkward Aesop, marched passed the local farmers and artisans, who backed off in a clear mixture of respect and fear. The steep cliffs circumvented the inlet while goats and eagles peered down with apprehensive curiosity.

In the village of Pythagoreion, they filled their pouches with fresh spring water from the underground aqueduct built by Eupalinos. Pittacus admired the marvelous tunnel concealed from the view of adversaries. Fertile crops and an adequate water supply were assured in the event of further hostilities.

As she sipped the restorative water, Sappho took in the intoxicating fragrances around her. The stringent scent of pine mingled with the sharp seduction of thyme, sage, and oregano, which was then sweetened by the redolence of lilacs and oleander. Lush collections of green leaves enclosed an explosion of white, pink, and violet petals curling and reaching for the sun. Ivy wrapped around tree trunks in a stubborn and determined spiral. Bees went about their business, undeterred by the strangers. The bees and the locals seemed to have a mutual agreement to live in harmony.

At their encampment, Aesop took the first fire watch and Sappho joined him as he piled on a few more logs and stoked the flame. After some mutual complaining about difficult paths and tired legs, they settled into a comfortable reverie. Sappho chewed on wild herbs and watched sparks racing toward the heavens.

"Returning to the Heraion provokes emotions," said Aesop as he gazed into the flame. "I was a slave here, the property of the men who tended to Hera. It was also where I met Doricha."

Sappho nodded with comprehension. "So you have bitter memories of slavery, but also warm memories of the kindness of your masters and Doricha's affections."

"Don't be offended," Aesop suddenly said. "But I'm glad that Charoxos and Doricha didn't come with us."

Sappho offered a sly grin. "You think I'm surprised to hear that?" she spurred. "I know your feelings about Doricha. Despite all my better judgment, she entices me too."

Aesop ruminated sadly. "When she cured my mutism, when she introduced me to Isis, I fell in love with her. So you see, when I see her with Charoxos…"

"I know," Sappho interrupted to reduce his pain of confession. "You're an old lover, one of many, and he's her new love." Aesop took a deep breath and then released a sigh. "Anaktoria, the 'army wife,'" she muttered.

"Excuse me?"

She recited the lines from one of her poems:

That man who sits there facing you, any man,

Listening to the sweetness of your voice,

The sweetness of your laughter.

I swear it, it sets my heart shaking in my breast,

For once I look at you, even for a moment,

I can't speak any longer, my tongue breaks down,

A fire burns inside my skin, my eyes can't see a thing,

A whistle sounds in my ears,

Cold sweat covers me, trembling takes hold of my body,

Just short of dying, yet I must endure,

His laughter next to you.

I'm a poor shivering child, greener than the grass.

Aesop felt a cold chill pass through him although he was close to the fire. "By the gods! You just spoke my pain! You do understand. Your agony in love must be double since you ache for both men and women."

----- ----- -----

Soon enough, the path opened to a walkway of blue marble with flanks of statues guiding them to the shrine. "The Sacred Way," announced Phaon. Despite their worldly skepticism, the small band was impressed. Old and new gods mingled casually with beautiful figures of young boys, dancing nymphs, and the favorite animals of Hera. Around the walkway, rabbits, ferrets, and smaller rodents scurried among the flora. Several snakes slithered across their path, taking no note of the travelers among them. The air was suffused with the songs of birds. Hawks hovered above the dense canopy toward the gentle slopes of the Samos Ampelos range.

As they proceeded to Hera's altar, they came to a wet marshland. A tortoise lumbered beside them and lizards flittered nervously away from the intruders. At a distance from their companions, Alcaeus addressed Sappho. "I'm curious about this mission. What are you searching for?"

She took a deep breath and tried to explain her motives. "I look around and have many questions. What is the force that brought all of this into existence? We speak of many gods and goddesses; but what force animates them? Across the Strait, in Miletus, the philosophers debate the essence of 'Arche', the primal fundamental element, the core of all else. Thales believes it's water, which flows through all life. Others point to Air, which pervades everything. Then, they speak of Fire, the spark of life. Anaximander introduced the concept of Apeiron, which, he claims, breaks into all the opposites of life. Light and dark, hot and cold, peace and war."

Alcaeus was intrigued. "What's your opinion?" he inquired.

"I don't claim any certainty, but I believe there is a primal source." She stared into his eyes. "I believe it's Love."

"Love?" Alcaeus was bewildered.

"I see the creatures of the woods entwined together. That's one variety of Love, Eros, and that fierce energy is worshipped by the adherents of Cybele. In my circle of participants, my thiasos, we offer praise to Aphrodite. She contains Eros, the beast of lust, with a more controlled desire." Alcaeus twitched nervously and Sappho couldn't resist the urge to tease him. "I'm sure you know Aphrodite," she commented with a smirk. He offered a weak grunt.

She continued. "Artemis, the Huntress, remains chaste but represents a love of children and beasts. She tries to protect women in childbirth, but she needs Hera's help." Her tone shifted. "Hera troubles me," she admitted. "Is she an aspect of Love or of obedience? She demands fidelity within the structure of marriage and is deeply vengeful when the rules are violated. But is that Love? Why are the goddesses so vindictive?"

"I see," said Alcaeus eagerly. "You seek to explore all the varieties of Love. You believe a primary power is to be found there."

166

She nodded and appreciated his sincere interest. "I can say, 'bird' and you'll understand. But look at all these birds. What is, 'bird'? Even more troubling, the various aspects of Love are often in conflict with each other. Perhaps that's the Apeiron, the essence of opposing forces."

Alcaeus took a risk. "I have Love for you, Sappho," he admitted. "That love is like Apeiron. At moments, I have the urge to take you, ravish you, release all my lust. Eros. But I also adore you. I want no harm to come to you. I would never hurt you or offend you. Then there are moments when, just being in your presence, I'm completely satisfied. I value the moments of sharing our poetry. Fire. It can warm the hearth, but it can also destroy a city."

"I understand," she assured him. "So Love is an Apeiron, a wild mixture of opposing forces. Is it *the* Apeiron? I need to understand all its variations."

"Let me take that exploration with you," he requested.

"That might be useful," she stated pensively. "The perception of both a male and a female."

"Are we also opposing forces?"

"I hope not," she replied. Alcaeus paused, open-mouthed. They shared a joyful laughter.

----- ----- -----

The Heraion was approached through a long stoa that led to the three walls of the temenos. The final section of the Sacred Path was covered and supported by concrete columns of the curled Ionic style. Hence the Sacred Path became a Sacred Stoa. To the side, a ritual was being performed at a smaller grove. They could smell the roasting pig and the solemn chanting of the adherents.

The Sacred Stoa ended at an open grove, encircled by pine, cyprus, and oak trees. Upon a great flat stone was a detailed rendition of Hera, the wife of Zeus. In contrast to the tight-lipped Hera of Attica, this one was still solemn but peaceful. The signs of weather and age added to the effect. Hera never forgave Paris for giving the Golden Apple to Aphrodite. Artemis had to hide her handmaiden Kallista from the vindictiveness of Hera by turning her into a bear. The women are always blamed; even if they were raped. Hera rarely forgave any one. But the Hera at Samos was humbled by age.

Sappho gazed at the goddesses' round diadem on her head, the scepter in her hand, the cow at her right and a lion at her left. Of course, she thought, both nurturing and ferocious. Her cape wrapped across her head like a covering and swept down her chest. Perhaps there was a time, Sappho considered, when people had to be separated from the beasts. Perhaps that could only be done with order. The archon Draco made similar arguments in Attica. So perhaps Hera's strict sense of order had a necessary time. Sappho would try to be more understanding. This goddess, born of Titans, was of a time of chaos. Perhaps, in her own way, Hera resents the domination of Zeus. She submitted only when Zeus threatens to drop her from Olympus. Perhaps she rages at the other women because she can't win battles with her husband. But, is it Love?

Numerous votive offerings were left at the altar. The remains of animal sacrifices were piled in a nearby pit. Ashes were gathered by devotees and scattered to feed the soil. Pine cones were everywhere. Seeds from various fruits were sprinkled around the statue. Simple pottery cups and bowls were piled to the side by attendants.

Several pieces of pottery caught Sappho's attention. The engravings were not from the Aegean or Asia Minor. The angular postures and profile glances, along with the human bodies and animal heads indicated Egyptian origin. Sappho recognized a similar style among the statues along the Stoa. She did not yet know enough about that. Perhaps Chamoxos and Doricha would enlighten her.

----- ----- -----

Cleis was reluctant to visit Hera once again. But, as she moved along the path, which was flanked by clusters of violet and white lygos blossoms, and arrived at the central courtyard, she noticed a different Hera. That sculpture was softened by age and presented with open arms and a gentler expression. That Hera was an earth mother from an ancient people. Despite her effort to remain strong, Cleis felt tears trickle down her face.

Sappho noticed her distress. "My child, what's hurting you?"

Cleis wiped her cheeks forcefully.

"The Arkteia," she replied. "And that poor girl who hung herself, my father selling me to the hoplite like a sack of grain, my mother accepting it like the will of the gods. The way Eurybiades 'consummated' our betrothal. Oh!" She buried her face in her hands and sobbed heavily. Sappho embraced the girl and rocked her tenderly. "My poor child," she hummed softly.

Between spasms of tears, Cleis uttered, "I wish you were my mother."

Sappho replied, "From this moment, you are my child. Aphrodite wills it."

As Cleis calmed down, she opened her heart further. "I want to be strong, I want to destroy those memories."

Sappho considered the girl's remarks. "Ah, yes. Memory. The realm of Mnemosyne. I've constructed verses about Memory and Time. Perhaps it's because of the few grey hairs I've noticed." She laughed gently.

"Would you recite them for me?" Their companions approached. "Please, I'm eager to hear them, too," Alcaeus stated. Pittacus, Aesop, Phaon and Antimenidas circled around like an eager audience. She relented.

She sang of a woman who had to depart from Lesvos and of the one left behind. The first woman paces on sleepless nights with memories of the sacred thiasos. In the next lines, the woman still in Lesvos watches a cloud pass before the moon, and thinks of her lost friend who sailed away like a cloud. She hopes she is not forgotten and offers to remind her friend on a distant shore: the beautiful times they had, the romps through fields of roses, crocus, and violets, their loving embrace beneath a chestnut tree. The final stanza offered a consolation. So long as memory survives, their love is alive. In memory is eternal youth and endless love. Memory conquers time and space. Despite the wide sea between them, they are together. Both are visited by the sparrows of Aphrodite.

Pittacus was moved by the poem and shared a memory. "I once had a war dog that I trained from a pup. In the chaos of battle, the dog was lost. It grew wild in the forests and mountains of Thrace." He brushed away the twigs near him. "Many years later, I returned to that land by way of the Hebros River. A pack of wild dogs were drinking from the river. One great hound rushed toward me and I prepared for a battle. But the beast wagged its tail and whimpered like the pup It remembered me. It was my dog! We were companions for a long time." He thought about the poem. "You're right, Sappho. The memory keeps him alive for me."

Aesop stood next to Pittacus. "Did you say it was the Hebros River? Do you mean the Evros?"

"Some call it that," replied Pittacus.

"That was my homeland," noted the raconteur.

The company took positions by the statue and silently contemplated the ripples of fate that define every life. Sappho had only created a few poems for Hera, but, at the temple in Samos, was feeling a creative inspiration.

Beside me now, I beseech you, Lady Hera,

Gracious in all your majesty

You whom House Atreus invoked to aid them,

When their glorious princes sailed to Ilion.

Now I entreat you, Oh, Goddess,

Teach men the power of peace,

Show them the path of Love

Forgive Paris, an impressionable youth,

Who gave the golden apple to Aphrodite.

19

EPHESUS

Phaon's scouts welcomed the passengers when they landed in the Anatolian city of Priene on Mount Mycale near the mouth of the Meandering River. Although a popular city, with several temples, and its own boule council, it suffered an earthquake in the last century and the Aegean continued to fill the harbor with silt. The city's leaders often spoke of relocation, but that would require a major works project with costly taxes, and the coastal site remained desirable for merchants and traders. Still, the sense of inevitability inspired many of the philosophers from nearby Miletus. The residents accepted swampy episodes with simple resignation.

After a period of animated bargaining, Phaon returned to his companions to announce the required fee, which the scouts would accept only in Athenian drachmas, Corinthian staters, or Lydian electrum. Pittacus said it was a fair price for the journey through the Mycale mountain range. In typical style, Antimenidas grumbled and his brother, Alcaeus, teased him about being miserly. When Aesop inquired who would guide them beyond the Mycale onto Ephesus, the answer was enticing.

"The Amazons, of course."

Cleis was thrilled beyond words. Sappho remembered those barbarian women with mixed feelings. They served well as trainers in self-defense, offered lively conversation, and enjoyed festivals and dancing. But they could be temperamental and easily provoked. They certainly liked her wine and drank it without water. Intoxicated Amazons were volatile.

Sappho advised the scouts that she only had the coins from Lesvos. She handed them several electrums from her home island. They bit the coins, judged their weight, and marveled at the ratio of gold to silver. Examining the coins further, they realized the face on the electrums was the same face speaking to them. One scout gazed upon her. "You're The Poetess!" he exclaimed with respect. "When Phaon told us he was bringing honorable guests, we had no idea. Of course we'll accept your coins from the land of Lesvos. Your island has a long history with Anatolia."

Phaon stayed with his ferry as the company proceeded to their first encampment in the Mycale range. Until their return, he would earn a considerable amount of electrums serving as a shuttle between Samos and Priene. Pilgrims often enjoy a journey instead of the local temenos, and he would profit from their missions. Antimenidas stayed with the ferryman as security.

----- ----- -----

The journey began with an ascent that left the group breathing forcefully; but it soon leveled off as the scouts brought them into a hidden valley with ample fresh water and few tree roots to maneuver. Long-horn sheep passed and paid them no regard. Goats evaluated the strangers suspiciously and then leaped along the mountain wall. The scouts used swords to slice away vines and thorns and selected flat sections for rest breaks. With relief, they came to the open meadow of the town of Anaia, which marked the halfway point of their journey. Townsfolk were eager to share their stores of olives, figs, goat cheese, grapes, and mazza. They were familiar with pilgrims traveling to the Artemision. One couple served as the leaders of the town and kept track of origins of wanderers. Lesvos and Athens impressed them. When Aesop spoke of his travails in Thrace and Egypt, they were enthralled. Once again, he had an enthusiastic audience. They knew of the heroic Pittacus and were excited about the two famous poets of Lesvos. Pittacus asked if the town faced harassment from marauders. They replied readily, "Not since the Amazons returned!" Cleis felt her heart skip a beat. The poets wondered if those warrior women would inspire creativity. Pittacus worried that they would be compelled to challenge a male hero.

In casual conversation, the townsfolk spoke of the Galli, who performed their rituals in a nearby cave. When the guests showed interest, they were told of those adherents of Attis, the god who is killed and then resurrected.

"It's a very ancient cult," the woman leader explained. "From what I know, Attis was born of the Great Mother, Cybele, in her earthly form as Nana. He was destined to marry a princess. But, when Cybele revealed her total beauty to him, Attis ran away from the wedding and went mad in the forests. That's when he un-manned himself."

Pittacus couldn't conceal a shudder. "What? Wait! Are you saying he castrated himself?"

The couple nodded their assent. The male elaborated. "That's why the Galli are eunuchs."

Pittacus protested. "But he was mad! Why imitate the horrendous act of a madman?"

"He was driven mad with total love and devotion for Cybele."

"How poetic!" declared Alcaeus sarcastically. "Should I write a lyrical poem, or an elegy? I'll certainly use a chorus for lamentations."

Sappho shushed him with a wave and inquired further. "The cult of Attis demands self-harm to demonstrate devotion. Do they ever show remorse for such a sacrifice?"

"Frequently," replied the male. "When the drugs wear off!" All the men agreed with a hearty laugh. Sappho contemplated the connection between sacrifice and religious piety. She had attended many rituals with goats, lambs, and pigs. In addition to the offerings, most of the meat was shared for a great meal. Tentatively, she asked, "What do they do with…the sacrificial parts?"

Nonchalantly, the woman replied. "Oh, I think they're left inside the cave. More wine?"

The man added perplexing details. "I've heard that, in some time, Attis himself was killed and The Old Ones ate him." Sappho and Cleis gasped. Aesop said he had heard of symbolically dismembered gods in Egypt. Pittacus was outraged. "Cannibalism!" he proclaimed.

"Perhaps in earlier times," they replied. "Now they use bread to symbolize the body of Attis. Our town baker serves them well."

"So, it's only a fable with symbols?" asked Aesop desperately.

"Please make it so," added Alcaeus.

"Sometimes they kill a bull instead," replied the woman. "They use the bull's blood instead of the blood of Attis."

"Yes, a taurobolium," noted Pittacus. "I've seen that." "Some cults have substituted red wine for blood," the wife noted. "The old tradition is changing."

When not horrified, Cleis was intrigued. "When does he mutilate himself and when is he killed?"

"We're not sure," answered the husband. "Perhaps it depends upon the location of the cult. Phrygia might be different from Pontus which might differ from Taurus. We know the stories but can't verify anything."

----- ----- -----

With fresh water and grapes for extra energy, the travelers resumed their trek. The lead scout informed them they had only one more mountain to cross before they would arrive at the field of the Amazons. Pittacus walked with him at the front of the procession. "I have heard of these Amazons," he muttered. "I know the tales of their Queen, Orithiya, and her invasion of Athens. They occupied the Areopagus before Theseus managed to evict them. Dionysus battled them at Ephesus and pushed them to Samos. The soil turned red with their blood and remains so."

The scout growled and scoffed at his concerns. "You believe stories men tell children, like your friend, Aesop. The Areopagus, the mound for Ares, would be a likely encampment since they honor the God of War. Someday, you must travel to Pontus and see their Rock of Ares. If Orithiya did invade Athens, she was trying to rescue her sister, Antiope. Your people sing paeans to thieves and murderers. Theseus and his mad cohort, Herakles, absconded with the belt of Hippolyte, slaughtered many of the women who welcomed them with kindness, and abducted the rest. The dirt of Panaema has always been red."

Pittacus replied calmly. "I remember the details. My concern is for the safety of my group. Will these women challenge me? If I fall, what will they do to my friends? They are man-haters!"

The scout roared with laughter. "You must not always listen to the liars of Attica! These warrior women fight men, compete with men, and sometimes kill men." He put his hand on Pittacus' shoulder. "I can assure you they do not hate men!" He winked at Pittacus and patted the warrior's back. "It's not just with iron that they can best you!" With a loud guffaw, he returned to the other scouts. Pittacus wasn't certain if he was reassured or more anxious.

"Their favorite goddess, Artemis; is she not The Butcher? Did she not kill any man who landed on her secret island? She turned Aktaion into a stag so his own hunting hounds would kill him! She's devious and bloodthirsty."

Again, the scout grumbled his reply. "She hunts," he reminded Pittacus. "She butchers whatever she kills. If the tale of Aktaion is true, then he was a fool. He was hunting in her sacred woods. He went to her secret pool. Why don't you give her as much indulgence as you do for Theseus or Herakles?"

----- ----- -----

With joyful surprise, the troupe discovered a well-developed town as they emerged from the last mountain range and faced a flatland below them. The scouts identified the region as Kusadasi – Bird Island. From their perspective on the hilltop, the travelers could understand the name, since one area did poke into the Aegean in the shape of a bird's head. Along the bay of the same name were numerous homes and shops. Merchants were loading their ships with figs, olives, grapes, spices, and oils.

The scouts halted the journey at a popular taverna in the area of Marathesion. A family had converted part of their home into a public house for food, drink, and lodging. "We will stay with you until the guides to Ephesus arrive," the lead scout explained. With mountains behind them and a wide view of the sea, the troupe enjoyed the local beverages and nourishment. Small rooms in the rear served as temporary lodging. The term, "temporary," could mean twenty minutes or several days, depending upon a tenant's purpose. "We will return to this taverna in two weeks for your return trip. Does that sound right for you?"

"Yes," replied Pittacus. "If I can believe what you say about our amazon guides."

The scouts laughed heartily. "We are the ones who should be concerned," he explained in jest. "You may fall in love and not return with the rest of our payment!" The scout then turned to Sappho and Alcaeus. "Surely you've heard of Myrine? Didn't she control Lesvos?"

"We've heard tales," replied Sappho. "In some fables, she and her sister founded Lesvos. Mytilene is supposedly the name of her sister."

----- ----- -----

Both Pittacus and Alcaeus were wary of some of the other lodgers in the taverna. "We think it's best if you and Cleis stay in the same room tonight," Pittacus advised Sappho.

"That's what we planned," she replied readily. "I wouldn't leave her alone. In her short time, she's been abandoned enough."

Alcaeus smiled at Sappho. "You truly love that girl, don't you?" he asked warmly.

"I love all my sparrows," she answered curtly. Then, more intimately, she qualified. "With my lyre and my stylus, I explore all the variations of Love. I sing paeans to the power of Love, I celebrate with epithalamia. But, when I look upon Cleis, I see the daughter I should have had. I recognize my own rebel spirit in her. I understand her craving to seek answers to limitless questions. She would be at home with the philosophers of Miletus."

"I understand," said Alcaeus. "She has a strong will. But I don't think her destiny lies with Miletus. She has a strong mind and could easily debate any wise man. But I think she'd prefer a horse to a philosopher's chair."

Sappho sniffed with annoyance. "What makes you think a philosopher can't ride a horse?"

"Ah, yes," quipped Alcaeus. "Once again, we merge opposites!"

Pittacus grew impatient with their prattle. "I'll take the first watch so you can rest your mind," he snorted sarcastically. Twice, an intoxicated customer and his female companion had to be cordially redirected to a different room. The owners of the house did well in their diversified business.

----- ----- -----

Cleis removed her chiton, which slid down her body and fell to the floor. She knelt to retrieve it, folded it carefully, and placed it on the night table. She then unfastened her purple headband and let her yellow hair fall freely past her shoulders. Sappho watched her from the bed and burned with desire for her young protégé. Cleis could inspire many poems. Despite her sensual reactions, Sappho pushed Eros aside and harvested a deeper affiliation for Cleis, as the girl slid into the bed next to her. She kissed the girl and they embraced under a thick blanket of wool.

"I love you, Sappho," Cleis whispered, and snuggled into her chest. Sappho stroked her golden hair and sensed a love neither Alcaeus nor Dika would understand. "I love you, too, dear Cleis, as a mother loves her child." They soon surrendered to Hypnos and slept peacefully entwined in each other's arms.

----- ----- -----

Stirred awake from a deep slumber with intricate dreams, the disruption sounded like another earthquake, which plagued the region. But Sappho soon realized it was the sound of horses galloping and snorting as they raced to the taverna. Cleis was also aroused by the rumbling and ran to the window. Sappho gazed upon the naked girl as she leaned out the window and the air sent a quiver through her hair that glowed in the morning sun. "They're here!" Cleis exclaimed with excitement as she turned to Sappho. "How should I greet them?"

Sappho laughed tenderly. "Welcome them like that and you'll be abducted," she quipped.

----- ----- -----

Some of the boarders dropped their breakfasts and hurried to the taverna entrance. Others slipped out from their rooms in disarray to witness the arrival. The scouts waited with their own horses at the hitching rail. The riders pulled up in a tumult of dust, stones, and commands. The women wore leather trousers and several riders wrapped their trousers with a chiton that was belted at the waist. Cleis noticed their leg greaves that reminded her of Eurybiades when he tried to comfort her. Three of the riders had quivers strapped across their shoulders and an attached bow. Javelins and swords were sheathed in their saddles. They wore pointed caps and carried circular shields on their arms. The shields were painted with images of roaring lions, soaring eagles, or lunging bears. Despite their aggressive appearance, they also wore long earrings and decorated headbands; and carried flutes and lyres in their saddlebags.

Most prominent were their tattoos. In Attica, only slaves and criminals had symbolic brands; but these warrior women inflicted the markings for decoration. The citizens of Lesvos were familiar with the custom but Cleis was fascinated. Besides their arms and necks, some branding occurred on their faces, to depict circles, dots, thunderbolts, and geometric patterns. Cleis wondered if the practice extended to legs, torsos and more personal intimate areas. She shivered to think of the pain such a practice would generate.

In one continuous motion, the lead rider swept her leg across her horse, dismounted, and hitched her stallion to the post. The other riders followed in kind. The lead approached the scouts, stopped in front of their leader, and smiled. In martial style, they took hold of each other's elbows and shared comradely greetings.

"Melanippe!" the scout shouted happily. "Always a joy to see you."

"You owe me a drink," replied the amazon. "I'm tired of mare's milk." She turned to Sappho. "So you're The Poetess." Sappho nodded and the warrior gazed upon Alcaeus. "The other poet from Mytilene?"

"Correct," answered Alcaeus. "Welcome, Melanippe."

The amazon appeared offended. "You dare to address me by my familiar name!" She glared at him without blinking. Alcaeus stammered an apology until she laughed heartily. "I'm playing with you!" She patted his back.

The other riders approached the taverna occupants, shook hands, and introduced themselves. Clyemne, with scarlet hair, carried a quiver and a short sword. Across her forehead were dots and studs made from gold. Marsepia of the golden hair, flaunted a javelin and several knives on her belt. Phoebe, with dark braided hair, was introduced as the second in command. Phoebe carried both a spear and a sword. Her bare arms displayed slithering snakes. Thermodosa, named after a warrior at Troy, also carried a quiver and bow and displayed lighting flashes at both temples. Derinoe wore a sword and held a lyre. She removed her cap and shook her raven dark hair with its streaks of blue.

Pittacus was impressed and offered his version of a welcoming compliment. "Six amazons and three hoplites. The country is safe!"

"Beware," warned Melanippe. "You wouldn't want to be humiliated in a contest with a woman." Pittacus accepted the challenge and the company roared in anticipation. The evening would include an arm wrestle.

Melanippe then noticed Cleis. "Who is this beauty?"

With Sappho's prompting, Cleis stepped toward the warrior woman. "My name is Cleis. I was born in Athens. I now live in Lesvos."

Melanippe studied the young girl thoughtfully. Cleis held her ground but was trembling inside. She couldn't take her eyes from the sunburst in the middle of the warrior's forehead. "I see. You live with The Great Poetess in Eressos." Cleis nodded nervously. "Has she inspired you?"

Cleis screwed up her courage. "Sappho has saved my life. She offered sanctuary when I had no one else. She taught me the love of Aphrodite."

"Has she now?" asked Melanippe, more like an accusation than a question. "Have you forgotten Artemis?"

Eagerly, Cleis answered. "Not at all! I love Artemis and never wanted to leave her protection." To drive home her defense, she added, "I still dream of Atalanta!"

Melanippe was touched by the girl's devotion. Sappho witnessed the interaction with apprehension.

----- ----- -----

Alcaeus came to Pittacus at the watch.

"I heard your songs," said the warrior. "Very clever and suggestive. I'm glad you kept the amazons happy."

"Get some rest," replied Alcaeus.

But the warrior was too restless to sleep and wandered into the drinking area. He slipped into a secluded corner, ordered a plate of appetizers, and had a high-handled kantharos filled with wine. With one sip, he knew they were no longer in Hellas, since the wine was not diluted. Several of the warrior women were seated at a table, telling exaggerated stories and playfully challenging the veracity of each tale. Aesop was entertaining several women with tales of magic creatures and animated animals. Other lodgers were discussing the current prices of produce and handiwork while many voiced concerns about the Persians. The family owners of the taverna were jovial and attentive and collected coins diligently.

Melanippe discovered Pittacus concealed in the shadows. "There you are! The noble Protector of innocent women! Come, join us if you dare!" Pittacus wanted to avoid an escalation but also had no inclination to offend their guides in a strange land. He brought his plate and kantharos to their table. "Such powerful arms!" Melanippe announced, gazing at his large biceps. "Your body speaks of many battles."

"Not that many," he replied modestly. "But I always do better than my adversary."

Aesop tried to dissuade the amazon. "He's a kind warrior. But once aroused, he goes mad!" Pittacus glowered at him. Melanippe was only further aroused.

The crowd roared their approval. Melanippe unsheathed her knife and displayed its handle to Pittacus. It was made of bone and had engravings. Near the base, two lions faced each other with a standing javelin between them. Further up the handle, curling lines were organized in a spiral. On the iron blade was the image of a rod with a snake twirled around it. "The legends are real," she murmured. "This dagger is from Troy." She pounded the blade into the wooden table. "Come, hoplite! Put your elbow there." Swords and shields were hammered to encourage the contest.

The rivals put their elbows together and grasped hands. At the sign from Phoebe, the skirmish began. Both contestants were encouraged with yells and howls. Aesop grabbed the opportunity to make a few wagers.

Melanippe didn't have the kind of muscles that bulged like those of Pittacus. Nonetheless, her strength was just as powerful although not as obvious. At one point, it looked like Pittacus had the leverage; but she pushed back and they reached a level of strenuous inertia. After thirty minutes, and despite the constant encouragement from the crowd, Phoebe asked them to call a drawer and both agreed. Several gamblers argued over the technicalities of their wagers. If you bet that Pittacus would win, do you lose if it's a drawer? The amazons, with their swords clashing against their shields, settled the debate: a drawer rendered all wagers void.

The crowd continued to grumble until they heard the strings of a barbiton. Sappho had been roused by the clamor and recognized the need for soothing music. Derinoe accompanied Sappho with her own lyre.

Come now, my holy lyre,

find your voice and speak to me.

Come to me once more, O you Muses,

leaving golden threads of melody.

Come to me now, you delicate Graces,

and you fair-haired Muses

The music, poetry, and wine had the intended effect. While the music lulled the crowd into a heavy stupor, Pittacus and Melanippe rushed into the shadows and crashed through the door of a vacant room. They said little but communicated with pounding breaths, eager hands, and hungry lips. Like starving bears, they devoured each other with erotic fury bordering on combat. In their explosive passion, Pittacus was convinced that amazons were not man-haters.

----- ----- -----

In the bright morning sun, Pittacus awoke from a sleep of deep exhaustion. He was grateful for the water krater and the fresh towels that he needed to wash off the residue of debauchery from his night of carnal indulgence. As he wiped his hair and face, he noticed the amazon warrior lying in bed and smiling at him.

"You know, I allowed the drawer," she muttered. "I knew that, as a leader of men, your authority would be damaged if a woman defeated you."

"That's funny," replied Pittacus, as he tossed the towel at her. "I allowed for the drawer. I didn't want the leader of our guides to carry resentment into a strange journey."

"Liar!" she exclaimed with a beckoning tone. "Typical man!"

He crawled onto the bed and slivered on top of her. "Am I typical?" he asked.

Melanippe ran her fingers through his damp hair. "Not at all," she replied. "I was impressed."

"So was I," he countered. "You have wonderful skills." He stroked the sunburst on her forehead.

Phoebe entered the small room as they kissed. "My queen, the riders are finishing breakfast and ready to travel." She nodded to Pittacus, who covered his nakedness. Phoebe laughed at his modesty. "No need to hide from me," she said.

Melanippe beckoned to Phoebe with outstretched arms. "Come here." Phoebe came to the bed and kissed her queen. "You let us sleep late, my dear."

"I assumed you both needed the rest." She mussed her hair. "But now, hurry up!" She exited with a giggle.

After years of combat, Pittacus was accustomed to rapid arousal and quick preparation. As he headed for the taverna, he encountered the leader of the scouts, who offered a friendly greeting. "You did well," he remarked.

Pittacus considered his words carefully. "The drink and the contest aroused our passions. We succumbed. I know you and Melanippe..."

"Don't bother," the scout interrupted. "No one owns that woman. She chose you last night."

Pittacus thought about that. "How many men has she slept with?" he asked with dismay?"

The scout grunted his reply. "How many women, and boys, have you slept with? Hypocrite! After your night, do you doubt that women also have desires?"

Pittacus held back an impulsive reply, took a slow breath, and said, "She's a marvelous woman."

The scout leaned in to share a confidence. "You know she let you call a drawer." Pittacus grumbled a reply but the scout clarified. "She knew not to injure the pride of a male lover."

----- ----- -----

Cleis strolled the grounds around the taverna. Sappho and Derinoe were sharing strumming techniques with their instruments. Derinoe was fascinated by Sappho's plectrum which was made from tortoise shell. Cleis was eager to ask Derinoe about the blue fringes in her raven hair. Marsepia and Phoebe were practicing their throws with spear and javelin, using an old tree stump as a target. Thermadosa and Clyemne were fashioning extra arrows and testing their accuracy by shooting apples off a tree. They never missed. The horses had been brushed and fed and were stirring impatiently at the hitching post. Aesop and Alcaeus were checking their provisions and securing their possessions in the wagon.

Cleis approached the golden-haired Marsepia, who greeted her affably. "Could you show me how to throw it?"

Marsepia smiled and handed the girl her javelin. Walking behind Cleis, she instructed her step by step. "Keep your palm up to the sky. Let it lie in the palm of your right hand. That's it. Put your hand back further. Good. Stretch out this finger. Look at your target. Let your left arm swing across your body. Keep the javelin at eye level. Go! Go!" Cleis ran and threw but missed the target several times. "Don't give up," said Phoebe. "Keep your wrist relaxed," said Marsepia.

Finally, after many attempts, Cleis managed to penetrate the stump. The onlookers applauded and cheered. "Very good progress," noted Marsepia. "Your left leg still has to shift your body weight. But you learn quickly."

Sappho turned to the sound of the cheers and witnessed Cleis running with the javelin and throwing it with a powerful vortex. The girl's expression, her motion, and her power supplied further inspiration for poetry. Alcaeus approached Sappho. "Your little sparrow is soaring like an eagle," he declared.

With a melancholy glukupikron, Sappho replied. "I can only hope my sparrow heeds the lesson of Icarus. Oh, Cleis, don't fly too high or too far too soon."

Melanippe and Pittacus emerged from the taverna. Pittacus approached The Poetess while Melanippe went to her horse. "Did you have breakfast?" asked Sappho.

"Honeyed vleeta," replied Pittacus. "And sweet melon. I'm ready."

Sappho nodded. "The amaranth here is better than our local wheat."

Pittacus squinted. "Was that a sneaky metaphor?"

Sappho laughed and headed for the wagon.

----- ----- -----

They traveled a path that cut through mountains along the coast. It was a strategic decision. Travel on the flat open lands would leave them exposed to marauders but the mountain passage was well-concealed and, being the high ground, easily defensible if necessary.

As their journey came to its final descent, marble roads and extensive architecture signaled entry into an ancient civilization. The oikos that blanketed the hills, and the stone streets that slithered through the agora, told of a city that survived the injuries of time. The residents had seen their share of invaders, conquerors, and marauders. Hittites had once erected a town there. Hellenes had established colonies along the coast for centuries. The Cimmerians had come and gone. Lydia was then ruling the region and Croesus was merging villages into manageable unions. The Amazons traveled down from Pontus and the Don River and had their impact. Pilgrims came to Ephesus from Thrace, Egypt, Palestine, and Asia. The people of Ephesus, the "Servants of Artemis", were never surprised by foreign visitors.

But the visitors were profoundly surprised by the temenos dedicated to the Cybele and Artemis fusion. The scent of burning herbs permeated the temenos. Galli, the castrated priests of Attis, chanted and danced along the stoa to the temple grounds. The Maenads of Dionysus swayed in serpentine frenzy to the sounds of flutes, tambourines, and horns as they waved the thyrsus and embraced any pilgrim in their path. Some wore deerskins, others donned horned helmets. Both the galli and the maenads were obviously intoxicated, but the catalyst could be any number of drugs. A few sober philosophers from Miletus or Crete were among the crowd, as were mystics from Asia and Egypt. Beggars also lined the border and electrums were thrown to them by travelers who were filled with inspiration or alcohol.

But when the travelers from Lesvos arrived at the temple mount, they were left speechless. Nothing in their prior encounters prepared them for the sublime magnificence of the Artemision. Double sets of stairs ascended to the temenos from all four sides. In the corners between the stairways were blossoms of all the colors of the rainbow. The inner temple was completely surrounded by a stoa of immense proportion. The columns were made from marble, an innovation none of the travelers ever saw at other temples. The roof of the stoa was engraved with numerous scenes from the lives of both goddesses. Touches of gold embedded in the stoa caused it to glow like a constant sunrise.

Torches at each space between columns were tended by priestesses, in long himations, with braided hair tied back and held in place by tiaras, each with purple amethyst in the center. At regular intervals, they threw incense into the flames and fanned out their arms in supplication.

Reaching the top of the stairway, the group entered the space of the hieron. They were startled by the screeching of guinea hens, free-spirited birds sacred to Artemis. Large hunting hounds were stationed at several columns while snake-dancers swirled and rotated with their reptiles. Everywhere, musicians filled the hieron with drums, horns, flutes, and lyres. The group passed large sculptures of animals sacred to the goddesses -- bears, wild boars, leopards, falcons, goats, and bulls – as well as statues of Cybele seated on her throne with lions on both sides, and Artemis soaring in her chariot pulled by robust horses. Paintings lined the walls. In one depiction, Acteon spied on the bathing Artemis, then changed into a stag and was attacked by his own hounds. In another composition, Orion is lifted to the stars.

Approaching the interior of the temple, where the great altars were located, they inhaled incense constantly and drank water from the large kraters that were available. It was easy to feel light-headed amidst the music and the dancing and the chanting. Entering the main hall, they were assaulted by frantic votaries with glazed eyes, tearing at their clothes in frenzied passion, writhing and jumping, twisting and screaming. Walking toward the great altar, Aesop encountered a group of maenads. The intoxicated women lured him into their revelry with their dancing, tambours, castanets, and singing. He seized the thyrsus and danced with it, chasing each maenad with the pine-cone end, until one of them grabbed the staff and wrestled him to the floor. Deciding he was thirsty, they poured water in his mouth. Pittacus and Alcaeus seized the clamorous opportunity to dance with the amazons. Sappho and Cleis danced with the galli as they lumbered to the great statue. Staggering off balance, Cleis reached the altar and stared at the sculpture. The Artemis from Brauron couldn't compare with the overwhelming multi-breasted earth mother gazing down upon her.

"Are they breasts?" Cleis asked herself. "They could also be gourds. Breasts and gourds can both nurture. They're certainly too large to be testicles of any kind!"

The large room started to spin. Cleis fell to her knees and tried to stabilize. A delirious man jumped onto the altar as the galli of Attis surrounded him and chanted. He was covered in red fluid that could be blood or wine. The fanatic tore off his clothes as the chanting intensified. Cleis' vision began to blur but she could tell the mad man had displayed a knife. With his other hand, he took hold of his genitals.

Details were cloudy. Melanippe was at the altar, with her sword, shouting, "No!" Pittacus grabbed the frenzied man and carried him from the altar. Phoebe was telling Sappho about the galli – or was it Gallus? – and spoke of toxic water. Phoebe grabbed Cleis and carried her outside to the open air. "The incense and the water," she was explaining. "They're intoxicating. It's not the goddess! It's the poisons!"

Cleis tried to organize the information into something she could comprehend. Pittacus was shouting. "The galli and the maenads were corrupted. I don't think the priestesses knew."

Aesop was trying to cleanse his body with fresh water. "That poor wretch!" he noted. "He would've been filled with painful grief tomorrow. You saved him." Pittacus replied, "It was Melanippe. The other amazons identified the taste of the water as Gallus, and the smell of the incense. They reported to her. She knew the old rituals." Alcaeus was enraged. "No man in his right mind would do such a thing!"

"Is this how the birthday of Artemis is celebrated?" asked Cleis as the facts began to collect for her.

"No!" answered the amazons in unison. "We returned to restore the glory of Ephos, the Queen who founded this land," declared Melanippe. "Ephesus, Land of Ephos. The ancient earth mother, Cybele, the goddess of fertility, has been corrupted by the fanatics of Attis and Dionysus! The celebration of sacred sex, the gift of the gods, should be a joyous tradition."

Sappho tried to explain to Cleis. "Sacred sex is a magnificent surrender to the power of the universe. In many temples, this communion receives great honor. But to mutilate and castrate is blasphemy. No religious belief should ever require such injuries. Cybele calls for celebration of human desires. Artemis chose chastity to maintain her freedom. In both cases, free choice is paramount. But, to intoxicate a person to the point of frenzy, and then to encourage mutilation? I reject such customs!"

Cleis was disheartened. "Is this where our journey took us? These two versions of Artemis have haunted me since Brauron. I'm still just as confused."

Clyemne brushed her crimson hair across the golden studs of her forehead. "When I traveled in Phrygia, I learned how The Mystery began with the number nine."

Cleis looked at Clyemne dumbfounded.

"Three sets of three," noted Sappho. "The Nine Muses. The nine moons for a woman to give birth."

"In the morning," Clyemne decided. "I'll speak of this when we have rested and recovered."

----- ----- -----

In the early morning, while most of the revelers were still recuperating from the madness of the evening, Sappho, Cleis, and Pittacus returned to the temple with amazon escorts. In the stillness of dawn, they could traverse the hieron undisturbed. The votive structures and depictions were worth the return trip. They saw Orion, the son of the god Poseidon, who could walk on water, but was accidentally slain by Artemis when they went hunting together. In an intricate sculpture, Acteon was turning into a stag with antlers and fighting off his own hounds while Artemis watched from behind a cypress tree. Another painting showed Artemis retrieving Iphigenia from the pyre at Aulis. Next to that masterpiece was the rendition of a giant swan. "Leto!" exclaimed Cleis. "The mother of Artemis and Apollo!" Sappho enjoyed her protégé's excitement. On further inspection, they found the twins huddled under their mother, hiding from the vindictive Hera.

Melanippe nudged Phoebe with her elbow. "Hey, isn't Phoebe the mother of Leto?" Phoebe grunted an assent.

Skillful painters must have worked on their backs to create the ceiling mural. On one side, Artemis stormed in upon her chariot drawn by powerful horses. On the other side, Cybele flew in her chariot drawn by roaring lions. She holds the globe of the world in her lap. The chariots were heading toward each other, perhaps symbolic of the blending of the two deities. Another mural depicted Cybele sitting on her throne atop the Taurus Mountains to the south. She pointed down to her priestesses who dance and sang with lyres, tambours, and flutes. Eagles soared from her mountaintop and lava flowed from an exploding summit.

Once again, the band arrived at the main altar. They stared at the enormous statue and struggled to comprehend her traits. Her circular turret crown resembled castle walls. Cleis questioned

Clyemne about the round objects on Cybele's chest. "Cybele, just like your Atalanta, was abandoned as an infant. She was suckled by leopards. As you know, felines have litters they feed with numerous teats."

Cleis nodded and accepted that explanation for the moment. Then she asked Clyemne about the issue of the number nine.

Clyemne was a patient teacher. "So many gods are born in Midwinter, in the month of Poseidon, when the light of the sun grows greater than the darkness of Night. The god's birth brings the sun." The group listened intently. "It takes nine months to give birth. Go back nine months and you have conception in the month of Elaphebolion, the time of Spring. But, there is a problem. In order to be born in Poseidon, the god must not be born yet in Elaphebolion. He must be unborn to be conceived every year."

Phoebe grew restless. "What has that to do…"

Clyemne continued quickly. "The god is born, the sun returns, when the world is in the dead of winter. The god is both unborn and conceived when the world flourishes. There's only one solution to the paradox. Resurrection."

"I see," said Sappho. "The god dies so he can be born again?"

"Yes," replied Clyemne triumphantly. "That was the idea that led to the cult of Attis! He's both the son and the consort of Cybele."

Cleis struggled to understand. "So Attis must die?" she asked.

"Death and Birth," explained Clyemne. "Attis must be killed so he can again be conceived. Adherents simulate the conception. His body is placed on a wooden phallus. It's a simple structure, just two pieces of wood. The wooden phallus then enters the almond-shaped cave, the womb of Cybele. Many people enter for the sacred rites of Spring."

Cleis grunted. "Sacred sex," she muttered.

Pittacus had heard enough. "Very primitive, but it does sound enjoyable. But how can you have sacred sex if you castrate yourself?"

"It's a very old belief," replied Clyemne. "Cybele was originally the monster goddess of the Taurus Mountains. Cybele was very powerful and also hermaphroditic."

"Cybele had both..." Pittacus was surprised to learn of a male/female goddess.

"The Olympian gods felt threatened by so much power so they removed Cybele's male parts."

Pittacus groaned in disgust. "So the galli castrate themselves to be like Cybele! Ridiculous!"

"Yes, the galli dress and act feminine and feline to honor Cybele."

Cleis grew agitated. "They call her Artemis. How can that be?"

Melanippe rushed with the answer. "There is an overlap. Both goddesses protect wild things, children, and women. Cybele rescued the abandoned Attis; Artemis rescued Atalanta and Iphigenia. They both favor bears and boars and deer. Cybele sits on her throne with lions; Artemis has her hounds. We brought Artemis to Ephesus to modify some of the brutal remainders of earlier times."

Sappho groaned sarcastically. "I think you have more work to do."

"How can the gods change?" asked Cleis.

"The gods don't change," answered Clyemne. "Our understanding of them grows. There's always more to learn about them. But the old mistakes are difficult to eradicate. Religious devotion is deep. The rituals become more important than the actual gods."

20

THE RETURN

The amazons knew the route well, and were able to bypass several smaller mountain chains on the way to Mount Thorax, where the Lydian scouts would reunite with the pilgrims. With their experience of the terrain, they soon arrived at the open field near Marathesion. The Poetess discussed with Alcaeus their plans to collaborate on several pieces that would detail their journey.

Melanippe, Phoebe, and Pittacus led the expedition while Thermodosa and Derinoe took the flank positions. Marsepia rode a relaxed rear with Aesop for company. Near the poets, Cleis rode with Clyemne and brandished a quiver and bow that had been designed for her. In exchange, Cleis offered Clyemne her belt from Brauron.

"You can't give me that," said Clyemne. "It's from your Arkteia. However you may feel about it, you must keep it."

Cleis scowled. "I've seen too much to accept what it represents."

Clyemne laughed. "At least you should display it proudly to show that you survived that ritual!"

Cleis thought of her friend, Antiope, and the sad girl who couldn't survive the Arkteia. "Yes," she replied sadly.

After a pause, Cleis removed her purple head band and handed it to Clyemne. The amazon studied the band. "Hmm. There are times when I want to conceal my studs, to avoid a confrontation. This would work. Thank you."

"I'm glad you can use it," said Cleis, rather squelched.

Her companion was aware of her malaise. "What troubles you, dear one?" The poets overheard the question and moved toward them. Phoebe also overheard, and guided her horse back toward the conversation, conveniently leaving Melanippe and Pittacus at the front.

Cleis looked at the archer with her golden studs, so fierce yet so tender. Then she gazed at Phoebe, with snakes rambling up her arms, so powerful yet warmhearted. The contradictions caused her to feel off balance. "You're women," she replied."

"Very observant," chided Phoebe playfully.

Cleis blushed and awkwardly giggled. "Let me explain. In Attica, people with tattoos are criminals or porne. But you're great warriors and you mark yourselves proudly. The obedient wives of Athens stay home, spin yarn, and cook. You warriors also know how to spin and cook, but you also ride horses, wield swords and javelins, shoot arrows. You challenge men as equals while Athenian women are modest and reserved. In Lesvos, the women are free to sing and dance and wear fine clothes. In Athens, the hetaerae do such things." The warriors nodded attentively and awaited her conclusion. Anxiously, she asked, "Am I a woman?"

Clyemne laughed heartily. Cleis was deeply hurt and she apologized profusely. "You are most certainly a woman," answered Phoebe with no pause. "A beautiful, smart, determined, resilient one at that. Never let the outside world define what you are!"

Cleis shared further concerns. "I failed in marriage. I abandoned my family. I sneaked in a boat with strange men. What's wrong with me?"

Clyemne offered a reply. "What kind of culture would force a woman to take such desperate actions? Look around at Scythia, Sparta, Lesvos, Lydia, Egypt. There is no single definition for being a woman. Those insane galli think it has to do with a body part. The oldest Cybele had both male and female attributes, but she was still the Earth Mother!"

Cleis had many thoughts about earth mothers. "Why were the ancient Goddesses overthrown by male gods? Look at Pythia. Gaia gave the oracle of Delphi to Themis and she passed it on to the titan Phoebe. Then Apollo arrived, killed the Great Pythons, and claimed Delphi for himself. In Dodona, Zeus evicted his own consort. In my homeland of Boetia, Apollo appropriated the oracle at Libadia. Zeus constantly deceives and humiliates Hera. The gods and the mortal heroes rape and abduct maidens, steal from other people and subvert their lands. But they're venerated. But the goddesses are demeaned as evil, jealous, and fearful."

Sappho interjected her opinion. "The tales are written by men. I plan to change that. With poetry and papyrus, ideas can spread to many places."

Clyemne pondered her announcement. "Is that your intent with your thiasos?"

"Exactly," replied Sappho with fire in her eyes. "By restoring Aphrodite to her true identity, equal to Inanna or Astarte or Isis, or any other Great Earth Mother, I can change ideas about women in general. By exploring the many aspects of Love, I might be able to change the way men and women relate to each other."

Clyemne was impressed. "There is much courage in your plan. I don't know about papyrus, but, if your words can reach many places, it sounds like magic. You have courage, Sappho."

Sappho eagerly replied to her. "There are many kinds of courage. For women, we must nurture the courage to say, 'No!', when the family or the city or the husband make unworthy demands. There is also the courage to speak your own thoughts rather than huddle in subservience. When you rebel against the order, you need the courage to face the unknown, like Odysseus, and react to circumstances wisely. There is also courage in challenging a single definition of beauty. Physical beauty is transient. I've noticed some grey hairs lately. It's inevitable. The most enticing woman will have to confront the curse of time. The hideous elder who feeds a hungry child is beautiful. In addition, every woman still faces the dangers of childbirth and motherhood, and the loss of loved ones."

"That's a lot of courage," noted Alcaeus deferentially. "To be an instrument of change can be a lonely journey. People grow comfortable with what they know."

"That's why you'll be helping me," replied Sappho.

The expression on his face amused the amazons, who were accustomed to facing challenges. But he told her, "Of course. I'll work with you."

Cleis remained silent through their exchange.

Up front, the leads rode silently, both striving to find the right words. The woods seemed to turn quiet as they passed.

Finally, Pittacus broke the impasse. "Melanippe, we're almost at the end of our adventure together. That leaves me with regret."

"Yes, me too," she replied. "It's time to end. I've been away from my husband a long time."

Pittacus was taken aback. "You're married? I had no idea!"

"Yes. I miss my family now."

"I thought...I mean...I didn't want you to break your vow."

Melanippe stared at the confused warrior and laughed. "I'm sure you understand the warrior bond. It's similar to your Sparta. Life is short and we are away from each other frequently. We're realistic about it."

"Realistic?" echoed Pittacus. "Let me offer more reality. After my time with you, I better understand Sappho's poetry. There are differences between Aphrodite and Eros. Our first intimacy at the taverna was pure fire! But, since then, I'm enthralled. It's why men fear women. You make us weak. But it's more than that. I understand now."

Playfully, Melanippe responded. "Perhaps our poets will sing about us. The Amazon and the General! Bold but tender, courageous but delicate!"

Pittacus frowned. "You mock me," he snarled.

"Not at all, my dear Pittacus," she replied. "Like the suitors of Atalanta, you're fascinated by a free woman. But you ache to crush the very freedom that beguiles you. For you, it's a painful paradox. I love you; but I won't be contained. You chase a receding rainbow."

Pittacus pondered her words like a man trying to undo an intricate knot. "You're Artemis unchaste, a paradox. Will you always love me?"

"Of course," she answered. They rode on in silence; but turned to smile at each other now and then.

----- ----- -----

When they arrived once again at the taverna in Marathesion, the scouts had already returned and were enjoying the local sociability. They put down their mugs and plates and welcomed the weary travelers with waves and cheers. Melanippe and Pittacus entered the taverna together, and the lead scout acknowledged them with no malice.

Melanippe approached the young woman who was a bit disheveled and sitting on the leader's lap. The woman cowered away from Melanippe; but the amazon stroked her hair and said, "No harm, dear." Glancing quickly at the leader, she made some inquiries. "I hope he learned something from me. Did he treat you well?" Anxiously, the girl nodded in the affirmative. "Did he take his time? Did he also please you?" The girl continued to nod. "Very good!" She leaned toward the leader and kissed him fiercely. "You've done well, my love." The girl bolted up and was about to leave when Melanippe reassured her again. "No need to run away. Would you bring me some wine?" Eager for any escape, the girl readily consented. "And not diluted!"

Sappho was moved by the amazon's behavior. "You're actually living the values I propose."

Melanippe winked at Sappho. "But what do we know? We're barbarians. Bar, bar, bar!"

Sappho was apologetic. "Not everything different is uncivilized. Furthermore, the so-called civilized person often acts in barbaric ways."

After a restful night, the pilgrims would be ready for the journey beyond Bird Island, to Anaia and, finally, Priene. Their muscles were stronger and they were more confident in their abilities.

----- ----- -----

They waited until the others were asleep. The fire gave off a comforting warmth in the crisp night while crickets chirped and owls hooted. The blur of tree bats was easily observed between branches.

Clyemne and Phoebe held down her outstretched arms while Thermodosa and Derinoe pinned her legs. "I must ask you one more time," whispered Melanippe. "Are you sure?"

"Yes," answered Cleis with a quiver in her voice. "Do it!"

"Two lightning bolts on each arm?"

"Yes. Yes."

"You understand, we have to keep you quiet." Cleis nodded. "Ok. Open your mouth." Melanippe nodded to Marsepia, who stuffed a cloth to stifle any screams. One more time, Melanippe asked her and one more time, she nodded eagerly. "Very well."

The cuts of the blade were done swiftly. Tears escaped from Cleis' eyes but she did not scream. Instead, she grimaced and made deep grunts. Wiping some of the blood, Melanippe applied the ash. Marsepia removed the gag while Clyemne stroked her hair. Melanippe applied a lotion to the scars, covered them with cloth, and tied them in place with leather strips. The amazons let her go and Cleis sat up.

"You didn't kick," noted Thermodosa. "Brave girl," proclaimed Derinoe.

Phoebe embraced her and whispered in her ear. "You have a great strength. But never provoke. Your power may intimidate some people who might try to diminish you. Fight only when necessary." Phoebe loosened her hold and kissed Cleis who readily accepted her affection.

----- ----- -----

The sun rose with radiant brilliance. The sights, scents, and sounds of late summer surrounded the taverna. The amazons were feeding and brushing their horses when Sappho stepped out into the morning air. She noticed Cleis comfortably among them. Clyemne's crimson hair was held back by Cleis' purple headband. Cleis was getting more instruction from Marsepia on javelin use. Watching the two women, with flowing golden hair, practicing the run and throw together, was a form of poetry. Sappho greeted the warriors brightly, but their reaction was subdued. Melanippe nodded cordially and Phoebe continued to gauge the condition of her spear.

"Let me assure you," Sappho declared. "You are always welcome in Lesvos. At least at Skala Eressos." The warriors thanked her. Cleis faced away from Sappho and adjusted some knots on a rope.

"Perhaps this is how amazons say good-bye," thought Sappho. "No emotional displays." But, then, Cleis came to her side.

"I need to take a walk with you," said the girl. Her tone sounded ominous. They walked toward the barn with its cows, goats, and chickens. Behind a wall of mooing, clucking, and bleating, they had some privacy.

After tossing some feed at the chickens and tugging the goat's beard, Cleis focused her courage. "Sappho, I love you, you know that. You saved me. I had no one and nowhere to go." She paused to take a gulp of rain water. Sappho waited anxiously while the girl returned the ladle to its bowl. "I've decided to ride with the amazons."

Sappho absorbed the news in frozen silence. In one way, she understood perfectly; but, in another way, she wanted to scream and rant. She chose her words cautiously. "Cleis this is what we spoke of. Remember? Apeiron? The law of opposites." The girl crinkled her brow, confused. "The amazons seem so free to you. They represent the extreme opposite of your upbringing. But, child, swinging from one pole to the other is not a solution!" Sappho felt desperate and twisted any logic to dissuade Cleis.

"Please, Sappho," pleaded Cleis. "It's decided." She tore open her chiton to reveal her tattoos. Sappho examined the double bolts on both arms, then seized Cleis by her shoulders, and wept. Cleis sought to reassure her. "I need to see Pontus and Amazon Rock."

Sappho shook her head. "It's a boulder hanging on a cliff and facing the Black Sea. It's also called The Rock of Ares! They worship the god of war!"

Cleis modified that perspective. "They honor martial skills, not war. Please understand. I must go to the Rock at Pontus. Maybe, then, my destiny will be clarified."

Embracing Cleis, the Poetess declared, "It's only a large rock; it's not an oracle!" But, she soon softened her tone. "If you ever change your mind, if you ever want to return, my home is always your home."

----- ----- -----

Sappho and her companions watched as Cleis and the amazons rode toward their mountains and disappeared as quickly as they had materialized such a short time before.

Alcaeus leaned into Sappho and commented softly. "She blends in so well with them."

Sappho agreed with a sad hum. "I feel the agony of a mother who has to let her child leave."

Alcaeus held her and rocked gently. "Glukupikron," he murmured. The hardened scouts and the warrior Pittacus were moved by the "sweetbitter" pain of her love and loss. For once, Aesop could find no fable or analogy to soothe her lamentations.

----- ----- -----

The trek through the Mycale range, and back into Priene, took on a somber mood. Aesop's chatter was forced and superficial. Pittacus tried to comprehend the reason for his own irritability. The scouts did their work in a business-like manner. Sappho would often examine a cluster of flowers or gaze upon soaring birds, desperately trying to capture the beauty; but it eluded her

During a rest break in Anaia, the townsfolk offered refreshments and were eager to hear of their expedition. Sappho wandered off to a solitary grove and lay prone on the soft forest carpet. Alcaeus approached her discreetly with his lyre. "May I play?" he asked her.

"Yes," she groaned. "Slow strums, deep notes." Each pluck pierced into her broken heart. Each deep tone resonated with her grief. "The memory remains," she reminded herself. "The love is eternal despite physical distance."

Alcaeus added further hope. "She wants to visit the Rock. Perhaps, once she experiences the harsh existence of Scythia, she'll return to Lesvos." He continued the slow deep strumming while Sappho sank into a dark cold realm that only poetry could describe. But the words were not yet formed. She sought divine assistance.

Oh, most adorned Aphrodite,

My blessed goddess with your eternal smile,

Remove the bitterness in my raving heart,

Bring me back to life.

Who, now, wrongs you, dear Sappho?

Which sparrow dared to escape the nest?

I beseech you, please release me from this longing,

Stand beside me, my goddess, my ally.

Sappho allowed herself to descend into the deeper crevices of her privation, soaking up every aspect of her lamentation, and tried to devise the right words. In her hand, she fondled a remnant from Cleis that was old and worn, her doll of Atalanta. The girl had clung to it through the Arkteia when all toys were supposed to be tossed aside. She had used it for comfort through the journey whenever her confidence failed her. But Cleis had finally detached from her totem and left it for Sappho.

----- ----- -----

A healing woman was applying lotions to Phaon's face. She assured him they would help with his scars. Antimenidas was in a private corner talking with two foreign hoplites.

"They tried to steal my ferry!" Phaon was making a dramatic impression on the healing woman. "All I had was my staff and a knife. But, over the years, I learned skill with the staff. The three thieves thought I was easy prey, but they were mistaken." He twirled and flipped his staff and let out a yell. "I have these scars but I still have my boat!" The crowd cheered and pounded on their tables.

Alcaeus approached the ferryman. "I thought you got those scars falling off a horse," he whispered.

Phaon grinned and whispered back. "Perhaps. That was after I beat those thieves."

Alcaeus nodded to the woman and dipped his finger in her lotion bowl. The scents were familiar: almond oil mixed with lavender and roses. Several more stringent herbs couldn't be identified. "Feeling better?"

"It has a comforting and penetrating power," he answered. "And so does she." He smiled at the healer who returned the glow.

"I'll leave you to it," said Alcaeus as he approached his brother's table, where a serious conversation was taking place. Their quiet tones and stern expressions led him to pause.

He was about to move away when Antimenidas motioned to him. "Alcaeus, come, sit. I need to speak with you." Alcaeus took the vacant chair. Introductions were abrupt and the tone remained the same. "I won't be going home with you," he stated flatly. "I have an assignment." Antimenidas explained that the men were recruiting for Nebuchadnezzar and the pay was exceptional. The other men discreetly left the brothers alone.

"I see," said Alcaeus with a solemn expression. "Mercenary work."

"It's what I do," replied Antimenidas defensively. "We can't all sit around and sing poetry. Besides, our clan needs resources. The time is approaching. Myrsilius grows more unstable. When Arion sang popular songs from Terpander, the tyrant began to rant. Arion now stays in Corinth at the court of Periander. If that tyrant's son, Lycopron, refuses to come home from Corcyra, Arion might actually be given the throne of Corinth!"

Alcaeus recalled the words of Sappho. "The poets have power. They impact the order."

"So it appears. You'll be pleased to know that our clan and Sappho's clan are united in their opposition."

"I remember that Sappho was deeply moved by Corinth's Temple of Aphrodite. The hetaerae there are renown. Corinth controls the Saronic Gulf and most of the Ionian colonies." Alcaeus returned to the main subject. "But, Antimenidas, you'll fight for Babylon! You would be the enemy of Charoxos and Doricha."

"I am no one's enemy," he countered. "I am paid for my service, just like a cobbler or a barrel-maker or a poet."

----- ----- -----

Phaon had done well with ferry fees during his friends' sojourn. Without Cleis or Antimenidas, he had room for extra passengers on the way back to Samos. One passenger turned out to be Thales, the "water" philosopher from Miletus. Another passenger, arguing that the sun was the ultimate source of life, was aptly called Heliopitus. Together, they carried on lively conversation beyond the Meandering River and across the Strait of the Mycale. Heliopitus also held radical astronomical ideas and claimed the sun, not the earth, was the center of the universe. Thales listened to him attentively and respectfully, using deductive logic to chip away at his premise with persistent questions. Thales was a firm believer that logic would expose truth.

Pittacus interrupted their discourse with a question. "What brings you to Samos?" Heliopitus said he was studying why the sun produced superior wines on Samos. Thales said he was attending a gathering near Panaimo.

"The Field of Blood!" exclaimed Pittacus. "When Dionysus and the Samians killed the amazons."

Thales grunted in disdain. "I prefer logic over myth. That battle supposedly happened thousands of years ago, when Titans roamed the earth. Right?" Pittacus nodded. "And yet the soil is still stained with their blood. Highly unlikely. Have you, General Pittacus, never seen red soil?"

"I have," replied the warrior. "It always intrigued me."

"Well, then, come with me to Panaimo. We'll use logic, rather than traditional belief, to solve the mystery."

21

DEPARTURES

As Phaon's ferry followed the coast of Samos and headed toward the Heraion once again, Pittacus noted another temple just south of their destination. He asked about it but only Heliopidus had the answer. "That's the Iraion," he explained. "In honor of the ancient goddess Ira."

"There's a goddess Ira right next to Hera's great temple?" asked Pittacus. "Samos is Hera's birthplace."

Heliopidus laughed at the general who was constantly trying to blend all the divergent pieces. "The gods assume many manifestations. In fact, Ira's old statue looks a lot like the Cybele of Ephesus."

"Another Earth Mother," noted Sappho. "Another female deity somehow lost to history."

"You're right," said Alcaeus. "We have to change that. Half the human spirit has been severed. Perhaps, because of that imbalance, we've suffered the consequences."

Phaon used his pole to direct the ferry gently into the harbor with its cacophony of merchants, craftsmen, farmers, musicians, acrobats, and porne. The oligarchy was well established as evidenced by carriages that were carried by slaves through the agora and guarded by hoplites. Samos was known for its exotic animals and, on display in cages, were a golden jackal, a viper, ferrets, and a hawk. Egrets perched overhead while dolphins frolicked near the boat.

Phaon took a deep breath to absorb the air that was filled with thyme, oregano, cypress, cedar, and lilies. "Anthemia," he sighed, stating the island's old name. "Flower blossom."

Pittacus was leaning over the gunwale talking with Thales while Phaon secured his ferry to the pier. Sappho needed to stretch her legs and purchase fresh fruits from the local vendors. Alcaeus remained in the boat thinking of new verses. The day drew into mid-afternoon and they were all getting hungry.

Sappho returned to the boat and asked about lunch plans.

Pittacus was first to reply. "My Lady, I'm going to stay here on Samos with Thales for a few days. There's something I need to do before returning to Lesvos."

Sappho sighed. "Our group keeps shrinking," she noted.

Pittacus placed his hand on her arm. "I'm glad I joined this expedition," he said. "All of us have grown closer and we dealt well with unfamiliar things."

"I hope to see you again in Eressos soon."

"Or Mytilene," he added. She smiled and nodded.

Pittacus embraced Alcaeus and Phaon as well. Aesop was already exploring taverna options. The general and the philosopher Thales set off west towards Panaimo. Heliopidus went with them to evaluate some of the wine vineyards.

"Four travelers left," Sappho noted to Alcaeus. "You, me, Aesop, and Phaon."

"Indeed," replied Alcaeus. "You lost a girl who was like a daughter. I lost a brother who seeks his fortune in the Babylonian infantry."

"Yes," Sappho confirmed sadly. "But, as poets, we gained a lot of inspiration. Personally, I could have accepted a little less."

Alcaeus nodded and took her hand. "Come! Let's get some food and drink."

----- ----- -----

Myrsilius had few allies left. Whoever offended him, or rendered wise counsel that he disliked, was soon removed from court. As a consequence, his counsel was more like an echo chamber than a gathering of elders with diverse perspectives. Occasionally, his young queen managed to soothe the tyrant and induce him to be more receptive to rational opinions. But his primary obsession was power, and he opposed any suggestions that implied weakness. That included the famous poets of Lesvos.

He grew impatient with his translators. "You said you understood the Aeolian dialect. What's taking so long?" He paced the chamber and continuously refilled his wine goblet.

The elderly scholars tried to explain the difficulties. "The grammatical structure is different. The placement of a word can also change its exact meaning. Aeolian is an oral language. Transposing to this new written form takes careful analysis."

Myrsilius pounded on his table, which caused his queen to startle and spill some drops of wine. Her handmaidens rushed to remove the stains from her gown. Timidly, the queen asked, "Don't we have Sappho's brother in court?"

Myrsilius paused in his rampage and considered. "Of course!" he realized. "Larichos." He called to one of his henchmen. "Bring that sweet boy to me!"

----- ----- -----

Thales and Pittacus traveled along the southern coast of Samos and entered a flat land between the mountain ranges of Ampelos and Kerkis. They arrived at a large plain with dirt that varied from scarlet to reddish-brown. "Behold!" proclaimed Thales. "Panaimo! Your Field of Amazon Blood!" His tone was clearly sarcastic.

Pittacus wandered into the plain, touching the ground at various points. "What's your explanation?" he asked.

"The water we drank near Ormos," replied Thales. "It tasted ferrous, eh?" Pittacus nodded. "Go ahead! Smell this dirt. Taste it."

Pittacus did as he was directed. "Yes," he noted. "Iron."

"You know iron. You use iron weapons though you probably prefer the alloys." Again, Pittacus agreed. "What happens to iron when left exposed?"

Pittacus nodded with enlightenment. "Rust," he murmured. "But why? Why is strong solid iron reduced by corrosion into rust?"

"We don't know," answered Thales. "Yet. But certainly water plays a part!"

Pittacus kneeled by the red dirt and let it run through his fingers. "Over these last few weeks, I've changed. Before the journey, I was wearied of war. But now, it's more than that. Now I am curious, I want to understand." He lowered his head. "I doubt the myths. I question the contradictions of the gods. I'm filled with uncertainty, but I feel…" He was at a loss.

"Free?" said Thales.

Pittacus gazed into the eyes of the philosopher. "Yes. I think so. Free."

"Sophia," said Thales. "The wisdom of logic, freed from gods, inspired by thought and not by any Muses."

"Is that heresy?" asked the general.

Thales smiled and looked upon Pittacus. "When you rule Lesvos, you can decide."

----- ----- -----

It was a long sail back to Eressos. His ferry was built for brief shuttles so Phaon avoided open water and remained along the Anatolian coastline. Through the Mycale Strait, he steered around northern Samos and between the peninsula of Cesme and the island of Chios. At the final stretch, within view of Lesvos, he accepted the open archipelago and kept a beeline for Sappho's home. As they passed the neck of Kalonis, they approached the familiar half of the horseshoe that was Skala Eressos. The end of any journey has its own glukupikron, with its sweet return home and the bitter end of a life experience.

Phaon bid his companions farewell at the harbor. Aesop had a mission to accomplish in Delphi and sought travel to Attica. As they watched Phaon negotiating with new passengers and Aesop making inquiries with several mariners, the poets knew the journey had concluded.

As they traveled up the Vigla, Sappho and Alcaeus were greeted by shepherds and goatherds who offered samples of fresh milk. A few farmers complained about foxes who were killing chickens. One artisan discovered another thermal spring and invited the poets on an excursion, which they politely postponed.

As they reached the summit and approached her family home, Sappho was filled with apprehension. Despite a glorious warm afternoon, the grounds were empty. There was no sound of laughter or singing. There were no students strumming lyre or playing aulos in the courtyard. The hounds welcomed Sappho with friendly but weary bays. She knelt to rub the loose fur of her Mollosus hounds and tug their sagging jowls.

Doricha came to the entrance of the portico and welcomed the poets with warm somber embraces. Sappho gazed at her sad eyes that emerged from layers of kohl. Ruby studs were attached to either of her nostrils. Her cheeks were rubricated with gentle brushes of ochre. Sappho was not repelled. In fact, she found her embellished features beautiful.

She held the priestess of Isis with such impassioned honesty that Doricha was startled.

They followed Doricha into the main lounge and were greeted by Charoxos and Larichos from their pillows. They were talking in subdued tones and taking slow sips from skyphos vessels, which Dika filled occasionally.

"Larichos!" Sappho was surprised to see her younger brother. He was devoid of cosmetics and jewelry, and wore only a hooded himation. "Charoxos!" She was deeply relieved to have her older brother home since the situation between Egypt and Babylon was corroding. She approached Dika, took her hand, and kissed her cheek. Scanning the chamber, she murmured, "Where are my sparrows?"

Charoxos beckoned for her and Alcaeus to join the circle. Dika put down her krater and also sat with them. Larichos began the conversation. "I came because Myrsilius needs a scroll that translates Aeolian into the common dialect. I told him you have one." The poets stared at each other anxiously. "That's right. He wants to decipher your words. He resents what he's understood so far. We dispersed your thiasos."

"What!" Sappho flare up in outrage. "You evicted them from my sanctuary! My hieron! By what right..." But Alcaeus took her hand and advised her to be attentive.

Charoxos explained. "We escorted them back to their families or to safe homes of their choice. They can't be here anymore. It is no longer a sanctuary."

Sappho was shocked. "What are you saying?"

"We have to leave Eressos, sister." Charoxos tried to remain calm as he spoke. "The tyrant's destiny is closing around him. But he won't leave the stage peacefully."

Larichos elaborated. "He intends to eliminate all his enemies." He stared at the poets. "You poets are enemies. Even Arion! When he recounted the silly tale of being rescued from pirates by dolphins, Myrsilius thought the pirates were a symbol for him and the dolphins were the rebellion! Arion is now with Periander in Corinth."

Sappho was ready to protest but Alcaeus asked, "What should we do?"

Charoxos answered sadly. "I can take you to the Saronic Gulf. With Periander's help, you can cross the land bridge at Megara."

"Yes," said Sappho. "Megara has traditional ties to the philosophers and poets of Miletus."

"One of the triremes of Corinth can easily get you to Periander's son, Lycophron, in Corcyra; or even to Syracuse." Charoxos then blinked. "Isn't Pittacus with you?"

"He had some purpose in Samos," replied Alcaeus.

"And your brother Antimenidas?"

"On his way to Babylon."

Charoxos punched his fist into his palm. "We need those warriors now! The time is ripe for Pittacus. The clans are united!"

"He's probably only a few days behind us," noted Sappho. "As soon as the madman is deposed, I will return and gather again my sparrows." She looked at Doricha. "You'll be the Mistress of the house."

"The priestess. Only standing in for you," she replied. "Both Isis and Aphrodite would curse me if I betrayed you."

Sappho looked around the room. She again kissed Dika, who was filled with tears. She proceeded to the portico and stared out to the courtyard with the altar of her goddess. She breathed in the fragrance of Eressos and listened to the chatter of millions of birds. "I will return," she avowed. "My thiasos will continue. The Love that surpasses pride, jealousy, vengeance, and greed, will once again be declared from this mound of dirt!"

As she packed, Sappho recounted some of the journey to Ephesus. It was the only time she had to share fragments.

22

PERIANDER OF CORINTH

As the ferry cruised onto the isthmus of Megara from the Saronic Gulf, the poets had their first glimpse of the Diolkos built under the command of Periander. The land bridge, composed of stones and earth, was flattened into a roadway and wooden rails had been embedded. Boats were then pushed the four miles west onto the Corinthian Gulf. Seafarers could avoid the treacherous route around the Peloponnese and cut right through to the Ionian Sea and the western colonies. With the help of paid hoplites, Periander kept the Diolkos safe from the brigands of Megara. Phaon marveled at how the project had opened the region to merchants from distant lands both east and west. Alcaeus was impressed by the military potential. Sappho was grateful for the convenient escape from the Aegean.

As they disembarked from the ferry, a hoplite of impressive stature came to the pier. His accent was Spartan and he was clearly one of the commanders. He noticed Sappho's cape, enhanced with engraved trim, and her fine sandals. "Welcome, travelers," he proclaimed. "I assume you came from Lesvos, Samos, or Anatolia? The fashion isn't Cretan."

"You assume well, hoplite," replied Sappho. "We journeyed from Lesvos."

"Good!" answered the hoplite. "The noble ruler, Periander, is fond of Lesvos and its poets." He studied the woman in front of him with braided hair and fine linen cloth. "Perhaps you're one of the poets?"

Sappho smiled silently but Alcaeus intervened. "Let me introduce ourselves. This is Sappho The Poetess. My name is Alcaeus."

"Aye, Sappho," replied the hoplite. "I know of your songs. You must visit the Corinthian Temple of Aphrodite. And you, Alcaeus, I know some of your songs well." He laughed. "Your fame in the taverna is great!"

Alcaeus had hoped his lyrical poetry was more impressive than his drinking ballads; but warriors need their uncomplicated amusements; and they paid well for the entertainment. "Perhaps we'll perform at the Temple."

The hoplite then introduced himself. "I'm Eurybiades of Sparta. I command this section." Sappho caught her breath and turned pale; but soon regained her poise. Eurybiades noticed her reaction. "Is the Lady not well?"

"It was a long journey under the Aegean sun. Perhaps you have some water?" The warrior offered his flask and she enjoyed two long draughts. "Thank you."

"May I be of further assistance?"

Sappho looked at the hoplite's large chest and powerful arms. Holding back the urge to attack with open claws, she answered politely. "We seek court with Periander. Can you arrange that?"

"I could," replied Eurybiades. "But, for a more efficient access, I suggest a meeting with Lais." When Alcaeus inquired, Eurybiades explained. "She is the most powerful hetaera at the Temple of Aphrodite. She's also a close friend of Periander. He enjoys the poetry of Arion, but Sappho would be honored highly." He saw the expression on Alcaeus' face. "Both of you, of course."

With the ferry well tied, Phaon joined the group. "Once I know you are received at court, I'll return to Lesvos. Doricha has another mission for me in southern waters. Crete and Egypt."

Sappho embraced the ferryman. "You've been a reliable friend. Even though your ferry is built for short trips, you've taken us on long journeys to Samos and Attica. And now, you will travel with Doricha to Egypt?"

"Doricha said she has to return to her temple there. I could never refuse Doricha's requests. Something about the journey is very important to her. Charoxos is letting me use his boat! He and Pittacus have a separate agenda."

Sappho was surprised. "Charoxos must trust you dearly. That boat is his livelihood." Then she reconsidered. "Or he must love Doricha so much to lose his better judgment."

When Eurybiades walked away, Alcaeus leaned into Sappho. "What happened? You turned pale when that hoplite introduced himself. I thought you were going to faint."

Sappho answered softly and close to his ear. "That hoplite is Eurybiades, Cleis' husband."

Alcaeus jolted with realization. It was his turn to examine the hoplite. "He's a very powerful man. Cleis never had a chance."

"And yet, he is very courteous and pleasant. We may be outraged; but he simply followed the traditions of his state." She placed her hand on Alcaeus' shoulder. "We'll be drinking wine with Eurybiades and Lais. Keep your wits. Do not be provoked to confront him. Remember our goal: to get Periander's help, travel on one of his trireme vessels, and find refuge in Syracuse."

"Of course," stated Alcaeus. "He'll be expecting us to stop in Corcyra and deliver a message to Lycopron. It's the least we could do in return for his assistance."

"Indeed," replied Sappho pensively. "It's odd. Periander ended the conflicts on Corcyra. He established a colony there and his people have done well. But these same colonists often demand independence from Corinth."

Alcaeus considered their motives. "Perhaps they resent the taxes imposed by Corinth. It's always economics."

----- ----- -----

There is a well-worn expression throughout Hellas: "Not everyone can afford the pleasures of Corinth". When the poets arrived at the Temenos of Aphrodite, on their way to Her Temple, they understood why. Proceeding through the skillfully engraved stoa on their way to the Temple, they were entranced by the hypnotic tunes of gentle musicians and soothing singers. Birds sang happily from perches and inside cages as floral incense blanketed the air. Dancers in loose flowing garments enticed visitors with their undulations while their jewelry rattled and their castanets clicked.

Inside the hieron of the Temple, the walls were bedecked with paintings of myths surrounding the Goddess. In one depiction, Aphrodite and Ares are in passionate embrace while the jealous Hephaistos spies upon them with iron chains. Nearby Hephaistos is placing a fateful necklace upon the tragic

Harmonia. On the other wall, Aphrodite is emerging from the foam of Cyprus, accompanied by her beloved dolphins and white swans. Nearby, Aphrodite is lamenting for Adonis as she stands on the Leucadian Cliffs with Apollo's Temple in the background. Closer to the altar is a rendition of Aphrodite gazing upon the Golden Apple while Hera and Athena covet the item as they glare behind her. On both sides of the Temple, hetaerae recline on their separate raised berms. Behind each berm is a private alcove, concealed by embroidered curtains with images of myrtle, sparrows, and roses.

The visitors were impressed by the compassion and sensitivity of the hetaerae. Several old men, contorted by serious war wounds, and gnarled by arthritis, were embraced lovingly by the priestesses, soothed by reassuring words, and guided patiently into the private chambers. Several loud and arrogant aristocrats were confronted with calm words, gentle persuasions, and relaxing massage. Occasionally, two priestesses would escort one visitor. Off to the sides, larger chambers were available for group events. Despite the hedonistic nature of the Temple, the encounters were treated like blessings from the Goddess of Love.

Instead of the heavier barbiton, Sappho carried a lyre into the Temple. Despite her reservations, Sappho was inspired by the sublime variations of the power of Aphrodite. Taking her lyre from her shoulder, she stood by the altar and gazed up at her Goddess, surrounded by roses and myrtle, swans and dolphins, apples and lilies. Sappho began to pluck the strings. Alcaeus heard the sounds and emerged from one of the alcoves with his own lyre. Absorbing the ambience of sound, scent, and motion, they blended with the Temple and joined with the Goddess in celebration of both human and divine connections. Despite her losses, beyond her lamentations, Sappho once again found her Goddess. Dancers and musicians followed their music. From a deep cavern of her most personal being, Sappho voiced tones of the earth and the rocks. Alcaeus accompanied her with flowing baritone notes.

The Temple resonated with their paean to Love. From behind the altar of the Goddess, a woman of ageless beauty emerged. Her long flowing hair caressed her shoulders and a large emerald was hanging on her chest from a golden necklace. Long earrings dangled from her ears while bejeweled bracelets jangled on her arms. Her chiton was Phoenician blue and her slippers were of silk from eastern lands.

Sappho looked upon the sacred hetaera. "Lais," she noted.

With a smile and a nod, the priestess replied, "Sappho."

----- ----- -----

In the private chamber of Lais, the two acolytes of the Goddess studied each other. They reclined on adjoining cushions and sipped sweet wine from kantharos while birds sang from cages and the midday sun streamed through circular windows.

"Your perception of Aphrodite is very gentle," the hetaera noted. "Sparrows and butterflies, roses and swans. You ignore the thorns on the roses and the aggression of your swans."

Sappho replied with delicate confidence. "In this world, there is far too much delight in the aggressive side. In my poetry, I hope to remind people of the sublime beauty of existence. We don't need more songs of war, but we starve for the call of Love."

Lais lean on her elbows and faced the Poetess. "The deer and the sparrows, the squirrels and the cats. Their love-making is fierce. The stag must subdue the doe. There is a natural beauty in the struggle."

"Animals can only communicate with their actions. A stag cannot speak of its desire. A jackal can't speak of the beauty of its darling." Sappho's conclusion contained the precision of pure logic. "People have words. We can affix those words to the necklace of poetry."

The hetaera stood up and gestured to Sappho. "Let me show you something," she said, and glided to a curtained wall. She pushed aside the curtain and revealed a cloth cover over a hole in the wall. Setting the cover aside, she invited Sappho to observe what was happening in the next room.

The man was clearly from Sparta. He stood near a large bed as two vigorous hetaerae ran toward him. With agile motions, he parried their advances, tossing them on the bed. The women were persistent and kept rising and attacking. They would slap the warrior, wrap around him, and tear at his clothes. He did the same to them. Sappho watched them scratch and bite. Finally, both women attacked the Spartan in a united assault. All three fell upon the bed and kept squirming and twisting. With no clothes left on her, one of the women sat on the Spartan and pinned his arms with her legs. She then wrapped a rope around his neck and tightened it whenever he resisted. The second woman removed the man's chiton. Her face was soon buried between his legs. The woman on top of him slapped the Spartan whenever he made a sound, and pulled on the rope. When he achieved his climax with a great moan, the man collapsed helplessly. The hetaera released the rope. Both women laid on the bed on either side of the Spartan, who began to laugh with joy. The women joined the laughter. They concluded their ritual with soft loving kisses and playful chatter.

Lais laughed when Sappho's expression blended fascination and outrage. "Wasn't Aphrodite in that room?" asked the priestess provocatively.

"He needed to break through the armor in his soul," replied Sappho. "Since a child, he was trained to fight and kill. He had to start there. But it was the ending he yearned for."

"Oh, Sappho!" Lais was condescending. "They struggled for dominance."

"Yes," Sappho countered. "But, finally, they were all happily submissive. Don't you see, Lais? Men control the narrative. They think of dominance and submission. There is another way."

Lais shook her head. "We will never restore the Goddesses. So we maintain them with Temples like this."

Sappho was undefeated. "We will also teach men how women make love. Instead of slapping, that man can learn the pleasure of soft touch. Instead of wrestling the women into submission, he can learn to embrace her with reverence."

"I admire your dream, dear Sappho," declared Lais. "But I think even Aphrodite likes it rough sometimes. She did copulate with the God of War!"

Sappho had a ready reply. "They were deceived by Eros!"

"I suppose that's where we disagree. You separate Aphrodite from her son. I see Eros as her reliable assistant." Lais took a final sip of her wine. "But you seek to improve the condition of women. I respect your endeavor. I'll take you to Periander." Sappho expressed her deep gratitude, but Lais gave her a warning. "He was a great man. He built the Diolkos and engineered the trireme. But now he grows old. He is haunted by the ghost of his wife, Lysida. He's quick to grow suspicious, so speak cautiously."

Sappho listened carefully to Lais and nodded compliantly. Lais leaned toward the Poetess and gently stroked her arm with a peacock feather. Breathing into her ear, she added, "Is there no room in your body for Eros?"

"My body responds to invitations when I am willing."

"Are you willing? Or do I frighten you?"

Sappho seized the initiative and kissed the hetaera, gently at first, then building in passion until their tongues and lips were dancing in a frenzy. Neither dominated but both were creative.

----- ----- -----

Periander, son of Cypselus, welcomed the poets onto his estate with open arms. With Arion at his side, the old tyrant requested the poets of Lesvos play together. Lais took his hand and suggested a respite before the concert. Periander could never refuse Lais, who was more like his mother than his lover. Soon, the company was seated around a large oaken table with trays of cheese and fruit, krates of wine, and goblets of water.

"So, what do you think of my Diolkos?" he asked eagerly.

"A marvelous achievement," pronounced Alcaeus. He held up his krater. "To the Diolkos!" Glasses were clicked and they drank in sincere praise.

In time, they adjourned to a smaller chamber and the three poets set up their instruments. Amusing ballads were interspersed with reflective lyrical compositions, allowing for relaxed laughter as well as introspective musings.

Periander reclined in Lais' lap and requested an elegy for Lysida, whom he called, "Melissa". The poets complied and Sappho accompanied the strings with deep lamentation. Periander went into a woeful rumination that was incomprehensible at moments; but the basic content was clear. "Procles, Lycopron's grandfather lies to him…Our relationship was filled with passion but never violence…I saw her again, my dear Melissa…" Lais stroked his forehead and whispered words of comfort. "Draco brought order to Attica, but now Solon plots against him. Even on Lesvos, Myrsilius is undermined by Pittacus…The wise men of Melitus understand…All is flux and change…I need my son. Lycopron is an honest man. I can trust him." Lais rocked the grieving old tyrant. "Our time is waning, like the failing moon! The Persians can't be stopped!" He turned to Sappho. "Will you keep your vow? Will you go to Corcyra? That rebellious horde doesn't deserve my son! Please, dear Poetess. He respects your work."

"Of course," replied Sappho. "But we have no boat."

"Hah!" Periander shouted with pride. "One of my trireme vessels will hasten your journey. The great sail and three levels of oars! The boat has the speed of Hermes!"

"It's true," said Arion. "I went with Periander to Lefkas. We arrived at those cliffs with the speed of the wind. The trireme can maneuver around any enemy."

"It's settled then," announced Sappho. "We seek refuge in Syracuse."

"You shall have it," declared Periander. "My ship will take you to Syracuse and my son will come home."

----- ----- -----

The poets and Phaon were fascinated by the disciplined exertion on the Diolkos. Three hundred men were pushing a trireme across the wooden rails from the Saronic Gulf toward the western coast of Hellas. Alcaeus volunteered to join the effort and he took his position in the line at the stern. Sappho studied the enormous vessel as it passed. She noticed the oar openings at the lowest level, the thalamitai. In any naval battle, those lower-deck passengers were the most vulnerable. If the ship were rammed, they would probably drown as the sea rushed into their quarters. The mid-level oarsmen, the zygites, needed the skill to coordinate with the oars of both upper and lower crewmen. The helmsman and boatswain occupied the top deck, the thranos, and handled the cables for the sails. The large main sail, in the center of the deck, and the jib at the bow, were reefed as the boat traversed the isthmus. Drummers kept the rhythm of the labor which was accompanied by communal grunts and howls. Onlookers harmonized with the rhythm.

"The trireme is a great asset for travel and battle, but it is difficult to maintain," Phaon explained to Sappho. "It rots easily and must be removed from the water at night. The crew becomes quite proficient in moving them over land. It was a trick they learned from the Egyptians who carried ships over land in battle maneuvers."

Sappho was deep in thought. "I met Periander in Mytilene during the royal wedding. He was an impressive ruler. The change in his demeanor was startling."

"Perhaps the rumors are true," said Phaon. "Did he kill his wife?" The ferryman paused before continuing. "Some say he desecrated her corpse with his lust." He grimaced with disgust.

Sappho grunted with doubt. "There are many conflicting rumors," she replied. "Was she pregnant when he kicked her? Did he push her down a staircase? Did she fall? Others say he stabbed her. No one doubts he did love her."

Phaon considered her remarks. "When the passion of love is combined with the passion of anger, it can be dangerous."

"Lais, the hetaera, said the same thing. And yet, from Ares and Aphrodite, we got Harmonia, my ideal, agape, universal love."

"Hmm." Phaon, often the skeptic, ventured a joke. "She wasn't loved universally. Someone gave her a cursed necklace."

Sappho disregarded that retort as she considered the condition before them. "Periander is a tragic figure," Sappho decided. "He loved Lysida and lost her. Instead of comforting him in his grief, people curse him and tell tales. Then his son abandons him to join the rebellion in Corcyra. I understand Glukupikron, the sweet-bitter entanglements of love. I'll offer him an elegy."

One hundred twenty-five feet of beams and planks, tenons and dowels, slid onto the Ionian coastline to the cheers of onlookers. Alcaeus, sweating and breathing heavily, returned to his friends with a sense of personal satisfaction. "There's something about a group effort that turns strangers into close friends." He picked out a few splinters from his palms, and ladled water from a krater. Taking the deep gulps of a man who earned his drink, he said, "There's a song in this."

Phaon laughed and then grew solemn. "I have achieved my mission," he announced sadly. "You have your boat for Syracuse." He leaned in and whispered to Sappho. "When I get to Samothrace, I'll bestow your honors on Harmonia."

"Thank you, dear friend," replied Sappho. She embraced him with the sincerity of pure love.

----- ----- -----

Arion and Alcaeus accompanied her with their strings as Sappho sang her elegy for Periander, who sat with Lais at his side. He remained sober for the farewell ceremony and carried himself with dignity. Lais had the poise of a queen as she sat next to her sponsor.

Sappho sang of the eternal love between Periander and his Melissa; a love which neither time nor death could extinguish. She sang of a love a father carries for a son, despite distance and discord. She sang of eternal memories of a young son and a beautiful wife, playfully frolicking in the meandering hills of Corinth. She proclaimed how those memories are immortal, kept forever in the realm of Mnemosyne.

The oarsmen boarded the vessel. Tier by tier, oars sprouted from the portholes and drummers began their incantations.

Periander handed Sappho a rolled papyrus. "When you engage Lycopron, please give him this parchment. It carries my stamp of authority. I make this pledge to my son: if he agrees to return to Corinth and claim his rightful inheritance, I will leave Corinth and seek my own exile in Corcyra."

Sappho was concerned for the old tyrant. "Periander, you can't do that. The people of Corcyra believe all the lies. They despise you. Such a proposal also puts your son in danger. Lycopron has represented himself as a member of the rebellion. Such an exchange would be viewed as a betrayal."

Periander nodded his consent. "I appreciate your wise council, dear Poetess. Your perception is correct. My agents have told me the situation is Corcyra is very unstable. Lycopron can no longer predict the mood of the crowd. He now stays in Lefkada. If necessary, he would find sanctuary in the Temple of Apollo."

Sappho considered that circumstance. "Lefkada! So close! Even with the trench your engineers have dredged, anyone could walk across the shallow water to that land."

Periander nodded warmly. "This is true. It pains me deeply for him to be so close and yet so far. I know your poem of the woman who laments for her loved one in Anatolia. The woman is still close but unreachable. Will you write a poem for me?"

Here was a powerful tyrant who conquered Corcyra, supervised the building of the trireme, constructed the Diolkos, and colonized most of Ionia. Yet he beseeched her like a defeated old pauper begging for a meal. She opened her heart to his request. "I will sing of a man's deep love for his lost wife. I will describe the Periander I know and have come to respect. I will describe the endless torments of a father for his son whose love has been torn asunder."

"Why do people choose to believe the lies instead of their own eyes?"

"An eternal mystery," she replied.

"I'll leave it to Lycopron to make his own decision. Will you deliver the message?"

"Of course," answered Sappho. "You have been very kind to us. I owe you so much more." She embraced him sincerely. Alcaeus also embraced the ruler and reassured him that his document would be protected.

Sappho then approached Lais. "May the Goddess protect us," she proclaimed. "Let us, one last time, summon her together." They held hands and closed their eyes. All those gathered went silent and time stopped ticking while the two adherents of Aphrodite offered their silent conjugation with the Goddess.

"We may honestly disagree about the ultimate nature of Love, or the boundaries of the Goddess of Love. But such disagreements must never cause hostility. We must always face each other with loving acceptance as we both seek wisdom."

Lais readily agreed. "We mortals should never be so arrogant to assume ultimate knowledge of a Goddess, who can have infinite manifestations. You can't find Love through intolerance."

Sappho nodded in consent. "When we meet again, our circumstances may be different. But our affection will endure."

23

UPHEAVALS

The old crone was tossed upon the floor of the Areopagus and the elders of the Council took their seats. The mood among the crowd was restive. Draco's laws had restored order but his justice was drawn in blood. The Eupatridae, hereditary aristocracy, continued to accumulate wealth at the expense of poor farmers, merchants and craftsmen. Draco extended the franchise only to free men who could produce their own panoply, giving military men most of the leverage. In cases of debt, the hated horos continued to mark off farmland and undermine a farmer's ability to pay back loans. Trade policies left the polis of Athens hungry while grain traveled to other lands. Draco's extreme punishments for minor transgressions provoked conflicts among the Archons, especially Solon, who used his poetry to call for moderations.

Many people in the crowd, particularly the women, knew the old woman. She had provided herbs and potions to reduce fevers in children, support women through difficult pregnancies, and relieve the pain of old injuries and infirmities.

In some cases, she helped the dying to depart peacefully. That caused her current dilemma, the accusation of murder. While his wife begged the plaintiff to not harm the mágissa, the man was filled with grief that he expressed in rage at the defendant, who had merely provided comfort in his mother's final days. "She acted in a kind manner, but it was a deception. Her plants and potions were poison!"

"Why would I seek to harm an old, dying woman?" asked the mágissa, who pleaded from her knees for mercy.

"Silence, witch!" declared Draco. "You gave her the dram and now she's dead. She may have died naturally, but we'll never know, since you hastened her demise."

Draco was set off balance by the ambivalent response of the crowd. In the past, they were bloodthirsty and called for action. But, instead, there was arguing among the gathering.

Solon spoke out. "I can see the man is lamenting the loss of his mother. Perhaps we should postpone this trial until emotions are settled and thoughts are clear."

Draco rose from his chair and waved his arms. "No mercy for murder!" he pronounced. He directed the guards to seize the woman, who continued to declare her innocence.

As the guards grabbed the old crone, a javelin whistled through the air and plunged into an oak near the rock of Ares. A woman's voice, strong and clear, summoned the Council. "You will not harm her!" All heads turned to the voice. The Elders, the Archons, Draco, and the assembly gazed upon a young amazon who approached the bima with a proud stature. She retrieved her javelin and the guards went for their swords.

Loud ululations resounded from the crowd and several other amazons aimed their bows.

Solon observed the wild warrior women with their tattoos, their riding trousers, and their pointed caps. He stood up and extended his arms in a gesture of peace. "Please, let's be reasonable. Athens has laws and the Council will proceed with justice."

The young woman with the javelin announced her rebuttal. "This is not justice! The conviction was decided before the trial began." She pointed to the mágissa. "I know this woman," she declared. "She is kind and loving!" She looked to the crowd. "Who agrees with me?" From the gathering, hundreds of people shouted their assent.

Solon approached the warrior woman with hands open in peace. "You know her?" He studied the double bolts on her arms. He looked upon her face. Recognition came upon him like an overwhelming deluge. "By the gods! Cleis?"

She smiled and replied. "We meet again, Solon, the wise archon who learned his poetry skills from my mistress."

The archon was stunned. "Why are you here?"

"Unfinished business," she replied. "Let us take the mágissa."

Solon went to Draco, who was fuming. "Draco, I know this woman. She grew up in Attica and is honorable."

Draco shouted to the crowd. "Do we let a few barbarian women command us? Do we surrender to mob rule?"

"Your rules are harsh. I've witnessed your justice before." Cleis walked to the plaintiff. "I can see you were a good son." The man shuddered. "You weren't ready to let her go. The loss is painful." He nodded and whimpered. "Your mother was in agony. This mágissa allowed her to depart with peaceful dignity.

Would you punish her for that gift?" The man broke down and sobbed deeply. Cleis held him and offered words of comfort.

Between sobs, the man addressed Draco. "I have been mistaken. Please, good Draco, rescind the sentence."

Draco did not like to be over-ruled. "The woman is free to go." The crowd cheered and applauded. "But you, amazon! Don't you ever disrupt my court again!"

Maintaining her poise, Cleis replied, "Law without mercy is not justice." She reached out for the mágissa, who ran to her with joy. As they left the bima, another voice called out. "Cleis!"

Cleis turned to the voice and saw a young mother holding a child. "Don't you know me?" she asked.

Recognition came to her. "Antiope!"

The mother smiled and embraced her friend. "How you've changed! Attica could never contain you!"

"It's still me," Cleis assured her. The other amazons surrounded them. "Let me introduce you to my companions. Clyemne, Derinoe, Marsepia, Thermodosa."

Clyemne laughed. "Your name is Antiope, eh?"

"I know," replied Antiope. "Cleis taught me all about my namesake."

Draco observed the happy reunion with trepidation. He had sharp political senses. The time was changing. He no longer felt secure in his role. He once felt like a great innovator; but he was feeling obsolete. Perhaps the amazon was right, he thought. Perhaps I brought law and order, but with insufficient justice and mercy. A display of force would be absurd, and might only hasten rebellion. When he left the Areopagus, Draco went home with the intention of seeking the advice of an oracle.

----- ----- -----

Pittacus addressed the assembly in Mytilene. "We have not been able to solve the problem of inequality," he proclaimed. "Once again, an oligos, a small group, has accumulated most of the island's wealth. I don't blame them. They benefited from the regulations of Myrsilius." He walked around the hall and stared into the eyes of council members. "Do you remember? When we overthrew the Penthilidae? We spoke of the dangers? If we only have two extremes --- the very rich and the very poor --- then we will soon be at each other's throats, blood will flow, brother will fight brother. Promises were made when Myrsilius took control. For fair wages and reduced debt, for protection of the craftsmen and artisans who leave their farms for other trades. But Myrsilius couldn't keep his promises; he succumbed to the greed of the oligos!"

The council broke into roars of dissonance as each clan, each faction, each family, argued for its personal interests. Myrsilius blamed the poets for spreading provocations.

"No," said Charoxos. "The poets merely report the situation. Their words should serve as warnings. Do we want Lesvos to fall into civil chaos?"

From the council, he heard the challenges. "What would you do to restrain the oligarchy?"

Pittacus had learned many things over the last few years. "Unless we secure peace, then war is inevitable. When people are respected, when there is an equitable distribution of the wealth, then people live in peace. But, if a small group controls the flow of wealth, there will be no peace. We all benefit when we all share the resources of our beautiful island. The merchants and craftsmen and artisans --- the people in the middle --- salvage our nation! When people have choices and receive just compensation, then everyone is secure. We must find that balance!"

There was wisdom in his words. Even the oligos is safer when they share the wealth.

"My sister now lives as a refugee from the land she loves!" Charoxos spoke with trembling passion. "Her songs speak truth. Her poetry offered wise counsel to men who forget their responsibility to the nation. Justice for all is protection for all!"

24

LEFKOS AND LYCOPRON

The trireme made a rapid excursion to Corcyra. During breaks, Sappho and Alcaeus spoke with the oarsmen. Most were slaves from the losing side of recent battles. Others were free men who had come upon hard times and labored to earn enough to start over. A few were adventurers, eager to experience every side of life and to travel to other lands. They all agreed that the three levels of oars had made their work easier. The poets were impressed with the diversity. Free men and slaves, citizens and foreigners, rubbed shoulders and sweat together. Sappho saw the possibility of something new; Alcaeus worked on a poem of "agape among the oarsmen." Sappho liked the idea.

The people of Corcyra welcomed the famous poets with open arms. From the boat, they entertained the crowd with lyrical delights. They walked among the throng, which included both native inhabitants and colonists from Corinth. Merchants mingled among them with dialects from Babylon, Egypt, Magna Graecia, and the mainland of Hellas. At a taverna, the conversation was lively and often political. Recognizing the poets as two more refugees from political oppression, the revelers spoke openly. Opinion about Periander divided them, as one group praised his noble accomplishments while the other group condemned his fierce explosions of anger, and repeated the rumors about his family life. Two Sabines voiced their disillusionment with all politics, and described their personal flight from Magna Graecia. The poets asked them about Syracuse. The answer was disheartening. In the Sabine report, Latinis, Samnites, Sabines, Romans, and Etruscans, competed and battled at every opportunity. Hearing of more strife and conflict, the poets considered a change in their ultimate destination.

They soon learned that rumors about Lycopron's relocation was true. How ironic it was that he left Corcyra, which was a safe distance from his father, and had resettled in Lefkada, at the doorstep of Periander! To keep their promise to Corinth, they'd have to travel back down the southern coast. Bidding the people of Corcyra farewell, they rode on the trireme back to Epirus. Although Periander had provided the vessel as a gift, the poets left payment for the oarsmen and their leaders. Gratitude was always more valuable than entitlement.

Paying a modest fee to a boatman with a raft, Sappho, Alcaeus, and her three Molossus hounds crossed from Epirus onto the small island of Lefkada. No sail was required. The man simply used his staff to push the flat vessel across the shallow waterway.

The Diolkos had converted the backwater colony into a major trading center between the Aegean and the Mediterranean. Languages from every land created a cacophony of dialects and accents while crops, garments, pottery, sculpture, drinks, and nuts were traded, and diverse electrum staters were exchanged. It was a simple matter to gather provisions for the twenty-mile trek to the Temple of Apollo and the Leucadian Cliffs.

During long junctures, the poets traveled silently over boulders and river banks, wetlands and forests, while the Molossus ambled at their own pace, sniffing every item of interest and chewing blades of grass and herb blossoms. At several points, the hounds froze in place and emitted a low gurgle. The provocation was usually a rabbit or ferret. They didn't even bother with squirrels. But, at one spot, the largest molussus stopped in front of Sappho to obstruct her path. The other two hounds froze at either side. At first, the provocation was obscure. Dead leaves and fallen tree branches concealed the object until it slithered in an undulating pattern. Sappho noticed the snake and Alcaeus identified it. "Viper," he stated in low bass. "A female. It's brown with dark brown zig-zag markings. Leave it alone and it will pass." She did as he directed and the snake meandered into the tall grass. The dogs relaxed and Sappho provided grateful pats which they answered with loving tongues.

Ironically, the Poetess of Aphrodite was then troubled by bees. Passing through a patch of sweet-scented blossoms, they were enshrouded by a thick swarm of bees. Despite the anxiety of the travelers, the bees did not sting. It seemed like Aphrodite's helpers were merely escorting her acolyte. They made no attempt to swat at the bees, an action which could have provoked a catastrophe. Instead, they accepted their buzzing companions as if the Goddess had furnished a test. Once they moved away from the sweet cluster, the buzzing subsided as the bees bid them farewell.

The next test, along a steep ledge, introduced a family of goats that were barely distracted by the weary explorers. In fact, while they grazed on mountain laurel, the goats were reluctant to make room on the narrow path. The dogs, however, motivated them with angry barks and threatening growls. Goats often attract flies; and that moment was no exception. Like poor Io, who was tormented by Hera's gadfly, and desperately escaped across the Bosporus, Sappho and Alcaeus had to suffer the irritation of the flies until they reached a natural pool and could splash them away. The hounds eagerly jumped in the water and drank heartily.

Halfway on their journey, they came to a flat grove with enough dry wood for a small campfire. The persistent repetitive, "hoot, hoot" of an owl resounded through the night as it scanned the woods in search of a nocturnal meal. With the hounds around them, the poets slept securely; but woke before daybreak to a morning rain. Since there was no lightning, they found shelter under several ancient oaks. They nibbled on some of their rations of fruits and grains, which they generously shared with the dogs. One hound captured two rabbits, which were quickly skinned and cooked. It was a satisfying breakfast.

Waiting out the rain, the poets worked together on the song for Periander. But Sappho was frequently diverted by troubling thoughts. Before the paean to Periander, she composed an elegiac poem that emerged from her own lamentations. Alcaeus understood. She had to purge her own sorrow with her words before any less personal creation was possible. He strummed gentle yet deep tones as Sappho breathed in the tender zephyr of the western wind and snuggled her hounds. Bats fluttered through the branches like restless spirits and the rain splattered upon leaves in a steady drizzle.

Like the restless ocean waves,

Love invades my life and then recedes.

Aphrodite arrives on white foam of passion,

Until the sad water quietly slips away.

My heart crashes against the rocks,

But I eagerly await the next onslaught.

The brush of Time paints grey the hair

That once shimmered with radiant youth.

The sculptor forces cracks in skin

That was smooth fresh clay.

In secret places, the old crone dreams

Of the vibrant girl she once was,

And hides her dreams from ridicule and scorn.

In pondering the contingency of existence, she recounted the Spartan tale of Apollo and his love for Hyacinthus. A simple game of discus ended in disaster when Apollo's throw struck the beautiful youth with a fatal wound. Some seek to blame Zephyrus, the west wind, but it's futile. In painful loss, we seek an evil cause to provide meaning for the catastrophe. Myths are created to explain why an earthquake or volcano devastated a town filled with devout citizens. Was it the work of an angry god, or a fact of natural life? Sappho asked the question but had no definite answer. She sang of the uncertainty and transitory aspects of her own life. In the blink of an eye, her thiasos was gone. In the brief moment of a breath, she left her home and her "sparrows". Instead of singing with a chorus by the altar to Aphrodite on her family estate, she was traveling on the cliffs of Lefkas in search of the disaffected son of an aging tyrant.

In her pain, she found insight. She considered the snake and the bees and the flies that hampered her; perhaps she was being tested. Composing paeans to a goddess from a comfortable portico might not be a true demonstration of devotion. Perhaps Aphrodite grew jaded with her dramatic renditions and needed greater proof of her fealty. Retrieving her own words, Sappho sang again of the different forms of Love. She had separated Eros from Aphrodite's more complex quality, with all its pleasure and pain. She knew about Philia, the love that grows with friendship. She experienced Storge, the natural love for family members. Many times, she had practiced Xenia, or hospitality, even with her slaves. Aphrodite's love was Agape, a pure universal love for all existence beyond the physical bodily passion of Eros.

With that insight, Sappho suddenly experienced a deep compassion for both Periander and Lycopron, how they both suffered from a barrier built of misunderstandings and distortions. She shared her revelation with Alcaeus, who felt energized by the radiance of her enthusiasmos. He changed the tempo of his lyre from a slow dirge to a dignified commemoration.

They worked on their lyrical composition with an energy that defied time. No longer fatigued by the ten miles of challenging ascents and natural obstacles, they worked until the sun, on the other side of the mountains, painted the sky; first pink, then blue. The rain had stopped and the air carried the scent of purification. Her personal epic was unfolding. Sappho was re-born.

----- ----- -----

It seemed as if Aphrodite had rewarded Sappho's epiphany. As they traversed a turn in their narrow path, they entered a field of butterflies. Bright gossamer wings fluttered in all directions as the delicate creatures drank the nectar of generous flora. The flying sprites even landed on the shoulders and arms of the poets who let them crawl on their fingers. The fragrance of fennel, thyme, lemon balm, and sage suffused the air. Alcaeus chewed on chicory roots as they proceeded through a field of red poppies and star-like arenaria with its five petals. Sappho was thrilled to discover a cluster of calla lilies, precious to both Hera and Aphrodite, and felt a renewed enthusiasmos as she walked upon a carpet of blue periwinkles.

When they arrived at their destination, they entered a green pasture with rolling hills. Looking over the pasture, they spied the famous white cliffs that dropped to a curved beach. From their height atop the cliffs, merchant ships looked like insects. The local residents swam in the crystal blue water as a soft zephyr cooled the hot afternoon. Flamingoes stood together in a small cove while hawks hovered above them and crows howled their complaints. Then, to Sappho's delight, a flock of sparrows soared above the beach and into the pines. She whispered to Alcaeus, "We'll be all right." He readily agreed.

"So, these are the Leucadian Cliffs," she noted. "The famous Leap of Faith for lovers and Leap of Truth for those accused of crimes."

"Indeed," replied Alcaeus. "This is where Aphrodite lamented her loss of Adonis." Alcaeus laughed. "How does an immortal goddess prove her love by leaping from a cliff?"

"I've been noticing that we both plunge into episodes of skepticism," she replied. "She may be immortal, but she wanted to experience the pain of a mortal woman."

"I see," he professed. "The gods miss out on some experiences because they're immortal."

Sappho smiled with admiration. "Alcaeus, you are growing very wise."

Nearby, at a stone promontory that jutted out from the cliff, stood the Temple of Apollo. After their journey to Cybele of

Ephesus and the Heraion on Samos, the temenos on Lefkada seemed prosaic and ordinary. But, as they got closer to the structure, they began to appreciate the architectural accomplishment. It was, after all, resting upon an outcropping of stone; yet, the Temple was level and balanced precisely. They found no stress cracks from uneven forces. The four-sided peripteros was surrounded by a stoa, supported by thick Corinthian columns of oolitic egg-white limestone, that allowed for unimpeded walks around the entire temple in any weather. As they approached the pronaos, the front porch of the Temple, the poets studied the semicircular tympanum above the doorway. It contained an engraved depiction of Apollo as the beautiful kouris of idealized male youth. Behind the naked god was a sunburst, indicating Apollo's identity with the light. In one hand, he held the Caduceus, the only remnant of the double Pythons that guarded the Omphalos, the central navel of the world. In his other hand, he held the lyre, a gift from Hermes.

Upon entering the naos, the central chamber, they were met by a grand statue of Apollo with the Python lying dead at his feet. Next to Apollo was his beloved Hyacinthus, holding the fateful discus.

As they approached the secretive opisthodomos, or back room, they passed a sculpted rendition of the Oracle at Delphi. She was sitting upon her tripod stool next to a fire pit that exuded smoke and incense. Inhaling the smoke had an intoxicating effect, perhaps to simulate the hypnotic fumes of Delphi. Two priestesses stood at either side of the door to the opisthodomos, holding donation trays. Apparently, the austere regulations of Delphi did not apply on Lefkada. The poets dropped several electrums in the trays and the women bowed respectively.

As the doors opened, the poets had to adjust their vision in the dark chamber. Gradually, they took note of small windows at the sides of the room that allowed a perpetual twilight. At the center of the room was a great statue depicting both Apollo and his sister, Artemis. They stood together like a proud royal couple. Their arms were stretched out with the palms of their hands facing upward. They apparently welcomed visitors with benevolence.

"The balance of idealized male and chaste female is impressive," noted Alcaeus. "But what does it mean?"

"I'm not sure," replied Sappho. "But I feel a deep rapport with the motif. Perhaps it harkens back in time to the Sacred Marriage of the Old Goddess and her Consorts. But it's a more contemporary rendition. Artemis has none of the primitive attributes of Cybele."

Alcaeus considered the implication. "Perhaps Apollo did not displace Gaia. Perhaps they joined."

Sappho struggled with that idea. "Why, then, is this statue hidden in the back room? Could it be that a balance of male and female energy is too radical for popular acceptance?"

Alcaeus offered another suggestion. "Some tell us that the Old Consort to the Goddess was sacrificed annually. Perhaps the artist wanted to join their energy but without the bloodshed."

"Perhaps the time for such a joining has not yet come. This may be a dream for the future."

"The dream could take centuries to become reality." The new voice startled the poets, who turned quickly to regard a tall man dressed in regal attire. "Perhaps even millennia. First we'll need male leaders to encourage a more feminine perspective."

Sappho examined the arrival. "You must be Lycopron," she concluded.

"And you're the great Poetess Sappho of Lesvos. Welcome." He turned to Alcaeus. "I know you. Her accomplice, the great Alcaeus." Their expressions of unease called for further explication. "The priestesses notified me. I've been expecting you. They are now restricting entry so we may speak confidentially."

They sat at the farthest end of the opisthodomos and spoke in soft tones. Sappho spoke of Periander's request and implored him to consider a reconciliation. But Lycopron remained adamant. Alcaeus tried to persuade the prince on political grounds and remind him of the benefits that accompany leadership over a successful state with a significant navy and numerous colonies.

"Your arguments are logical," replied Lycopron. "But such an arrangement would be impossible. The people of Corcyra hate Periander as an invader and a conqueror. The colonists want to be free from Corinth. I was welcomed to the colonies because they know of my animosity for my father. If they even suspected betrayal, they would turn on me violently. The very idea of Periander going to live on Corcyra or Lefkada…Hah! Madness!"

Alcaeus placed his hand on the man's shoulder. "I understand. Your pain runs deep and your mind whirls with memories you retain and stories you've been told. We were inspired to create poems describing your struggle. May we?"

Lycopron saw an opportunity to spread the word of his dilemma to the world. "Yes, go ahead. Weave your words. Create a tapestry of my family's tragedy."

In the inner sanctum of Apollo's temple on the Leucadian Cliffs, the poets placed their instruments upon their laps and suffused the sanctuary with the sounds of strings. Sappho sang a solemn song of inextricable longing between a father and a son, torn asunder by a great tragedy and the slander that built a wall between them; each brick composed of fabrications, distortions, exaggerations. Her poem went on to commemorate the great technical and military achievements of Periander; and how he helped to transform Corinth into a major trading center for the entire world. However, her song described how the man, in his faltering years, perceives himself as a total failure because of the loss of his son's love.

Lycopron listened to the Poetess intently. His expression frequently changed. In one moment, he sat grimly with pursed lips. Another moment, his jaw dropped and his seemed to shudder. At one point, he lowered his head and stared at the floor. At the end of the song, he stood and walked to the rear wall with his back to the poets. "You have great skill with your poetry," he muttered. "Such words can shake kingdoms, or melt hearts." He turned quickly to face them. "Your sensitivity transcends personal pain. It causes me to experience…I don't know how to describe it."

"Agape?" Alcaeus suggested. Sappho smiled at her companion.

"I've heard that term," replied Lycopron. "A higher level of Love." The poets nodded in accord. "The last stanza, Sappho. Please repeat it." She did so eagerly. "Of course," he said when she concluded. "All the wealth and power are worthless without…" He stopped speaking and trembled. Putting his hands to his head, he begged them to leave the opisthodomos. He needed time to be alone and contemplate.

----- ----- -----

The women left Attica and galloped into the fertile plains of Boeotia, passing the famous land of Thebes and traveling around the southern bank of Lake Copais, with Mount Parnathis hovering above them like a watchful god. They had to stop frequently to accommodate their elderly companion, but no one seemed to mind. It gave Cleis extra time to prepare for her visit. Villagers observed the five amazons with trepidation as they ambled into their territory in a casual gait. They used an alibi Cleis taught them: that they were on a pilgrimage to Delphi.

When they arrived at the farmstead, they calmed their horses and approached with stealth. Menares was standing next to the hated horos that designated the land as collateral until debts were paid. Damiskos was leaning on a cane and letting his son do the talking. Menares was arguing with a well-clad gentleman, probably a dignita who served as representative for the eupatrid creditor. In contrast to Menares' simple chiton, the dignita's himation was embellished by a chlamys that he attached at his shoulder with a peronal of engraved silver.

"We can't honor the debt unless we can produce more crop." Menares was trying to engage in a reasonable negotiation.

But the dignita grew impatient. "You georgoi are all alike!" he roared. "Eagerly accept the loan but reluctant to meet your obligation!"

Damiskos sought to have the dignita understand. "We seek a loan and then find it difficult to pay the debt for the same reasons." Menares added his clarification. "Not enough rain, or too much. A cold spring or a summer that burns the fields. In a good season, we readily re-pay. Almonds are a very thirsty crop. The wheat is fragile. But we are doing well with the beans, the lentils, and the amaranth."

"Beans?" The dignita was indignant. "There are some cults who believe beans are poisonous. Not good for that business! The debt must be paid or we'll have to seize the land."

Barnyard dogs began to bark and the dignita noticed the unexpected guests. "What is this? An invasion?" Menares and

Damiskas turned and faced the band of amazons with startled trepidation.

"Foreclosure won't be necessary." Cleis approached the men with a straight back and confident stride. The creditor and the farmers looked upon the women with bewilderment and intrigue.

Menares stared at the woman who just spoke. Her tattooed arms and riding trousers appeared so alien to him that he couldn't make the association.

She removed her cap and stared at her brother. "Menares, have you forgotten me?"

"How do you know my name?" he asked. Then he paused, stared at the amazon. His eyes went wide and his mouth dropped open. "Cleis?" Tears came to his eyes. "Cleis!" He wanted to embrace her, but, noticing her quiver and sword, was uncertain how to behave. So Cleis took the lead. Damiskos trembled with surprise and Cleis took his shoulders to keep him steady. The other amazons smiled and wiped away tears as they watched the family reunion.

The dignita knew the name. "Cleis? The runaway wife? Eurybiades will be glad to hear of your return!"

She approached the nobleman with dignified contempt, with her hand on her sword. "Do you intend to tell him?" Her glare was piercing and threatening.

"Perhaps not," he replied with a snarl. "I haven't decided yet."

Cleis barely contained her anger. "Do as you wish, thief. You can also let him know that I free him from his commitment to me."

The dignita remained arrogant. "YOU free HIM?"

Cleis opened her pouch. "Open your palms," she commanded. He did as she ordered. Cleis dropped staters and electrums onto his open hands. The coins were from Lesvos, Corinth, Athens, and Aegina. "That should satisfy the debt," she sneered. "And a bit more."

The dignita was overwhelmed. "Yes. Yes."

Cleis walked to the horos and tried to kick it over. As it began to loosen, she attempted to pull it up from the ground. Menares went to her assistance and the siblings, together, liberated their family farm.

Clyemne walked to the dignita. With her hands on her hips, she asked him, "Why are you still here?"

"Wait!" said Cleis. "He can leave after he gives me an acknowledgement of debt paid in full."

The dignita was eager to escape from the wild warrior women. He took out the original note and wrote, "Paid". He then signed the bill and applied the creditor's official stamp.

Cleis examined it carefully. "If you deceive me, you'll never write anything again." The dignita bowed in respect.

Menares faced the dignita. "Get off our land!" The gentleman was eager to honor that request. He rode off in a rush and the small group cheered and laughed.

Menares examined his sister. "You're...you're Atalanta!" The amazons laughed heartily.

There were many things to discuss. First, Cleis wanted to see her mother. Menares bowed his head. "Mother has grown very ill. She's weak and feverish."

Cleis hurried to the home. "We have a healing woman with us from Athens. Maybe she can help mother." She introduced the mágissa.

The mágissa addressed Damiskos directly. "I suppose you keep your good wife indoors most of the time?" The man nodded. "She needs the sun and the light. The Athenian men seek to keep their wives as pale beauties but they go off and play with the rosy-cheek hetaerae."

Menares was impressed. "You have made many friends." Cleis grunted with a small grin and strutted to the house.

The small band followed her to the farmhouse for a well-deserved dinner and a sharing of many tales. The mágissa brought her sack of herbs and potions.

25

DRACO'S DEPARTURE

Charoxos put into harbor at Piraeus to make several trades and purchase provisions. He was eager to reach his sister with the good news. Pittacus had finally made his move and Myrsilius was exiled. The clans had united behind Pittacus. She and Alcaeus were free to return to Lesvos. In the interim, Charoxos and the loyal slave had become close friends. In yet another irony, the slave accompanied Charoxos to share the news.

In a symbolic gesture, Charoxos purchased a fresh supply of papyrus. The poets would probably have much to say. He also found some of Sappho's favorite fruits and desserts. Back at Eressos, Larichos was on a mission to retrieve her "sparrows" for her thiasos.

As they were loading the boat, they witnessed an aristocratic procession marching onto an imposing vessel. The crowd was pushed back by a squadron of hoplites, but that did not prevent them from using their voices. They shouted and jeered, cursed and ridiculed, as the prominent dignita passed them. When the luminary boarded the craft, he addressed the raucous mob.

"I stopped the blood feuds! I gave you written laws! No longer could silver and gold buy a judge's decision." He tried to shout above the noisy throng. "I pushed the Cylon invaders from the Acropolis and sent them back to Megara." The people always enjoyed a good show. They had been entertained by the trials and, at the pier, they relished the departure of a fallen archon. "The laws are written! Anyone can read the steles!" They no longer listened. His time had passed. "Now I retire to Aegina." The crowd cheered. "I have done my part to establish order in Attica." He waved at anyone who was still interested, and then disappeared below deck.

Charoxos was amazed. "That's Draco! Is this possible?" He asked several people what was happening and received joyful answers. "Solon is now archon!"

The slave also knew Solon. "The man who attended Sappho's thiasos, and she taught him how to play the lyre?"

"Yes!" replied Charoxos. "When Doricha returns from Egypt, and we bring back the poets, and Larichos gathers Sappho's acolytes, we will have a grand celebration!"

----- ----- -----

Doricha arrived in Egypt and entered the Temple of Isis in Byblos. She received a warm welcome from her devotees. Doricha paid homage to gods as she passed each statue: Horus, with the head of a falcon, wore the double crown of a united Egypt. At the base of his statue is the symbol of the great eye, which can see everything and protect his people. In doing battle with his evil uncle, Set, Horus fights for the better side of humanity. His parents stand on either side. The green-skinned Osiris, wearing his large crown with its two ostrich feathers, held in his hands the shepherd's crook and the threshing flail, uniting the shepherd and the farmer. On the other side of Horus stood Isis, wearing the diadem of a full round moon framed by cow horns. Emerging from the front of her crown was a cobra, with arched back and piercing eyes. On her necklace of lapis lazuli was a scarab painted red. Osiris, the dying god, is rescued by his sister/lover, Isis, the goddess of resurrection, who held in one hand an ankh, the symbol for life. Like her brother, she also held ears of corn. The gods of Egypt forever united polarities. Upper and Lower Egypt, Life and Death, shepherd and farmer, sun and moon. Her younger sister, Nephthys, was cohort to Isis in funeral rituals, and was the unlucky wife of Set. Nephthys stood behind the family triad and bore a crown in the shape of a house. Her falcon wings were wrapped around her. Nephthys had her hand on Isis' arm. Her wails of lamentation served the transition for the journey of death. Nephthys assisted Isis in restoring Osiris and played no part in Set's evil actions. At least among the gods, a female could be an individual who was distinct from her husband.

The old priestess, Doricha's mentor, emerged from a rear chamber and embraced her adherent lovingly. Doricha spoke of her journeys to Attica and Lesvos, and of the turmoil among the Hellenic states. The old woman shared her trepidations for Egypt as well. They entered the rear sanctuary and shared some tea. Doricha then revealed her reason for the visit. Eagerly, the older woman took hold of the nine volumes of papyrus.

"The work of Sappho must be preserved from the changing torrents of time."

"I understand," replied the mentor. "You have grown very wise, dear child. Some things must exist beyond the transitory states of king or pharaoh, conqueror or zealot." The woman pushed aside a rug with intricate tapestry and revealed a trap door in the floor. She retrieved a copper box and brought it to the surface. Opening the box, she displayed other sheets of papyrus with the stories of the gods and records of the pharaohs. "Sappho's poems will be safe for the centuries."

Doricha nodded. "It might take centuries for people to appreciate what she did for all women."

----- ----- -----

SOURCE MATERIAL

hirty years ago, it might have been impossible to write this historical novel. The research alone would have required visits to numerous libraries and book stores all over the world. Today, with Wikipedia and other online sources, it was possible to collect all the necessary historical facts and connect the dots. The internet helped me to breathe life into Sappho, Alcaeus, Cleis, Solon, Pittacus, Draco, Periander, Myrsilius, Aesop, Rhodopis, and all the other characters who appear in this tale. As papyrus supplied the poets of archaic Greece with a new form of social media, digital technology today allowed me to bring The Poetess and her contemporaries into modern relevance. I also relied upon the research of several diligent authors:

Berkowitz, Eric, "Sex and Punishment --- Four Thousand Years of Judging Desire," CounterPoint, Berkeley, CA , 2012

Kleinman, Paul, "Philosophy 101," Adams Media, Avon, MA 2013

Krznaric, Roman, "How Should We Live? --- Great Ideas from the Past for Everyday Life", BlueBridge, Katonah, NY and Profile Books, England (as "The Wonderbox"), 2011

Mayor, Adrienne, "The Amazons --- Lives and Legends of Warrior Women Across the Ancient World," Princeton University Press, NJ, 2014

Powell, Jim, "The Poetry of Sappho", Oxford University Press, 2007

Snyder, Jane McIntosh, "The Women and the Lyre", Southern Illinois University Press, 1989

Walker, Barbara G., "The Woman's Encyclopedia of Myths and Secrets," Harper & Row, 1983

Wilson, Lyn Hatherly, "Sappho's Sweet Bitter Songs", Routledge, NYC and London, 1996

Cover: "Sappho Embracing Her Lyre", by Jules Elie DeLauney, c.1851.

Other Novels
by Steven R. Green

Beyond The Lock (previously, "Interlock")

Menage3

Menage 3B – Baby Makes Four

Captives in the Shadows

Website: www.stevenrbtgreen.com

Books available online from Amazon, Kobo, Nook (Barnes & Noble), and SmashWords.